"Tell me th
missed this

Her first impulse was to deny Kane's words, to tell him that she had been perfectly satisfied with her life before the Agency tapped her for this particular assignment.

She'd thought she'd been happy arguing with her neighbor, tending her lawn, fighting with common criminals and making arrests. But she'd been fooling herself, and she knew she'd never be able to fool Kane.

"Yeah, I missed it," she replied grudgingly. "But that doesn't mean I'm coming back. I agreed to this one assignment, and that's all."

Kane reached out for her hand and twined his fingers with hers. "We were good together, Cassie. We stopped a lot of bad things from happening in the world."

"But I couldn't stop you from taking that bullet for me, could I?" she said. Hot tears burned her eyes, and she was appalled that this still had the power to hurt. "If I hadn't been your lover, if we'd just been partners like we were supposed to be, then you wouldn't have nearly died. Sorry, I can't let you take that risk—ever again."

Dear Reader,

Welcome to Silhouette Bombshell, the hottest new line to hit the bookshelves this summer. Who is the Silhouette Bombshell woman? She's the bombshell of the new millennium; she's savvy, sexy and strong. She's just as comfortable in a cocktail dress as she is brandishing blue steel! Now she's being featured in the four thrilling reads we'll be bringing you each month.

What can you expect in a Silhouette Bombshell novel? A high-stakes situation in which the heroine saves the day. She's the kind of woman who always gets her man—and we're not just talking about the bad guy. Take a look at this month's lineup....

From *USA TODAY* bestselling author Lindsay McKenna, we have *Daughter of Destiny,* an action-packed adventure featuring a Native American military pilot on a quest to find the lost ark of her people. Her partner on this dangerous trek? The one man she never thought she'd see again, much less risk her life with!

This month also kicks off ATHENA FORCE, a brand-new twelve-book continuity series featuring friends bonded during their elite training and reunited when one of them is murdered. In *Proof,* by award-winning author Justine Davis, you'll meet a forensic investigator on a mission, and the sexy stranger who may have deadly intentions toward her.

Veteran author Carla Cassidy brings us a babe with an attitude—and a sense of humor. Everyone wants to *Get Blondie* in this story of a smart-mouthed cop and the man she just can't say no to when it comes to dealing out justice.

Finally, be the first to read hot new novelist Judith Leon's *Code Name: Dove,* featuring Nova Blair, the CIA's secret weapon. Nova's mission this time? Seduction.

We hope you enjoy this killer lineup!

Sincerely,

Natashya Wilson
Associate Senior Editor, Silhouette Bombshell

Please address questions and book requests to:
Silhouette Reader Service
U.S.: 3010 Walden Ave., P.O. Box 1325, Buffalo, NY 14269
Canadian: P.O. Box 609, Fort Erie, Ont. L2A 5X3

GET BLONDIE

CARLA CASSIDY

Silhouette®

BOMBSHELL™

Published by Silhouette Books

America's Publisher of Contemporary Romance

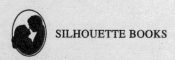

SILHOUETTE BOOKS

ISBN 0-373-51317-8

GET BLONDIE

CARLA CASSIDY

isn't a secret agent or martial-arts expert, but she does consider herself a Bombshell kind of woman. She lives a life of love and adventure in the Midwest with her husband, Frank, and has written over fifty books for Silhouette.

Dedicated to my editor, Julie Barrett.
Thanks for all your work on this project.
Long live Bombshell heroines!

Chapter 1

The tough punk was known as Snake on the streets of Kansas City, but in reality his name was Sammy Watson and he had a long string of outstanding warrants. As he warily faced Officer Cassandra Newton beneath the dirty glare of the overhead street lamp, he appeared more like his street name than his birth name, hissing and coiling in preparation for a fight.

Cassie threw a glance toward the patrol car parked nearby. Her partner, Asia Malone, leaned against the driver door, eating a candy bar that looked minuscule in his massive hand.

A roar from Sammy yanked her attention back where it belonged just as the young man charged her like an enraged bull. With graceful agility she sidestepped the attack, then turned to face him as he stopped and turned back toward her, his breaths coming in short, quick gasps.

"Come on, Sammy. It's been a long day. We can make this easy, or we can make it hard," she said as the two circled each other.

"I ain't making nothing easy on you. No bitch cop is going to take me in."

"Don't get her riled, Sammy boy," Asia called out. "I know what she's capable of and it isn't pretty."

"Shut up, you big, black pile of crap," Sammy screamed. With a surprisingly quick movement he pulled a knife from his pocket. "Come on, Blondie, let's tango."

Cassie sighed wearily. It had been a long day of minor irritations and this kid pulling a knife on her was the last straw. Sometimes young, ignorant creeps just needed to get their butts kicked.

She drew a deep breath and centered herself. Her first kick, sharp and crisp, sent the knife flying out of Sammy's hand. The second one, delivered to the side of his head, sent him crashing to the ground on his hands and knees.

She put her boot in the center of his back and with a minimum of pressure flattened him to the ground. "Didn't anyone ever tell you, Sammy…" She slapped cuffs on him and yanked him to his feet. "…I hate to tango."

She shoved the cuffed prisoner toward her partner. "Thanks for the help," she said dryly to Asia as he popped the last of the candy bar into his mouth.

He grinned, his white teeth gleaming in the dark of the night. "Poetry in motion," he said. "You know how much I love to watch you work."

"Yeah, well you get to do the paperwork when we get back to the station."

They loaded Sammy into the back seat of their car and within minutes they were on their way back to the Kansas City, Missouri East Patrol Station House.

"I'm going to kill you," Sammy yelled from the back seat. "You're dead. You are one dead cop." He kicked the seat for emphasis.

"Give it a rest, Sammy," Cassie said. "You've got enough warrants against you that you'll be on Medicare when you finally see freedom again."

Sammy fell silent, apparently contemplating his future behind bars.

"Ah, Cassie, for years I hoped to be partnered with a person who was bigger than me," Asia said.

She eyed him with a wry grin. It would have been next to impossible to find a man bigger than Asia. At six foot six inches tall and almost three hundred pounds, Asia had once told her he'd gotten his name because his mother had sworn she was birthing a continent when he'd come into the world.

"I never managed to find a partner bigger than me, but I definitely hit easy street when they put you with me." He laughed, a deep, robust sound that filled the car. "Hell, I love it that I got a partner who can kick ass better than me any day of the week."

Cassie loved having a partner whom she trusted and respected. Asia, along with his wife Serena and their four children were so wonderfully normal. And in her thirty-years on earth, Cassie had had very little normal in her life.

"Hey, Serena's making that rice dish you like so much on Sunday. She asked me to ask you if you want to come over around two and eat with us."

"I thought you hated that rice dish," Cassie said as they pulled into the underground parking area.

"I do. I'm planning on sneaking a couple of steaks on the grill." He grimaced as Sammy began yelling and kicking in the back seat. He looked back at Cassie. "You go on, get out of here. It's past time for us to be off. I'll process this schmuck and you can head home."

"Thanks, Asia." She bounded out of the patrol car and headed inside to get her personal belongings. It had been a long day and she was exhausted.

The station was relatively quiet. Wednesday nights were usually easy ones. The cops called it the midweek recovery day…the perps of the city were either resting from the past weekend or preparing for the next.

As she made her way to the desk she shared with Asia and four other patrolmen, her fellow cops greeted her.

"Hey, Cassie, we heard another one bit the dust." Officer Gomez held up two thumbs.

She grinned at the attractive Hispanic man. "We got lucky, spotted him strolling down the sidewalk like he didn't know he had eight warrants against him," she replied. Gomez laughed and shook his head.

"Looks like you've got a secret admirer," Jim Johnson, a vice cop said as he finger-combed his scraggly beard.

"What do you mean?"

He pointed toward her desk at the back of the room. "It was delivered just a few minutes ago by some over-night delivery service."

A long-stemmed white rose stood in a slender gold bud vase. A blood-red ribbon was tied to one end of the rose and the other end to a cell phone.

The sight turned Cassie's blood cold. No way, she thought as she moved on leaden feet to the desk. No way in hell were they going to sucker her into coming back. She didn't care what was happening. She didn't care what was at stake.

She leaned a slender hip against the desk and untied the rose from the compact phone. She knew the phone was impossible to trace and the favorite mode of communication for three groups of people…terrorists, drug dealers and the agency. This one hadn't come from any drug dealer or terrorist.

She stared at the number pad. All she had to do was hit the redial button and she'd be connected to somebody who would tell her what they wanted her to know.

She didn't want to know anything. The phone would only be active for a little while, then the activation would be stopped and she'd toss it in the trash.

Irritated by the mere sight of it, she grabbed the vase and the phone and threw the entire mess into the garbage can next to her desk.

"Ah, somebody is really in the doghouse when pretty

flowers and a free cell phone don't even work," one of the officers teased.

She only wished it were something as simple as a boyfriend in her doghouse. She unlocked the desk drawer and retrieved her car keys from the jumble of items inside. Forget it, she told herself as she walked to her car parked behind the station house.

She had a relatively uncomplicated life now. She wasn't about to risk it all to go back to work for the agency. She'd left that life five years ago and had never looked back. When they didn't immediately get a phone call from her they would know she was out of the game permanently.

The agency had a name...SPACE...acronyms that stood for Special Personnel Against Criminal Elements. It was a secret, covert group run by John Etheridge, head of Homeland Security for the United States.

Cassie had been recruited by the agency when she was at the Police Academy in Los Angeles. She'd given SPACE four years of her life, working dangerous assignments all over the world. But she'd left the agency five years ago and vowed she'd never go back.

As she got into her car she drew a deep breath of the early summer night air. After so many years on the West Coast, Cassie had grown to love the Midwest's four seasons.

Early summer scents brought with them a curious blend of pleasure and bittersweet pain. Kansas City was the city of her early childhood, a childhood that had ended abruptly and inexplicably on the streets of Los Angeles when she'd been eleven.

She consciously shoved thoughts of her past aside as she started her car. She tossed her hat into the back seat of the car, then began the thirty-minute drive from the station house to her ranch in the northern suburbs.

She yawned and checked the clock on the dash. Almost one o'clock. If she and Asia hadn't spotted Sammy the Snake on the street, she would have already been snuggled into bed and fast asleep.

When she finally pulled into her driveway, she cut the engine and tapped her short nails against the steering wheel. A restless energy had begun to build inside her as the vision of that darned white rose played and replayed in her mind.

If it were earlier she'd have gone to the gym and worked it out. She could always throw some jabs on the punching bag in her spare room, but it was too late and she'd promised Max she'd meet him for breakfast early in the morning.

White Rose. It had been her code name. Another life, she thought. That life had nothing to do with the one she'd carved out for herself over the last five years.

She got out of the car and walked up the sidewalk to her front door. She couldn't help but feel a burst of pride. Her sidewalk…her front porch…her home and nobody could ever take it away from her.

She would never again sleep on the street or in the shelter of a cardboard box or beneath the thick concrete of a highway overpass. She would never again go to sleep and be afraid of what the night might bring…of what the next day would bring.

Security. It's what she'd finally attained in the last five years and nobody and nothing would make her risk it. She unlocked the front door, stepped inside and disarmed the security system.

When she closed the door behind her, she knew she wasn't alone. She didn't hear a sound, smelled only the scent of lemon oil and glass cleaner from her cleaning frenzy earlier in the day, but she knew in her gut someone had either been inside recently or was still here.

The living room was dark except for a thin stream of illumination that seeped through a crack in the front curtains from a nearby street lamp.

Moving slowly, stealthily, she reached with her right hand into her pocket and pulled out the knife she'd had since she'd been thirteen years old.

The intricately carved handle fit perfectly into her palm and when she tapped the button on the side the switchblade shot out with a faint sound. Not exactly police issue, but she never left home without it.

She shifted it from her right hand to her left, grabbing the sharp point as adrenaline pumped through her. She could hit a target faster, more accurately with the knife than she could with her gun. The knife had kept her alive for many years on the streets.

Her living room was sparsely furnished, as was the

rest of the house. There was just enough light to see that there was nobody in the living room. Everything appeared to be just as she had left it when she'd gone to work at three that afternoon.

But the hair stood up on the back of her neck as she quietly advanced from the living room into the kitchen. It was darker and more difficult to discern what lie waiting in the shadows.

She stood in the doorway, willing her breathing to still, the sound of her own heartbeat to silence. Beneath the hum of the refrigerator motor she heard nothing to indicate there was another living, breathing person in the room.

Maybe she was mistaken, still charged with residual energy from the scuffle with Sammy the Snake and from receiving the unexpected communication from the agency. Maybe she was just imagining the nebulous presence of another invading her personal space.

But it had been innate instinct, intense imagination and an almost paranoid level of caution that had kept her alive until now. She'd learned through the years that when any of those three emotions went into action, it was best not to ignore them. And at the moment all three were screaming inside her.

Slowly, not making a sound, she made her way down the hall. The door to the bathroom was closed, as were the doors to the two spare bedrooms. But the door to the master bedroom at the very end of the hall stood open. She never left the doors opened.

The minute she stepped into the doorway of the bedroom she saw him…a tall dark figure standing near the window. An intruder who didn't belong in the sanctity of her home. The instinct of survival kicked in and she raised the knife to throw…at the last minute a flash of recognition altered her aim.

The knife shot through the air and hit the wall with a sharp thud. Cassie flipped on the light switch to see the handsome dark-haired man standing against the wall, the knife embedded in the Sheetrock an inch from the left of his head.

"Losing your touch?"

"Not likely. If I hadn't recognized you at the last minute your ear would be pinned against the wall. What are you doing here, Kane?"

She didn't bother to ask him how he'd entered her house. There wasn't a locked door or a security system invented that could keep Kane McNabb out if he wanted in.

He moved with a languid grace away from the window and sat on the edge of her bed. "You didn't call."

"You're right, I didn't." She walked over to her knife and pulled it out, satisfied to see that a little putty and touch-up paint would easily heal the wall wound.

"Aren't you intrigued?" Kane asked.

She turned back to face the man who had once been her partner and lover for two years. He hadn't changed much in the past five years. Like a chameleon, he had the ability to look like a debonair man of means, a disreputable drug lord or a high-ranking foreign government official. He could be whatever the agency wanted him to be. The last time she'd seen him he'd been pale, lifeless and unconscious in a hospital room bed.

Now his eyes were dark and brooding and a remembered flutter of heat ignited in the pit of her stomach. She tried to ignore it. "No, I'm not intrigued. I'm tired." She bent over and untied the laces of her black boots, then kicked them off.

"You should hear the details before you make any decision."

"I don't need to hear the details," she replied coolly. "I'm not interested…and get off my bed. In fact, get out of my house." Now that she was closer to him she could smell the scent of his familiar cologne.

To her irritation he didn't move a muscle. "We need you, Cassie. This is big…really big."

"I don't care. I told you I'm not interested. Now, get out." It was bad enough the agency wanted her back, it was sheer manipulation by them that they'd sent Kane all the way from the L.A. office to recruit her back. It made her more adamant about staying out of all of it.

He stood and moved toward the bedroom door. "So I guess it doesn't matter to you that within two months' time tens of thousands of men, women and children will probably be dead and you may be the only person on earth to stop the carnage." He shrugged. "Pleasant dreams, Cassie." He left the bedroom and she slammed the door shut behind him.

"Good riddance," she muttered as she removed her flashlight and billy club from her belt, then took off her service revolver. As she placed the knife and gun in the drawer next to her bed, she tried not to think about what he'd said.

Tens of thousands of men, women and children, and she was the only person on earth to stop the carnage. She was sure Kane had added on that last part in an effort to appeal to her ego, but it hadn't worked. The agency had hundreds of agents, including other females as effective as she was.

She sat on the edge of the bed and worked the tie out of her hair, allowing the long blond strands to spill free around her shoulders. Damn them. And damn him for intruding back into her life.

Her fingers moved to the top of her light blue uniform shirt, but instead of unbuttoning the buttons, her hands fell back into her lap. Tens of thousands of men, women and children. What could possibly be brewing in the underworld? Was it a terrorist plot of some sort? Certainly the world was ripe for such potential.

Damn them, she thought once again as she rose from the bed and yanked open the bedroom door. The scent of brewing coffee had just begun to make its way down the hall.

With a new rise of irritation welling up inside her, she followed the scent to the kitchen and turned on the light. Kane sat at the table, two cups in front of him awaiting the brew…and obviously her.

She wasn't sure what she hated more, the fact that he'd found her special stash of vanilla-flavored coffee or that he knew her so well he'd anticipated her inability to remain completely uninvolved on all levels.

She threw herself into the chair opposite his, unsure if she was angry with him or angry with herself for playing right into his hands.

"I'm not promising anything, but I'll admit, you've piqued my interest."

He nodded and stood to grab the coffee carafe. "Ever hear of Adam Mercer?" he asked as he filled their cups with the fresh brew.

"Adam Mercer?" She frowned. "Isn't he some sort of rich philanthropist?" She watched as he returned the coffee carafe to the machine. Kane moved with an almost feline grace that belied the strength and power she knew him capable of.

He returned to the chair opposite hers and wrapped a hand around his coffee mug. "Adam Mercer…fifty-four years old, wealthy as Midas and the behind the scenes leader of a grass roots coalition called MAD."

"MAD…as in Men Against Drugs?" Kane nodded and she racked her brain to think of everything she knew about that particular organization. It was easier to focus on the matter at hand than to sort out her emotions about seeing Kane again. "All I really know about the organization is that they run several shelters around town."

"They run a hell of a lot more than a few shelters,"

Kane replied. He paused a moment to take a drink of his coffee, then continued. "At the moment MAD runs dozens of shelters in cities all across the nation. They also maintain several rehabilitation centers specifically geared toward substance abuse."

"What does this all have to do with the death of thousands of men, women and children?" she asked impatiently. Kane McNabb had always liked the sound of his own voice.

"Adam Mercer and his organization has lobbied for law changes, provided drug education and paid for antidrug advertising. The agency began to monitor the group when it realized that MAD was gaining not only huge political support, but also amassing a cultlike following with the movers and shakers of the country."

"Just get to the point, please."

"Patience was never one of your strong suits." His dark eyes gave nothing of himself away. "Bottom line…three years ago Adam lost his only daughter to a drug overdose. He lost his daughter, then months after that his wife left him and we think he's gone off the deep end. The man has lost his mind to hatred and an obsessive need to wipe out all drug use."

He paused to take another sip of his coffee. "Several months ago a new kind of marijuana and cocaine hit the streets. It was called Blue…Blue grass or Blue snow…because it has a faint blue tinge to it. It's better, purer and stronger than anything that's hit the streets in years."

"I heard a couple of vice cops talking about it," she said and sat up straighter in her chair. "They said it was the most potent stuff they'd ever seen, but if I remember right, nobody ever figured out where it came from."

"A month ago it dried up. You can't find any Blue on the streets anywhere in any city right now. The demand is huge, but the supply is gone."

"So what does this have to do with Adam Mercer?"

"He supplied the original Blue, then he pulled it off the market to create an enormous demand."

Cassie stared at Kane in disbelief. "That doesn't make sense. You just told me the man is over-the-top antidrug and now you're telling me he's become a drug czar providing the best dope in America? That's crazy."

"Yeah, but there's a method behind the madness," Kane replied. He shoved his coffee mug to the side and leaned across the table toward her. "He's managed to create a huge supply of Blue and our sources tell us in the next couple of months he intends to flood the market with more Blue…except this time the drugs will be highly lethal. He'll kill the users, put the dealers out of business and rid the world of the scourge of drugs."

Cassie leaned back in her chair, stunned by the ramifications of what he'd just told her. "But that's insane," she said softly. "It's not only insane, it won't work. The minute people started dying, we'd be able to get an alert to the public about the tainted drugs."

"You know that and I know that, but apparently Mercer has lost touch with reality." Kane's dark gaze held hers. "He's crazy all right, but also highly intelligent."

"So what are you doing here talking to me?"

"We need somebody to get inside the organization...get up close and personal to Adam Mercer."

"And what makes you think I can get up close and personal with him?"

His gaze slowly slid the length of her. "Because Adam Mercer has a weakness for sexy, long-legged blondes."

The heat that had flickered to life in her stomach moments before intensified beneath his gaze. "So how would somebody go about meeting Adam Mercer?"

"Mercer frequents a nightclub called Night Life. It's an upscale kind of place and his last two relationships have been with waitresses that work there. We've got a contact there and whomever we send in will have a job as a cocktail waitress."

There was no way she was going to get roped into this, she told herself. "There are plenty of other women in the agency that can do this. I'm not interested."

She stood and carried her cup to the sink, where she emptied out the coffee, shut off the coffeemaker and turned back to him. "Get somebody else. I have a nice, uncomplicated, complete life here. I don't intend to screw it up."

"Okay, if that's the way you want it." He shrugged his broad shoulders. "I just thought maybe you'd be personally interested in this particular job."

She eyed him warily. "What do you mean...personally interested?"

He finished the last of the coffee in his cup and also stood. "Adam Mercer and his team have worked with drug addicts in this city and others for years. Sources tell us he maintains a data base with the names of all the people he's helped in the cities where MAD works. It's possible at one time or another he ran into your mother. It's possible he might have some information about both your mother and your brother."

"Get out." She was grateful her voice contained nothing more than the cold command, grateful that there was no indication of the emotions his words had stirred.

"Cassie…"

"I mean it, Kane. Get out of here now."

He placed a piece of paper on the table, then moved to the back door and grabbed the handle. "Twenty-four hours, Cassie. You have twenty-four hours to make up your mind. That's the address where you can find us." With these final words he slipped through the door.

She reset her alarm system, then stalked out of the kitchen and into the spare bedroom that held nothing but her punching bag.

She pulled on the lightweight red gloves, then the padded foot protectors. She drew several deep, cleansing breaths in an attempt to gain control of the emotions that threatened to surface.

Thoughts of her mother always brought with them a strange combination of bittersweet longing and anger. Mingling with those two emotions was a tinge of reluctant excitement as she thought of going back to work for the agency.

However, the most threatening, confusing emotions she felt at the moment concerned Kane McNabb. She'd thought she'd forgotten him. She'd worked so hard to forget everything about him. But seeing him again had forced memories back into her head…the memory of lying in his arms, of feeling his body against her own, of seeing him almost die.

She delivered a roundhouse kick to the bag, then followed it up with a flurry of punches that left her half-breathless. Damn them.

Damn them for contacting her again and for manipulating her with her past by making Kane the contact. As if it wasn't bad enough seeing him again, he'd given her the one compelling reason she'd find it difficult to say no.

Chapter 2

Cassie didn't wake up on the wrong side of the bed. She woke up on the wrong side of the world. She'd slept restlessly, her sleep filled with nightmares that weren't so much the fantasies of unconsciousness, but rather memories she'd spent her adult life trying to forget.

The morning was heralded in when her neighbor, Ralph Watters started his lawn mower. Like clockwork, every Saturday morning at precisely eight o'clock, the man began yardwork.

Cassie might have gotten used to the monotonous whir of the mower, but Ralph didn't stop there. After the mower he cranked up a weed eater and after whacking weeds to an inch of their lives, he used a high power blower to blast ever speck of grass, dirt and dog crap off his driveway and sidewalk.

Many an early Saturday Cassie had fantasized about taking that blower and blowing old Mr. Watters into the next subdivision.

She might have forgiven the man his fanatical fixa-

tion with noisy machines if he wasn't such a cantankerous old fart whose pastime was making Cassie's life
miserable.

She pulled herself out of bed to the growl of the
nearby mower and padded into the kitchen to get the
coffee started. Surely a cup of coffee and a hot shower
would help the foul mood she felt building inside her.

Moments later she stood beneath a hot spray of
water, trying to forget her late-night visitor, trying not
to remember the words Kane had spoken to her.

Drugs and death. The combination was certainly not
anything new, but the scenario Kane had painted had
been chilling.

And if that wasn't incentive enough for her to join
the team, Kane had found it necessary to dangle the car-
rot of the possibility of gaining information about her
mother and her brother.

She stepped out of the shower and, wrapped in a
towel, went back into her bedroom. Sitting on the edge
of the bed she pulled open the drawer in her nightstand.

Inside were several items…a box of tissues, a half-
eaten bag of M&M's, a manila folder filled with papers
and a small silver trinket box. It was the trinket box she
withdrew and placed on the bed next to her.

She rarely opened it, almost never took out the item
it contained, but she opened it now and stared at the thin
gold chain and gold heart-shaped locket that rested inside.

When she'd been twelve years old she'd nearly
lost her life protecting the necklace when an older

street kid had tried to take it away from her. The neck-lace was the only link she had to the mother who had abandoned her and the little brother who had called her Ci-Ci.

The teenage punk had managed to yank the chain from her neck, but he'd dropped it. When he bent down to the sidewalk to swipe it up, Cassie discovered the power she had in her legs. She'd already spent a year on the streets, alone and afraid, surviving by instincts she didn't understand and didn't question.

As the punk had bent over she'd kicked him, con-necting with his upper chest. He fell to the sidewalk, his breath whooshing out of his lungs like air from a de-pleted balloon. Pumping with adrenaline, she'd kicked him one more time in the ribs, then had scooped up her necklace and run like the wind.

She'd never had the chain fixed. It was still broken and was too small for her neck now anyway. She picked up the locket and held it for a long moment in her hand. It was cool, and yet burned her palm as if on fire.

Her mother had given it to her the week before they'd left their home in Kansas City to travel to California to start a new life. Cassie had been thrilled with the unex-pected present. Of course, she hadn't known at the time that it was a going-away present and she would even-tually be left behind while her mother, her brother and her mother's boyfriend went off into the sunset.

She opened it and stared at the two tiny photos held within. The one on the left side was of a blond woman with too much makeup and a desperate kind of hunger

in her smile. On the right was the image of a little boy
with a blond crew cut and laughing eyes.

She touched the picture of the child with her index
finger. Billy. He'd been five when her mother and her
mother's boyfriend had dumped her out of a battered
pickup on the streets of Los Angeles. The last vision
she'd had of him was of his sad little face peeking out
the grimy back window of a pickup truck.

"We'll be back in an hour." Cassie could still hear her
mother's voice as the pickup zoomed away.

Back in an hour, yeah, right. She shoved aside an
ache that never completely went away and snapped the
locket closed. She threw it into the trinket box, then
placed the box back in the drawer and slammed it shut.
That hour had stretched into forever.

For just a moment she was that child again, standing on the street corner waiting for her family to return.
She could taste the fear that had twisted up from her
stomach. She swallowed hard and shook her head to
dispel the images.

In a moment of weakness she'd told Kane about her
past. And now she hated the fact that he knew her Achil-
les' heel.

She hastily pulled on a pair of red workout shorts, a
matching sports bra and a large white tank shirt. It was
Kane's fault that she was in a foul mood since opening
her eyes this morning.

Kane McNabb was just as sinfully handsome now as
he'd been five years before. The two of them had made
a terrific team. Like synchronized swimmers, they'd

worked with one mind, swimming the waters of danger in perfect rhythm.

They'd spent two weeks in Libya posing as husband and wife scientists in an effort to learn how close Qaddafi really was to obtaining nuclear weapons. They'd pretended to be brother and sister for several weeks to infiltrate a cult in South Carolina.

Their assignments took them far away from home or as near as their own city as they took care of problems that fell through the bureaucratic cracks of other agencies.

He'd also been the best lover she'd ever had. But that was the past and the past was best left alone.

After two cups of coffee she felt lucid enough to get behind the steering wheel of her car. Max would be expecting her between now and noon for their ritual Saturday morning breakfast. If anyone could put her right with the world again it was Max Monroe.

Before she left the house, she grabbed the address that Kane had left on the table the night before and shoved it into the bottom of her tan purse.

The June sun was already hot despite the early hour as Cassie left her house by the front door. As if on cue before she could reach her red Mustang in the driveway the sound of the lawn mower came to an abrupt halt.

"Ms. Newton…Cassandra." Ralph hurried toward her, his bulldog features in a pregrowl expression.

Cassie hesitated. She had two choices…quickly jump in her car and drive away or stand and bicker with her pesky neighbor. Before she could make a choice he stood directly in front of her. Procrastination would one day be the death of her, she thought with a sigh.

"I've been trying to speak to you for the past week," Ralph exclaimed, his jowls flopping with each word. "Haven't you received any of my notes?"

About every other day for the past two weeks Ralph had been taping notes to her front door. She could wallpaper her bathroom with all the notes he'd left.

"Mr. Watters, I've read your notes, but we have nothing more to discuss." Cassie tried to keep her voice pleasant.

"I want that tree cut down." The tree he referred to was a lush sugar maple just inside her property line in the backyard. Ralph was obviously not a member of the Hug a Tree Association.

"We've been through this a dozen times. I'm not cutting down that tree." She smiled in an attempt to soften her words.

"That tree is a nuisance. It sheds seeds all over my property in the spring and leaves in the fall."

"But it's a beautiful tree and it provides wonderful shade," she replied.

"Then what about that bush?" He pointed to the bush next to her front porch.

"What about it?"

"It's dead," he exclaimed.

"It's dormant," she countered.

He snorted. "If I was that dormant they'd have me in a coffin and buried six feet under." A spot of spittle flew out of his mouth and landed on his chin. He swiped at it with the back of his hand and drew a deep breath. "I'm just trying to be a good neighbor here, you know, keep the neighborhood looking nice."

Cassie had to fight the impulse to snort back at him. "And I appreciate it. Have a nice day, Mr. Watters." Before giving him an opportunity to reply she slid into her car and started the engine with a roar.

She backed down the driveway, then threw the car into first gear and popped the clutch. Tires whined, then grabbed with a squeal as she peeled down the street.

An utterly childish display, Cassandra Marie Newton. Still, she smiled in satisfaction as she imagined Ralph's outrage at her antics. Sometimes being childish was mentally healthy.

She shoved thoughts of Ralph Watters out of her mind as she made the fifteen-minute drive from her home to Good Life Gardens, the assisted-living facility where Max lived.

Built with a flair of Spanish-flavored architecture, Good Life Gardens was an immense sprawl of buildings on twenty acres of lush, treed acreage. When Cassie had moved Max from California, it had taken her months to find a place she thought worthy of Max's presence. Good Life Gardens had lived up to her expectations.

The complex was enormous, but Max was never difficult to find. If he wasn't in his apartment, all she had to do was check the common areas, and wherever there was the biggest gathering of little old women, Max would be in the center.

Max loved the women, but Saturday mornings were

devoted to the little girl he'd met on the streets of Los Angeles, the teenager he'd taught everything he knew, the woman he loved like a daughter.

Cassie could smell the scent of cooked breakfast sausage before she reached his door. The savory scent brought back memories. The first meal Max had ever cooked for her had been sausage and eggs.

She'd been almost fourteen and after three years of living on fruit swiped from an open market and whatever could be found in Dumpsters and trash cans, those eggs and sausage had seemed like a gift from a God she'd begun to think had forgotten her.

She rapped on the door twice, then turned the knob as Max's deep voice boomed a welcome. She found him in the kitchen pulling a tray of golden-brown biscuits from the oven.

"Juice is in the fridge, coffee's made and breakfast will be ready in another ten minutes or so."

"And good morning to you, too." Cassie walked over to him and bent to plant a kiss on the top of his head.

He grinned at her. "It will be a good morning if this new egg casserole recipe lives up to its ingredients."

Cassie poured herself a tall glass of orange juice then sat at the small oak table and watched him finish the breakfast preparations.

Max Monroe, known as "Mad Max" in his Hollywood stuntman days was still handsome at almost seventy years old. His hair, so black and shiny when she'd first met him, now sported shiny strands of silver. His features were ruggedly handsome and his brown eyes snapped with the gift of laughter and an exuberant love of life.

Too many movie stunts had put him in a wheelchair. Although he wasn't paralyzed, crushed and shattered discs in his back caused him excruciating pain when he tried to stand on his feet. A yearlong bout with a whiskey bottle had made him nearly lose his mind.

He'd always said that finding Cassie had saved his life, but she knew the truth. If it hadn't been for Max Monroe Cassie would have probably been in jail, or on drugs, or a prostitute…or dead.

Although Cassie had continued to live on the streets of L.A. until she was seventeen, Max had taken her under his wing. He'd taught her everything he knew about physical strength and skill, about martial arts and achieving death-defying feats.

He'd also educated her so that she could get her GED and build something of her life. He'd been her savior and she would die for him.

They didn't speak until breakfast was ready and Max had wheeled himself to the table opposite where she sat. "You got that look," he observed as he passed her the plate of biscuits.

"What look?"

"You know, the one where you look like you want to tear somebody's head off and spit down their neck. Old Ralph giving you a hard time again?" he guessed correctly.

Cassie laughed, already feeling her foul mood transforming into something more positive. "The man is relentless." She pulled apart a biscuit and began to slather each half with butter. "Out of all the neighborhoods in Kansas City, out of all the people I could live next to, I get Mr. Rogers with an attitude."

Max laughed and shoved the plate of sausage patties closer to her. "You take the man too seriously."

"Too seriously? He wants me to cut down that beautiful tree in my backyard. Now this morning he asked me what I was going to do about one of the bushes by my front porch."

"You mean that dead bush?"

"It's dormant, not dead."

Max raised an eyebrow and eyed her wryly. "He's a lonely old man."

"Maybe he wouldn't be so lonely if he wasn't such a pain in the neck," she retorted.

The last of her irritation faded as they began to eat and indulged in small talk. Max told her about his lady friends and the most recent social activities he'd attended and she talked about her plans to redecorate her living room.

It was the kind of benign chatter between two old friends that was comforting in its utter banality.

It wasn't until they were clearing the table that Cassie decided it was time to move out of the small talk arena and into what was really on her mind. "I had a late-night visitor last night."

Max made no reply. He knew her well enough to know she'd tell him what she wanted him to know in her own time.

"I thought it was a burglar and almost took his nose

off with my knife, but it was Kane." Even just saying his name aloud caused a wistful regret to sweep through her.

"Been a long time," Max said.

"Yes, it has." She sighed. "The agency wants me back."

Max motioned toward the coffeepot. "Pour us each a cup and let's go into the living room and you can tell me all about it." He disappeared out of the small kitchen.

Cassie poured the two cups of coffee and followed Max into the bright, airy living room. One entire wall held an entertainment system that contained a huge television set and Max's movie collection.

In the sixties and seventies Max had worked as a stuntman in over a hundred action-adventure and Western films. No matter how small or large his part, he owned a copy of every movie he'd ever been in.

The little old ladies who lived in the complex loved movie night when they all gathered in a great room and watched one of Max's movies as he narrated his part in the film.

Cassie set his coffee cup on the tray next to where he sat, then placed her own on the coffee table. But she didn't sit. Talking about Kane, talking about the agency made her far too restless.

"Tell me," Max said as she paced back and forth before him. "What do they want from you?"

Briefly she told Max what Kane had told her the night before, about Adam Mercer, his suspected plans and his deadly drug called Blue. It sounded just as crazy now as it had when Kane had explained it to her the night before. It sounded so crazy it had a terrifying ring of truth to it.

Max listened without expression, occasionally taking a sip of his coffee and nodding his head. "So what exactly do they want from you?" he asked when she'd finished.

"They want me to go undercover, get close to Adam Mercer and find out when and where the tainted drug shipment is to arrive." She flopped down on the sofa.

Max finished the last sip of coffee and set his cup down. "I wish you were still doing stunt work. I'd worry much less about you."

She smiled at him affectionately. "You know I just did those movies to pay for college. I never really wanted to be a movie stuntwoman," she replied. Between her eighteenth and her twenty-first birthday, Cassie had done stunt work in a number of movies thanks to Max's training. "You know my goal was always to be a cop."

"I know, but you would have been one of the best stuntwomen in the business." Max shook his head, his eyes filled with reflections of the past. "I'll never forget that first time I saw you. I'd heard about you for weeks. All the security guards were talking about the kid who kept sneaking onto the lot."

Cassie smiled at the memory. Max had been working as a stunt coordinator on a movie on the Embassy Pictures studio lot where Cassie had been hanging out.

She loved the lot, where magic abounded in warehouses filled with furniture and scene backdrops, old costumes and various props. Although security was tight around the lot, Cassie always managed to find a way inside.

She'd watch the action as the various movie scenes were shot, join the lunch lines for the hearty fare served in the cafeteria and pretend to be one of the extras until somebody caught on to her. Then she'd scamper like a rat, afraid that if she were caught, afraid that if somebody found out she had no parents, no home, she'd be sent to a foster home. She had heard too many horror stories about foster care from other kids living on the streets to want to try that avenue.

"That first time I saw you running down the lot, then darting into that alley and climbing the fence like a monkey, I knew you were something special. You had physical abilities I'd only dreamed of possessing."

She smiled. "And the first time I saw you I thought you were some kind of pervert trying to pick me up for nefarious activities."

Max laughed again then sobered and clasped his hands together in his lap. "Don't forget, it was your stunt work that brought you to the attention of the agency."

"I know." She frowned thoughtfully. It hadn't just been her stunt work alone that had brought her to the attention of SPACE. She'd just finished the police academy and was enrolled in criminology courses at the community college when a man from SPACE had contacted her about working for them.

"So when do you start?"

She stood once again. "I haven't decided if I'm going to do it yet."

"Yes, you have." He smiled, the smile of a man who knew her too well. "If you hadn't already decided to work with the agency, you wouldn't have told me about any of it."

He was right. She walked over to the sliding glass doors that led out onto a tiny patio. Beyond the patio was a tall wooden privacy fence.

She stared at the fence for a long moment as she contemplated going back to work for SPACE. She knew the kind of calculation that went into each assignment the agency made. If they had tapped her it was because they believed she was the best agent for this particular job.

She was a cop, sworn to protect her community and this was even bigger than her community. How could she turn her back and walk away? The possibility that she might discover something about her mother and brother's whereabouts would be a nice by-product.

"Kane thinks it's possible Adam Mercer might have information about my mother," she finally said.

"Is that possible?"

She turned from the sliding door to face Max. "I suppose. We know that ten years ago she left California and came back here to her roots. We also know that she was arrested on possession charges here in Kansas City. But no one has heard from her since. I'd say it's quite likely she and Adam Mercer could have crossed paths at one point or another, though. It's also a rumor that Mercer keeps records of all the addicts he helps."

"Then you have to do this, Cassie," Max said. "You might finally get the answers you've been seeking."

"Maybe." She knew better than to get her hopes up. She'd gone into police work in the first place in the hopes that the job might help her find her missing family. She needed to know that they were okay, especially the baby brother she'd adored.

She'd hired a private investigator just last year to try to find her mother and brother, but his search had yielded no results. Even though she was angry with her mother's choices, she needed to know why she'd been thrown away.

"You'll never be completely at peace until you resolve the issues from your childhood."

"Have you been watching Dr. Phil again?" she teased.

"You need to heal the wounds of your inner child."

"Okay, enough already."

"You also need to resolve your feelings where Kane is concerned. You need closure on several levels," Max finished.

Cassie wanted to argue with him, to tell him that he was espousing a bunch of psychobabble. But his words shot straight to her heart, to all the wounded areas that existed inside her, and as much as she hated to admit it, she knew he was right.

Chapter 3

Cassie compared the address on the slip of paper Kane had left her to the one on the front of the downtown brick six-story building. The addresses were the same although the sign on the building proclaimed the establishment on the ground level to be Eddie's Employment Agency. The floors above the employment agency appeared to be empty.

The building was in an area of Kansas City that hadn't yet seen the efforts of revitalization of the downtown area. The buildings on either side appeared abandoned, storefronts boarded with plywood that sported the usual colorful and obscene graffiti.

The street was relatively deserted considering it was just after noon, but she wasn't surprised that SPACE would choose this kind of area for a mobile base.

During the four years that Cassie had worked with the agency, she'd frequented a number of "fronts" in a number of cities used for conducting business. They were usually set up in areas where there was little foot traffic and where it wasn't unusual for stores to appear and disappear in short time.

It had been explained to Cassie at her recruitment that because much of what SPACE did pertained to national security and many of the agents found it necessary to work outside of the law, the agency was top secret.

The agency had been dealing more and more with domestic matters following 9/11, while other agencies like the CIA and FBI focused more on terrorists.

Cassie didn't know where the home office of the agency was, but she suspected it was somewhere in Washington, D.C. She'd always worked out of mobile offices like the one she had just left.

In truth, she knew very little about the agency, although Kane had once told her part of the history. It had begun in the mid-eighties as one of many covert agencies run by the government to deal with problems both foreign and domestic that might need special handling. The agents didn't have to worry about the restrictions that often bound the hands of law enforcement and were highly trained both physically and mentally for all circumstances.

Cassie wasn't sure how their recruitment ordinarily worked. She'd come to the attention of somebody because of her stunt work in several movies. Apparently an extensive background check had been run on her and they liked what they saw. It didn't hurt that she had no family. In fact, Kane had told her the agency preferred their operatives to have no families.

Ancient history and in a few minutes she would be back in the fold of the agency she'd left behind.

She remained in the car for a long moment, staring at the old brick building. It wasn't too late to change her mind, to turn her car around and forget everything that Kane had told her the night before.

She could go back to her ordinary life, arresting bad guys, bickering with her cantankerous neighbor and having breakfast with Max.

All she'd have to worry about were the nightmares that would plague her as she thought of the danger hitting the streets in the form of a deadly drug.

In truth, she had no choice. She hated nightmares.

She got out of her car and approached the building, aware that once she opened the door and walked inside the relatively peaceful life she'd built for herself would be transformed into something much different.

The interior looked like a hundred other employment agencies. Plastic orange chairs lined one wall, a table provided a place to fill out applications and a water cooler occasionally gurgled from its position in one corner.

A receptionist at a small metal desk looked up from the magazine she'd been reading. "Hi, can I help you?"

"I'd like to fill out an application," Cassie said.

At that moment a door behind the receptionist's desk opened and a tall gray-haired man stepped into view. "Cassie, it's good to see you."

"Hello, Greg." Cassie smiled at Greg Cole, the man who had recruited her into the agency years ago.

"Why don't you come on back. I've been hoping you'd show up."

A sense of déjà vu filled Cassie as she followed him down a long hallway and into a private office. He motioned her into one of the two chairs that faced a large, mahogany desk.

She sank down in one of the chairs, suddenly feeling much like she had nine years ago when she'd had her first private meeting with Greg. Excitement and anxiety battled each other inside her as she waited for Greg to get settled in the chair behind the desk.

Once he was seated, he smiled at her again. "You look good, Cassie."

"It's all that good, clean normal living I've been doing," she replied and felt herself begin to relax. The old, familiar excitement was quickly taking over the anxiety. She recognized that she was not only back with the agency physically, but emotionally as well.

Greg Cole was a distinguished-looking man about fifty years old. With his steel-gray hair and blue eyes, clad in a three-piece tailored pale gray suit he looked like he'd come from the same mold as a thousand other successful businessmen.

But Cassie had seen Greg put a bullet between the eyes of a paid assassin yards away. She'd seen him scale a twenty-foot fence like a monkey climbing a tree. Greg was much more than a man behind a desk pushing papers.

"Something is agreeing with you," he said. "We've heard good things about you since you've been away from us. Eight commendations, a folder full of civilian praise for you and a stellar record that proves you're better than most police officers."

So they'd kept tabs on her since she'd left the agency. Somehow she wasn't surprised. "I try to be the best at what I do."

"You were one of the best agents we ever had when it came to working the streets."

That had been Cassie's specialty. Her early experiences on the streets of L.A. had given her an insight into the language, the nuances, the underbelly of that world that few people truly understood.

It was something that couldn't be taught, but had to be experienced and it was part of what had made her valuable to the agency. She'd been useful in information gathering from the streets, able to tap into gangs, drug dealers and weapon deals by knowing who to listen to and what to say.

"You know what they say, you can take the girl off the street, but you can't take the street out of the girl," she said.

"I don't know about that, you manage to clean up pretty well." Greg's smile not only held genuine affection, but respect as well.

During the time she had worked for the agency, Greg had always been the superior she reported to and she'd never doubted the man's integrity and belief in all the agency stood for. She hadn't left because she didn't believe in their work. She'd left before she could completely destroy one of their top men.

However, she also knew that Greg's loyalty was to the agency and agents were expendable when it came to protecting SPACE.

He leaned back in the chair and patted his breast pocket absently. Cassie smiled, realizing the pocket that had always held a pack of cigarettes was empty. "How long since you quit?"

"Six months, but old habits die hard. Kane filled you in?" She nodded and Greg continued. "It's an insidious plot devised by a devious man."

"Sounds like a nutcase with a nutty plan," she said.

"Perhaps, but it's a mistake to go into this and think Adam Mercer is just your garden variety nut. He's far too intelligent, far too resourceful to be written off so easily."

A knock on the door interrupted the conversation. "Come in," Greg called and Cassie half turned in her chair to see Kane enter the room.

Instantly she felt every muscle in her body tense. She hadn't expected him to be here.

"Cassie," he said and nodded in her direction, then took the chair next to hers. She nodded back at him, then returned her attention to Greg.

Shock had gotten her through last night's unexpected meeting with him but seeing him again now brought forth feelings she hadn't expected...or wanted.

There was that initial blaze of physical attraction that had always burned inside her for him. It was an attraction built not only on the mysterious forces that worked between a man and a woman, but also on memories of their explosive lovemaking and the intimacies they had once shared. But she also felt guilt…for what had happened on their last assignment. And for leaving him and the agency behind.

"Kane, now that you're here we can all go over the game plan," Greg said.

She shot a quick glance at Kane who, despite being seated, radiated with an underlying taut energy. He didn't return her gaze. Kane smelled the same as she remembered, a wonderful blend of wildness and spice. But she didn't remember his eyes being as dark, as brooding as they were now.

"We have to stop this shipment." Greg looked at Kane, then to Cassie.

She shook her head ruefully. "It seems strange. You're asking me to save the people who under normal circumstances I'd be arresting…drug users and dealers."

"That's true and yes, we find ourselves in an unusual position here. But it isn't just the guilty we're trying to protect. Innocent lives will be affected if this drug gets on the market. We're talking about first-time users, college students who succumb to peer pressure, even kids who mistakenly get hold of it."

"We can worry about the dope dealers and users later," Kane said. "Right now the man we need to get off the streets is Adam Mercer."

"Why aren't the local authorities taking care of this?" Cassie asked. She'd never been certain what criteria were used to determine if the agency would get involved.

"We took it over due to the special circumstances of the potential for thousands of deaths," Greg explained. "We're coordinating with DEA."

"Okay, so what's the plan?" Kane asked.

As Greg outlined how it would go down, what would be expected of her and the dangers, Cassie wondered what Kane was thinking.

He'd always been difficult to read, but there had been a time when he'd shared more of himself with her than she suspected he ever had anyone else. And she'd simply turned her back on him and walked away. He had to hate her now…or maybe their relationship had never meant enough to him to warrant that kind of intense emotion.

She'd halfway hoped that he was simply the contact man and would have nothing else to do with the actual operation. But the fact that he was here told her she'd have to work directly with Kane. They couldn't fix old wounds now. Not after all this time.

She focused her full attention back on Greg. "One thing you have to understand, Cassie. You'll be deep undercover and that means little or no backup."

"I understand that," she replied.

"You sure you're up to it?" Kane asked. "I mean, it's been a long time since you've played this kind of game."

Her back stiffened as she sensed him questioning her competency. "I'm in better shape physically and mentally now than I've ever been. Just because I haven't played the game in a while doesn't mean I've forgotten how to play."

"Then you're in?" Greg asked.

"I'm in."

"Kane will be your contact. Is that going to be a problem?"

For the first time Kane looked at her and in his dark gaze she thought she saw the hint of challenge. "No problem here," he said.

"Fine with me," she replied and looked back at Greg.

"Good, then we're set to begin." Once again Greg went over the plans, detailing the work that would be done before Cassie went undercover.

It was nearly two hours later when she left Eddie's Employment Agency and headed for the station house. She needed to arrange for time off her job, which shouldn't be a problem as she had plenty of vacation time accrued.

She knew that within the next couple of hours Eddie's Employment Agency would be shut down. All the equipment would be moved and there would be no evidence that a business had been there.

She pulled into the parking lot behind the station house but remained in her car.

She'd have to come up with a logical reason for requesting time off. If she didn't, Asia would wonder what was going on and she knew how relentless her partner could be if he smelled any kind of a mystery.

A rush of adrenaline filled her as the full realization of what she'd agreed to hit her. White Rose was back in action.

Kane sat in a car parked in the lot of a Motel 6 located on the north side of Kansas City. He tapped his fingers on the steering wheel then checked his watch.

Quarter until eight. Another fifteen minutes and she should arrive at this location. He'd never known Cassie to be late.

He leaned back against the headrest and thought of the woman who had been his partner five years ago.

Cassandra Newton had been the best partner he'd ever had. She'd not only been exceptionally bright, but tough as nails as well. She had amazing physical ability. She could punch like a man, kick like a kangaroo, and had moves that would made Jackie Chan turn green with envy.

She was almost as deadly with a gun as she was with her knives and she had a natural cunning that made her a survivor. She'd been a hell of a partner. She'd been the one lover he hadn't been able to forget.

He leaned forward and switched the air-conditioner fan from low to high, his thoughts still consumed by Cassie. He'd kept tabs on her over the past five years even though he knew if she found this out she'd despise him for it.

He knew she liked her toast light, her pizza with mushrooms and her coffee black. He knew she worked out at a gym near her home four or five times a week, that she'd received nearly a dozen commendations as a police officer and that she hadn't dated anyone in the five years since they'd been together.

He knew all that about her, but he didn't know why she'd walked out on him and the agency when he'd needed her most. An edge of anger rose up inside him and he consciously shoved it aside. He couldn't let their past complicate the job they had to do now.

The streak of color he'd enjoyed in the sky lasted only minutes, then was gone in the purple shades of early night. There were only a few cars parked in the spaces in front of the motel rooms. Business wasn't booming for this particular motel.

He tapped his fingers once again on the steering wheel as he waited impatiently for her to show up.

He hadn't wanted to bring her back in. She'd managed to do what so many agents found impossible…build a normal life as a productive citizen. He hadn't wanted to screw things up for her, pluck her from her ordinary existence and place her into danger.

However, Cole had insisted that she was the right woman, the only woman for this particular job. Kane knew there was nothing Cole would like better than to pull Cassie back into the fold, to get out of her "retirement" and working once again for the agency.

But, Kane had to admit, Cassie was the best woman for this job. She was not only Adam Mercer's type, but she knew the city. If she was going to work it, then Kane wouldn't allow any other agent to work with her but him. He knew her. He knew how she thought, how she worked. He knew her strengths and her weaknesses. There was no way he'd allow any other man to back her up.

Deep in his heart, he'd known she would take the job. Cassie was an adrenaline junkie. In this they were on the same wavelength. And if that hadn't been incentive enough to bring her on board, he'd known the information about her family would entice her. He'd felt guilty about using that particular card to get her back into the game but he knew it was a shoe-in.

When she'd first joined the agency a search had been conducted for the mother who had abandoned her and the brother she'd never seen again. But even the agency, with its far-reaching tentacles and information highways couldn't find the scent of a ghost.

He sat up straighter in his seat as he saw Cassie's red Mustang approach, then turn into the parking lot. She pulled up in front of room 115 just as she'd been instructed and parked.

She slid out of the car, her long blond ponytail keeping time with her subtle hip movement as she strode from the car to the door of the motel room. She carried nothing with her but the motel room key, but he knew beneath her short skirt and blouse she had no less than two knives hidden. Cassie never went anywhere without her knives.

He knew the minute she spied him. Her gaze met his, then slid away as if she didn't know him. But her back stiffened and her gait appeared less fluid.

Working with her again was going to be both exhilarating and torturous. She was the most complicated woman he'd ever known, independent and competent and yet exuding a vulnerability that she seemed unaware of and would anger her if she became aware of it.

Working with her again would have been so much easier if they hadn't shared a past…an intense past both as partners and lovers.

She didn't seem to suffer any regrets about walking away from him. In the brief time he'd seen her two nights ago in her apartment and again yesterday in Cole's mobile office, she'd been cool and collected.

Again a burn of anger built inside him, but he forced it down. There was no place for anger…or any other kind of emotion where she was concerned. Emotion was dangerous. He had to remember that, it might make the difference between life and death.

As she disappeared into the motel room, he shut off the engine of his car and got out. It was just after eight but the lateness of the hour hadn't done much to ease the heat and humidity of the day. Early June and already records were being broken. July would be a killer unless the current weather pattern broke.

From the trunk of his car he removed a suitcase, then headed toward the motel room where Cassie would be staying for the next couple of days.

If Cassie thought this was going to be all business, she was in for a shock. Because he still had questions she'd never answered. Questions that would finally let him close the door on their past.

Let the games begin.

Chapter 4

Cassie stepped into the motel room and looked around, knowing she had only moments before Kane would come in. A quick glance around the room showed it to be like any other budget motel room in the city.

Two beds covered with identical shabby gold spreads, shag carpeting that was probably older than Cassie's thirty years. A small table took up the space of one corner and a television was bolted to the top of a set of dresser drawers.

This would be her home for the next couple of days, until Kane deemed her ready for the undercover task ahead of her. She would not be lounging in bed and ordering up room service. She would be spending her time learning everything there was to know about Adam Mercer and whatever persona they had chosen for her to become.

She heard a brisk knock on the door. Kane. She drew a deep breath, steeling herself for what lay ahead and opened the door.

He breezed past her and dropped the suitcase he carried on top of the bed closest to the door. She closed and locked the door behind him, then turned to face him.

"Ready to begin?" he asked.

No hello, no how are you. All business. If that's the way he wanted it, fine with her. "Whenever you are," she replied. She sat in one of the chairs at the tiny round table in the corner of the room.

He opened the suitcase and withdrew a thick manila folder. "You took care of what you needed to in order to disappear for an extended period of time?"

She nodded. "I'm on vacation with the police force and I told my partner that I was leaving town to chase down a lead on my mother and didn't know when I'd return."

Kane tossed the folder onto the top of the table and sat down in the chair opposite her. "Everything you need to know about Adam Mercer and everything you need to know about Jessica Sinclair."

"Jessica Sinclair?"

"That's your cover. You need to learn everything in that folder backward and forward. I don't need to tell you that your life might depend on it."

The file was thick, filled with information she'd need to know as well as she knew her own name. "How long do I have before I go in?" she asked.

"Three days. You'll spend three days here memorizing those things, getting into character, then we'll move you to your new living quarters and you'll start your new waitress job at Night Life on Saturday night."

He pulled a new cell phone from his pocket and placed it on the table. "I'll be your only contact. Speed dial one to connect with me day or night. The phone is legit and registered under the name of Jessica Sinclair."

His eyes were dark, enigmatic as he gazed at her. "For the next three days you're going to be dependent on me for everything. I'll bring you your meals and whatever else you might need while you're here."

She hated this part, the utter dependency on anyone and especially this person. But she also knew the necessity for it. Before she could respond to him, a knock sounded at the door.

"That must be Carolyn," he said. He got up, ignoring the question on Cassie's face.

He opened the door to allow in a short, squat dark-haired middle-aged woman carrying two small suitcases. She set the suitcases just inside the door and threw herself into Kane's arms. "Kane, my darling man, it's been too long. You're just as handsome as ever." She gave his cheek a playful love slap.

"Carolyn, you little bundle of dynamite, you make my heart pound with desire," he replied, causing the plump woman to giggle like a schoolgirl.

Kane had the capacity to charm a nun into bad habits…or out of her habit when he wanted. Of course, in the time Cassie had spent with him so far there had been none of his easy charm directed at her.

And that's the way I want it, she reminded herself. Strictly business, the way it should have been when they'd worked together before.

"Carolyn, this is Cassie Newton," Kane said as Cassie stood. "Cassie, this is Carolyn McIntyre, makeup artist extraordinaire."

"Oh, my, Cassie Newton, it's such a pleasure to meet you." Carolyn grabbed both Cassie's hands in hers and squeezed tightly, her eyes sparkling in obvious admiration. "I've heard so much about you from people in the agency. You're a legend."

Cassie laughed with a touch of self-consciousness. "I don't know about that, but it's nice to meet you, too, Carolyn."

"Carolyn is going to give you a makeover," Kane said. "You've spent time on the streets in your job as a police officer. It's her job to make you look different enough that nobody will recognize you as Cassandra Newton or Officer Newton."

Carolyn reached up and grabbed Cassie by the chin, her green eyes narrowed in concentration as she turned Cassie's face first one way, then the other. "Good bone structure…nice skin…we'll have to do something about the eyes and the hair, both are too distinctive."

Carolyn whipped around to face Kane. "Out," she said and pointed to the door. "No good artist ever works in front of an audience."

Kane opened his mouth to protest, but Carolyn was having nothing to do with it. She grabbed him by the arm and propelled him toward the door. She moved like a minitank, with determination and purpose, not stopping until Kane was out the door. "Come back in three hours or so and you can see the finished result."

Three hours? What in the heck did the woman intend to do to her? Cassie wondered.

Carolyn turned back to face Cassie and rubbed her hands together in a gesture of extreme anticipation. "Now, we get to work."

Was it Cassie's imagination or did Carolyn have the slightly demented look of a mad scientist?

Two and a half hours later Cassie stood in the bathroom in front of the mirror and stared at the reflection of a stranger.

Carolyn wasn't just an artist, she was a wizard and had managed to transform Cassie into someone else.

Gone was her trademark long ponytail. Instead her hair had been cut to shoulder length and feathered around her face in a sort of long shag.

Contact lenses changed her eye color from blue to deep green and the makeup Carolyn had applied had subtly changed the shape of her face, giving her higher cheekbones and a slightly exotic look.

While Carolyn had worked, she'd chattered nonstop about skin and hair care. "Never sleep in your makeup," she said. "No matter how late it is, no matter how tired you are, always clean your makeup off to let your pores breathe."

Cassie was about to go undercover on an assignment where the stakes were high and a mistake could mean her life and Carolyn was worried about her having clean facial pores.

Still, even though the woman had chattered like teeth

on an icy night, she knew her business. Cassie didn't look like Cassie, but she had to admit, she liked the new look.

The bathroom, on the other hand, looked like a war zone. Carolyn had pronounced herself an artist, and apparently her palette was not only Cassie's face but also anything in a ten-foot radius.

Base powder speckled the sink, along with an array of various eye-shadow colors. A contact lens hung on the faucet, like an errant eye glaring askew. It had taken Cassie twenty minutes to finally get the hang of putting something foreign in her eyes.

The remnants of her hair littered the floor, looking one-dimensional and boring compared to the silver highlights Carolyn had added to her new do.

Yes, Carolyn had done a heck of a job, but apparently cleanup wasn't in her job description. Cassie had managed to tidy up most of the sink when she heard the door to the motel open, then close.

She turned and saw Kane entering the room. He walked to the doorway of the bathroom, stopped abruptly and stared at her. "Amazing," he said softly. "You look absolutely amazing."

For just a moment his gaze felt hot…hungry on her and heat ignited deep within her. But as quickly as it had appeared, the look in his eyes disappeared and a cold, hard darkness took its place. "At least nobody should recognize you unless they know you pretty well."

He turned and walked over to the bed and once again opened the suitcase he'd brought in with him earlier in the evening. "You'll find everything you need for the next couple of days here…pajamas, clean clothing and toiletries. If there's anything else you specially need or want, let me know and I'll see that you get it."

"All right."

"It's late. I'm going to get out of here and let you get a good night's sleep." He motioned toward the folder on the table. "You have a lot of work ahead of you." He moved to the motel room door and opened it. "I'll be back first thing in the morning. And Cassie…welcome back." With these words he turned and left the room.

Welcome back, indeed, she thought. She walked to the door and locked it then peeked out the heavy, puke-green curtains. What was it about motel rooms and that particular color of green?

Her car was gone, magically taken away to erase any connection between Jessica Sinclair and Cassandra Newton. In place of her sweet little red Mustang was a banged-up blue Escort. She'd miss her little muscle car, just like she had a feeling she would miss her old life before this was all over.

She turned away from the window and sat on the bed next to the suitcase. She didn't want to think of Kane, but she couldn't help it. His familiar scent still lingered in the room, haunting her with memories of their shared past.

They'd begun their relationship as partners, two committed people working for the good of the country. They'd flown to exotic locations, worked both in squalor and in splendor. By the end of that second year of their partnership, their relationship had become personal.

It had been a tumultuous affair, filled with the danger of their jobs and an explosive passion neither had been able to deny. The most difficult thing she'd ever done in her life was walk away from him. But she was determined that she stay personally removed from him.

The air-conditioner unit in the wall clicked on and began a loud hum. She opened the suitcase to see what was inside. As Kane had said, she found clean, comfortable clothing, the usual toiletries and a cotton nightshirt. All in her size. In the bottom of the case she found a tube of pear-scented moisturizing body cream.

He'd remembered.

She clutched the bottle to her heart and closed her eyes. A well of emotion pressed tightly in her chest. One of her nightly rituals was to apply the sweet-scented cream to her arms and legs. It touched her more than she cared to admit.

She tossed the tube on the nightstand and stood, eyeing the folder that sat waiting for her on the table. Better to focus on work than on her softening resolve to keep her work with Kane strictly professional.

"Where did you go to high school?" Kane barked the question from his position in a chair at the table.

Cassie paced back and forth in front of her unmade bed, thinking that he sounded like a drill sergeant. "Lincoln High school," she replied.

"What was your mother's name?"

"Mary…Mary Sinclair and my father was Joseph.

They died in a car accident when I was eighteen and my brother, Jimmy, was eight."

"What was your address in Des Moines?"

Cassie stopped her pacing, frozen as she drew a blank. She stared at Kane with frustration.

"Bang, you're dead," he said.

He was right. It was the kind of lapse in memory that got you killed when you went undercover. She sank down on the edge of the bed, exhausted both mentally and physically. They'd been at it for the past three hours, Kane firing questions and her answering.

"You're right," she said tiredly.

"We'll take a break, eat some dinner, then start again."

She wanted to protest. What she really wanted to do was curl up in bed and sleep for about ten hours. She'd stayed up most of the night studying the information in the file, then had gotten up before dawn to study some more.

"I feel like a college student cramming for finals," she said.

He rose from his chair. "Yeah, but in this case if you flunk your final, you might lose your life."

"I know…I know."

"So what are you hungry for?"

"I don't care as long as it isn't another hamburger." He'd brought her a burger and fries for lunch. "Surprise me."

She immediately wanted to call the words back as a muscle in his jaw ticked and his eyes darkened.

"I'll be back," he said and left the room.

Cassie rubbed the center of her forehead where a headache threatened to take hold. Surprise me. How many times in their past relationship had they said those words to each other…a hundred? A thousand?

"If we get out of this alive, want me to tell you what I'm going to do to you?" he whispered when they'd been trapped in a cooler on a ship smuggling explosives to the Philippines and left to die.

"No, don't tell me. Surprise me," she'd replied.

"Want to know what I'm going to do with you when we get back to your place?" he'd asked, his eyes lit with fires that had burned her from the inside out.

"Surprise me," she'd whispered breathlessly.

She now got up and began to pace once again in an attempt to erase the past from her mind. So far, Kane certainly hadn't acknowledged that they'd shared any kind of a past. He hadn't asked her why she'd left. He apparently had moved on.

It was important that she do the same.

All she had to do was get through these three days in the motel room. After that she'd be undercover and immersed in the job. There would be no time for thoughts of Kane, no time for entertaining any regrets that might plague her even temporarily.

He was back within twenty minutes, bringing with him Chinese takeout. He opened the containers as she got out the paper plates and chopsticks.

Moments later they were seated at the table across from each other, eating in silence that quickly became oppressive and heavy.

"Has the agency kept you busy in the last couple of years?" she asked, unable to stand the silence any longer.

"Fairly busy." He speared a piece of sweet and sour chicken with one chopstick. Cassie swallowed a smile. He was adroit at almost everything else, but had never mastered the art of chopsticks.

"Domestic or foreign?" she asked, trying to draw him into something that resembled a normal conversation.

"Both. Did you follow the Brahm's case?"

"The guy in New York selling arms to Iraq?"

He nodded. "We were in on that. It took almost a year to build the case."

"Tell me about it," she urged, eager to keep the silence at bay.

To her relief, he did. As he told her the details of the operation that had taken place two years before, his eyes lit with animation and he appeared to relax.

Cassie found herself relaxing as well as the tension between them disappeared at least for the moment. As Kane explained the various operations he'd been a part of for the past five years, Cassie asked questions to keep him talking.

She had always enjoyed Kane when he spoke with passion and conviction, and that's what he exhibited whenever he talked about the job. The darkness left his eyes and his features softened.

Clad in a pair of tight jeans and a black T-shirt, there was a look of danger about him. His dark hair was carelessly mussed, but that only added to his attractiveness.

As he filled her in on his work over the last five years, she found herself wondering about his personal life. He told her where he'd been and what he'd done for the job, but he didn't mention anything about the days, weeks and months that he wasn't working on an operation or in recovery from his bullet wound.

When they'd been together, they'd spent much of their off time in Hawaii indulging in their passion not only for each other, but for scuba diving.

"You still diving on your downtime?" she asked.

With that simple question she shattered the mood. Shutters dropped over his eyes and he shoved his plate away from in front of him. "No, and that's enough idle chatter. Time to get back to work."

If she thought he'd been relentless in his drilling of her before, there was a new intensity now. He fired question after question at her, his expression revealing satisfaction when she answered and disapproval when she faltered.

He was a hard taskmaster, pushing her harder and harder until she finally cried uncle. "Enough," she said and collapsed on her bed. "That's enough for tonight. I'm exhausted and my brain shut off about an hour ago."

"Actually, an hour and a half ago according to my assessment."

To her surprise, one corner of his lips curved upward in a half smile. It was like a gift after their grueling hours of work.

She felt herself responding to his smile, not just with

a smile of her own but with a warmth that suffused her entire body.

"You did better than I expected with just a night of study," he said as he got up stiffly from his chair and stretched his arms over his head. "I have no doubt at all that by Saturday morning you'll be ready to go."

"I appreciate the vote of confidence," she said, pleasantly surprised by his words.

"I've never doubted your abilities when it comes to the job." He dropped his arms and held her gaze. She held her breath as she waited for him to say something more. There were unspoken words in his tired eyes and her heart quickened as a new tension sprang up between them.

"I'll see you in the morning," he finally said, then opened the door and disappeared out into the night.

She locked the door behind him, then took a long hot shower and pulled on her short-sleeved nightshirt. She kept her mind carefully blank as she sat on the edge of the bed and applied the lotion to her arms, legs and throat. The scent of pears filled the air and her heart filled with a loneliness she hadn't experienced in years.

As she crawled into bed and shut off the light, the air conditioner kicked on. As she listened to the monotonous hum, the loneliness swelled inside her.

It wasn't an emotion she'd experienced often in her life. She could only remember two other times. The first had been on that initial day and night she'd found herself alone on the streets of L.A. At eleven years old she hadn't understood the deep ache and in any case it hadn't lasted as the need to survive was far more important.

The second time she'd experienced this kind of lonely had been in the days and weeks after she'd walked away from Kane and the agency that had brought them together.

Even though she'd known she'd made the best choice for herself and for him, that didn't stop her from missing him. She'd missed his smell, the cast of his smile and the way he looked at her when he wanted her.

She'd missed him, but she'd gotten over it. She'd gotten over him.

Maybe she was just feeling lonely because she missed her house, her things and her life. Surely it was a temporary emotion and would go away once this crazy job was done. The job, yes, that's what she needed to focus on. Getting it done without getting killed, then forgetting Kane and the agency for good.

With this reassuring thought in mind, Cassie fell into an exhausted sleep.

Chapter 5

"Go away!" Cassie shouted the words from her comfortable burrow in the bed. The room was dark and her sleep had been dreamless and she sure wasn't in the mood to face a new day.

The irritating knock fell again on her door and she fought the impulse to grab one of her knives, throw it, and see if she could impale Kane's fist on the other side of the door. It would be wasted effort. Even if she succeeded he'd only knock again with his other hand.

"All right, all right," she yelled and pulled herself upright in the bed. She looked at the clock, shocked to discover it was almost ten. She'd grown quite fond of the puke-green curtains that blocked the light of day in the early mornings.

She stumbled from the bed and to the door. She unlocked the chain and bolt, opened it to see Kane, then turned and hurried into the bathroom. She didn't want to hang around and greet him in her nightshirt.

Shock rippled through her as she saw her reflection in the mirror. She still wasn't used to the new look.

At the moment it wasn't the new look that startled her, it was the fact that she looked like a zombie.

Red eyes stared back at her from the mirror, eyes that felt gritty from lack of sleep. The T-shirt she'd slept in bore tomato sauce testimony of the 2:00 a.m. piece of pizza she'd both eaten and managed to slop down the front of her.

For the past twenty-four hours she'd been on a marathon cram session, but unlike college students who crammed for an exam, she hadn't resorted to junk food and caffeine pills to keep the adrenaline flowing. As far as she was concerned pizza wasn't junk food and massive quantities of liquid coffee beat pills any day of the week.

Yesterday had been like the day before, with Kane spending hours in the room drilling her with questions about the woman she was about to become and about Adam Mercer. He'd been relentless, cold and demanding as a drill sergeant.

Under normal circumstances, she would have protested, but she knew he was working her hard to save her life. Along with trying to stay focused on the job and the questions he asked, she had to keep her mind away from him as a man.

She'd been almost grateful when he'd finally left the night before near midnight. At least with him gone she relaxed a bit more. She'd continued to go over the file for several more hours.

By 5:00 a.m. she had crashed, falling into a hard, dreamless sleep. Groggy and cranky were the two words that came to mind as she assessed her current mood. She changed into a pair of shorts and a T-shirt she'd left in the bathroom the night before. She washed her face, brushed her teeth, then ripped a brush through her hair to tame the errant blond strands. There, she felt better ready to face the day.

She left the bathroom and walked to where Kane sat at the table. Before him was manna from Heaven, two large foam cups of coffee and half a dozen various kinds of doughnuts.

Sinking into the chair opposite him, she reached for one of the coffees at the same time. He didn't say a word to her until she'd taken a couple of sips. Smart man.

"Good morning."

"I think it will be once I get about a gallon of this coffee in me," she replied.

"You were never much of a morning person," he said and reached for the only chocolate frosted doughnut in the bunch.

"If you take that one, I'll have to kill you."

He quirked a dark eyebrow up in amused indulgence and grabbed a glazed instead. "Drink your coffee, it will make you human."

The problem was at the moment she felt far too human. Seeing Kane again, spending time with him brought to the surface memories of the often playful, always hot sex they'd shared years before.

"So what's the plan?" she asked, needing to keep her mind focused on the present and not on the past. That's the way she survived all the pain and hurt of her child-hood…day by day.

The half smile that had lifted one corner of his mouth disappeared and he leaned forward, his eyes glittering as he studied her intently. "The plan is up to you. If you need a day or two more to prepare that can be arranged."

Cassie shook her head. "No." She gestured toward the thick manila folder on the nightstand next to the bed. "I know the material backward and forward. You know that. I didn't miss a single question yesterday when you were grilling me. Another day or two won't make me any more prepared. I'm ready now."

Kane reached for another glazed doughnut, then apparently changed his mind and dropped his hand on the table. "You realize you're going in utterly alone. No wires, no cameras, and no real backup. If things go south you're on your own unless you can contact me and, depending on the situation I might not be any good to you."

An edgy adrenaline rush pumped through her veins, a rush she hadn't felt since the last time she'd worked for the agency. "Things won't go south," she said with a touch of bravado. "But if they do I can take care of myself."

For a moment their gazes remained locked, their past a haunting specter between them. She broke the eye contact. "I can take care of myself," she repeated.

"Then we proceed with the plan." He pulled a set of keys from his pocket. "This is the key to your new set of wheels."

"I don't suppose it just happens to be a Jaguar." She already knew it was that crappy old blue car in the parking space in front of her motel unit.

"Dream on. It's a ten-year-old Ford Escort with a hundred forty-five thousand miles on it."

"Des Moines, Iowa plates?" she asked, even though she knew it was a dumb question. Of course SPACE would see to it that every aspect of her new identity held up.

Kane nodded. "Licensed and tagged to Jessica Sinclair." He held up the next key on the ring. "The key to your apartment. You already know the address from the file. This third key is to a safe house. I'm staying there. It's a fifteen-minute drive from the safe house to your apartment. I can make it in seven."

"You must not be driving a ten-year-old Escort," she said dryly.

"I've got news for you. Not only are you driving an old clunker car, your new apartment isn't exactly the Ritz, either."

"Somehow I figured as much," she replied and once again reached for her coffee cup.

Kane pulled a small spiral notebook from the breast pocket of his navy shirt. He ripped off the top sheet of paper and handed it to her. "This is the address to the safe house. Memorize it."

She took the paper from him and looked at it: 7207 N. Oak. The safe house was only a couple of miles from her home address. Home. She hoped her neighbor wouldn't do anything to her property before she got back to her home base.

She gave the paper back to him and watched as he placed it in the ashtray then struck a match and lit it on fire.

"A bit dramatic, don't you think?" she asked as flame transformed the paper into ash.

He grinned, the first full grin she'd seen from him. "You know I love this covert stuff."

She laughed, unable to help herself. The grogginess that she'd awakened with was gone, swallowed by the rush of anticipation. Although she would never admit it to Kane, she still loved "this covert stuff."

"You start your waitress job at Night Life at eight tonight."

"Don't remind me," she groaned. "Nothing Adam Mercer can throw my way can possibly be more dangerous than me trying to juggle a tray full of drinks and serve them to patrons. It's been years since I did any waitressing."

"You'll be fine," he assured her, then stood. "You can leave here whenever you're ready." She stood as well. "You have the cell phone to get in touch with me if necessary."

She nodded and walked with him to the door. Once there he turned to face her once again. "Take care, Cassie. We don't know for sure what Adam Mercer is capable of, but we do know that nobody has seen his last girlfriend for a little over a month."

"Nice of you to leave that little tidbit of information until now. Why wasn't that in the files?"

"We were hoping to locate her whereabouts before we handed the file over to you. But so far that hasn't happened. I just want you to remember that Adam Mercer is a crazy man on a mission and that makes him dangerous. Get in, get the information we need and get out."

He hesitated and Cassie felt herself holding her breath, unsure what to expect from him. The moment stretched taut between them, then he reached up and touched her cheek with the pad of his warm fingers. "Be careful and I'll be in touch." He dropped his hand abruptly and turned and left.

She closed the door, her cheek burning from his touch as her breath whooshed out of her. She scrubbed at her cheek as if to erase the warmth of his touch.

It was time to move. No time for introspection, regrets or fear. Once again she headed for the bathroom, this time to shower and dress and prepare herself to crawl into the skin of Jessica Sinclair.

An hour later she stood once more in front of the mirror studying her reflection. Her makeup was perfect, hair all in place, and glittering green contacts weren't hanging off the end of her nose or on her eyebrow but were where they belonged.

Jessica Sinclair was twenty-five years old and from Des Moines, Iowa. She'd been raised in a rough part of town and at eighteen when her mother and father had died had become the soul guardian for her eight-year-old brother, Jimmy.

Brother and sister were close but struggled with poverty, few opportunities and bad breaks. The final bad break had come six months earlier when Jimmy had been caught between warring drug dealers in a drive-by shooting.

He'd been shot in the head and had died instantly, leaving Jessica alone, grieving and with a burning anti-drug sentiment in her soul. She'd moved from Des Moines to Kansas City to put the past behind her and start a new life.

Playing the role of Jessica wouldn't be much of a stretch for Cassie. In many ways their lives mirrored one another's. Cassie knew the grief of losing a brother, had known early on the heartache of being alone along with the anger over how completely drugs could destroy lives.

She smoothed a hand down the worn sundress that had been in the suitcase as part of Jessica's wardrobe. "Hello, Jessica," she murmured to the reflection of the green-eyed woman in the mirror. "Get in, get the information needed and get out." Sounded simple.

Fifteen minutes later she was in the car, cursing the fact that the air conditioner blew hot air as she drove to the apartment in the riverfront area.

The area where her apartment was located was a part of Kansas City that had suffered an identity crisis for years. When the first settlers had arrived, it had been in the riverfront area where they had built the first city buildings and the place had been the hub of the city.

As years passed and Kansas City grew, the city moved south, leaving the river front area to eventually become eight blocks of abandoned buildings.

In more recent years there had been several attempts at rejuvenating that part of town. In the late seventies the riverfront area had thrived with a new resurgence of popular nightclubs and restaurants.

For about four years the River Quay had been "the" spot in Kansas City, then several organized crime factions moved in and fought for control. The area died a dramatic death as shootings occurred in bars and there were murders daily.

As recently as ten years ago a group of businessmen tried to breathe in new life. Lofts were renovated and unique little shops opened, but the people didn't come and once again the riverfront was abandoned.

The only constant in the area was the city market vendors who set up each morning in a common area to sell their fresh fruit and vegetables. People came from all over Kansas City and beyond to buy the wares, then returned to their safe suburban neighborhoods.

The building where Jessica lived was across the street from the city market area. The four-story brick building extended little welcome, but rather radiated an air of abandonment and hopelessness. It would be a place where neighbors didn't visit and didn't ask questions. It was the kind of place Jessica could afford. It was the perfect cover.

A small parking lot in the back of the building offered parking for tenants only and Cassie pulled her car into one of the many empty spots.

She grabbed the suitcase from the back seat, and after discovering the back door of the building locked, headed around to the front door.

The lobby was minuscule with a single elevator door next to a set of stairs. She punched the up button and heard the elevator whine and creak, squeal and rumble ominously as it approached. When was the last time it had been inspected?

Stairs. She didn't mind the stairs. She headed up. The stink of age and despair clung to the walls, along with the scent of urine, smoke and stale cooked food.

On the third floor she found apartment 3B and used the key to enter what would be her home for the next few weeks.

It wasn't as bad as she'd anticipated. It was a studio apartment with a large closet, a kitchenette and a tiny bathroom.

The few pieces of furniture were obviously thrift store offerings. The blue flowered sofa was faded and worn in spots and cigarette burns and nicks decorated the coffee table. Bookcases built using the plastic cubes from discount stores lined one wall and held an array of knickknacks that drew Cassie's attention.

A life. That's what the bookcases held. The life the agency had formulated as Jessica's life. There was a picture of a young boy who could only be Jimmy in the center case. A little stuffed teddy bear, a porcelain angel figurine, several romance books and candles filled the rest of the cases.

Cassie set her suitcase down on the sofa and checked out the closet, where a meager wardrobe awaited her. In the bathroom she found cheap shampoo and soap and a jug of strawberry bubble bath.

She hung the clothes from the suitcase and put the suitcase itself into the closet floor, then placed her make-up in the drawer in the bathroom. The next thing she checked out was the cabinets in the small kitchenette and the refrigerator.

Cheap TV dinners and boxed macaroni and cheese and bologna sandwiches looked as if they would be the meals of choice. Not exactly terrific cuisine, but exactly what a woman like Jessica could afford.

From the refrigerator she walked over to the single window in the apartment and peered outside. The apartment window offered a bird's-eye view of the city market area. At this time of the day the place was busy.

Trucks were pulled up, their back doors open to display their goods. People crowded the market place, bartering with vendors and picking over fruit for the biggest and best.

Her gaze not only took in the city market, but the general area that surrounded her apartment. She didn't look so much as she assessed.

A drain pipe ran up the side of the building next to her window. Good. If any nefarious character came to her apartment door, she'd have an escape route. The city market area was littered with Dumpsters and in a matter of life and death, Dumpsters could make good hiding places. Although it would take a dire situation to get her Dumpster diving for cover.

She turned from the window. She had the afternoon to wait until her job at Night Life. Maybe she'd rearrange the furniture, make the place feel more like her own. At least doing that would help her work off some of her nervous energy.

The afternoon passed swiftly and it was just after seven when she once again stared at her reflection in the slightly distorted mirror on the back of the bathroom door.

It was Jessica Sinclair that stared back at her. Clad in a simple cotton dress that was slightly faded from too many wash days, she looked the part of a young woman struggling to survive. She hoped to Adam Mercer she looked like the woman of his dreams.

It was vital that she capture his attention, stoke his desire for her. She wouldn't be able to help stop him if she couldn't entice him into a personal relationship.

Cassie had never done the bar scene, but she knew that the club called Night Life was a popular singles hang-out. Some of the other single women cops had talked about it, said that despite the club's uptown atmosphere and high-dollar drinks, it tended to draw slick guys who were players and well-to-do alcoholics.

"Time to go to work, Jessica," she said softly to the woman in the mirror.

She had only taken a step out of the bathroom when she froze, her gaze riveted to the opposite wall of the room. Icy currents slithered up her spine, bringing with them a horrifying chill of terror.

The bug was huge…a leathery-shelled dark monster with long antennas that could easily pick up a New Jersey radio station. It cast a shadow on the wall as big as her fist. A cockroach.

Breathe, her brain commanded, but the sight of the creepy insect had stolen her breath and frozen her in place. It was a monster from her dreams, a horror from her past. Breathe.

She drew a deep breath through her nose, then released it slowly through her mouth. At the same time her hand crept to the knife in her pocket.

There were few things that could make Cassie's knees weaken and her blood turn cold…bugs of any kind was at the top of the list. She knew it was a silly phobia for a woman of her credentials. But if she had her wish, she'd kill every last one of them and screw up the ecosystem.

With a snap of her wrist she released the knife and it hit the wall with a sharp thud, giving an instant autopsy to Mr. Cockroach the intruder.

The only good bug was a dead one. She walked over to the wall and removed her knife, then wiped the end clean with a tissue and tucked it back into the sheath.

"Hell of a life you have, Jessica Sinclair," she muttered as she grabbed her purse and car keys. By day she killed cockroaches and at night she served them drinks.

Chapter 6

The vendors had gone home for the day, leaving the city market area a large expanse of asphalt decorated with trash and the Dumpsters she'd spied from her window earlier.

A man with a scraggly beard and clad in a pair of filthy pants and an overcoat stood on a crate in front of one of the Dumpsters, digging into the contents like an old prospector looking for gold.

Of course this area would attract the homeless, who could find a meal every night in the trash. She watched him for just a moment, an empathetic sadness swelling inside her.

The homeless was the nation's shame, a problem that she knew had no easy answer. She had met enough lost souls when she'd been younger to know many of the homeless chose that lifestyle, whether because of mental illness, or other reasons.

Would she have remained on the streets had she not met Max? She liked to think she wouldn't have, that one way or another she would have pulled herself up and off the streets and found legitimate work and built a life for herself. But in truth she wasn't sure of the answer.

She was grateful that the drive from the apartment to the club wasn't far. The night air was warm and not only did the car's air conditioner not work, but neither did the radio. Bummer.

Surprisingly she wasn't nervous. Kane had once told her that she was the only person he'd ever worked with who managed to remain cooler than Kane himself in the midst of a job.

It was true. Although she hated to admit it, Cassie was comfortable when under pressure, when in the middle of a crisis. Perhaps it came from those years of living on the streets, never knowing where danger might lurk, fighting for every morsel of food and fearing the night and the vulnerability of sleep.

Night Life was located on the second floor of a downtown building. An Italian restaurant was located on the bottom floor. A discreet neon sign flashed a top hat and cane, advertising Night Life as Kansas City's club of choice.

She walked into the building lobby to see two wide staircases leading up to the second floor along with two elevators. The Italian restaurant was on the left and a fancy boutique, closed for the day, was on the right.

As she waited for the elevator to take her upstairs, she thought about what she knew about Night Life. Owned and operated by a man named Jackson Tyler, the club had a high cover charge, a drink minimum and expensive prices in an effort to keep out kids and riffraff.

In her work as a police officer Cassie had learned that riffraff didn't necessarily mean without money. She'd met plenty of well-to-do people who could be considered trash.

The restaurant filled the air with the savory scents of spicy tomato sauce and pungent garlic and onion. She wondered how late they were open, if it would be possible to get takeout when she got off work.

The elevator arrived with a soft *ping* and the doors slid open. She stepped inside for the brief ride up. She had no idea what arrangements had been made with whom for her job but was confident that it was all taken care of.

The elevator arrived and she stepped out. Straight ahead of her the entrance to the club beckoned with bright lights, loud music and the sound of laughter.

A burly young man stopped her at the door to collect the cover fee. "I'm here to see Jackson Tyler," she said. "I'm supposed to start a waitress job in half an hour."

"Hang on." He raised a hand and motioned toward a man standing nearby.

As she waited, she peered inside the club. From this vantage point it looked typical. A DJ played on a stage and in front of the stage a lighted dance floor held two dozen or more gyrating figures.

Across the back of the right side of the place a polished bar stretched seemingly endlessly. The bar stools in front of it were filled with men and women.

Round tables and chairs filled the rest of the space and waitresses scurried back and forth between tables delivering drinks with friendly smiles. The uniforms they wore weren't too bad, although a little low cut at the neckline for Cassie's taste.

She turned her attention to the squat, dark-haired man who approached her. "Jessica Sinclair?" She nodded and he stuck out a hand. "I'm Jackson Tyler." He released her hand. "Come on into the back with me."

She followed him through the throng of tables and people to a door just left of the stage. They went down a long hallway with doors on the left and right to the end and into a large office where the music was barely discernible.

He motioned her into the seat opposite the desk. "I've got some paperwork you need to fill out," he said as he eased down behind the desk and opened a manila folder. "You know…tax stuff." He slid a sheet of paper and a pen across the desk.

It was the usual withholding information everyone filled out when taking a job. Cassie filled it out with Jessica's name, address and social security number, then slid it back to Jackson.

"You come with good references," he said. "If you show up on time, work hard and have a good attitude, you and I will get along just fine."

"Sounds reasonable to me," she replied.

"Good, then I'll just have one of the girls take you to the locker room, get you a couple of uniforms and orient you." He pressed a button on an intercom and almost immediately a knock fell on the door.

An attractive red-haired woman stepped into the office. She smiled first at Jackson, then at Cassie. "Cassie, this is Dana Williams, one of the best waitresses that's ever worked for me. She'll show you the ropes." Cassie stood, knowing she was being dismissed.

"Hi, Cassie, nice to meet you."

"Nice to meet you, too." Cassie followed her out of the office and back down the hallway to another door. They entered a small room with a bench and lockers and a rest room. "This is where we stow our personal items," Dana said as she unlocked and opened what appeared to be a storage room door.

She pulled out two uniforms on hangers. "Size eight?"

Cassie nodded and took them from her. "Thanks."

"And here's a lock for one of the lockers. The combination is on the tape on the bottom. Just memorize it then throw the tape away. I'll just wait outside for you to get dressed." She gave Cassie another friendly smile, then slipped out into the hall.

It took Cassie only minutes to wiggle into the short black skirt and the deep scoop-necked white blouse. She was grateful she'd worn hose and flat black shoes. She also was glad that the uniform allowed her to wear the two knives she rarely went without…one in her bra and the smaller knife against her upper thigh.

She'd just finished stowing the extra uniform and her purse in the locker when Dana stepped back into the room. "All set?"

Cassie hesitated, then nodded and smiled. "Maybe

just a little bit nervous," she admitted, thinking it's exactly what Jessica would say.

Dana smiled reassuringly. "Trust me, you don't have anything to be nervous about." They walked back down the hall toward the main room. "One of the biggest problems is that sometimes the music gets so loud it's hard to hear the drink orders. The other problem is that sometimes some of the men have a little too much to drink and decide they want more than what's on your tray…if you get what I mean."

"I get it," Cassie replied.

"Usually it's not a big deal, but if the guy gets too obnoxious, you can call for Sam or Jake. They're the two bouncers and both of them are big as bulldozers. They don't take any trouble from anyone."

"That's good to know." They reentered the main room where the DJ was playing an upbeat song that Cassie didn't recognize.

"The good news is the tips are great here. Just be friendly with everyone and you'll do fine," Dana reassured her.

For the next fifteen minutes Dana explained how things worked and which tables would be Cassie's for the night. She introduced Cassie to several of the other waitresses and the bartender, then cut Cassie loose to do her job.

For the next hour Cassie served up drinks, bantered with customers and kept an eye out for Adam Mercer. By 10:00 p.m. there was still no sign of the wealthy anti-drug guru but she was shocked to see Kane seated at one of her tables.

"What are you doing here? I thought you said no backup." She kept her features pleasantly schooled, as if he were just another customer to serve.

"Just wanted to check this place out." His gaze traveled the length of her. "I don't like the uniforms."

She smiled. "Funny, I don't remember asking your opinion. There's a two-drink minimum. Is your favorite poison still scotch and soda?"

"That will do."

"No sign of Mercer."

Kane checked his wristwatch. "It's early. He'll be here. He rarely misses a Saturday night."

She nodded and turned to get his drinks. As she waited for the bartender to fill her orders, she found herself watching Kane from across the room.

He was clad in a pair of charcoal-gray dress slacks and a black and gray pin-striped shirt. With his dark hair and eyes, he looked successful, handsome and just a little bit dangerous. It was an irresistible combination and Cassie realized she wasn't the only woman in the place eyeing Kane.

Two young women at the bar whispered and pointed in Kane's direction at the same time a tall blonde approached his table.

Cassie was shocked by a sudden surge of jealousy that swept over her as Kane gestured for the woman to join him at his table. She turned back to face the bar, wondering where the emotion had come from.

It was ridiculous. She wanted nothing to do with him other than working with him. He had every right to pursue any woman he wanted to and she had absolutely no right to be jealous.

She grabbed her tray of drinks and delivered each of them to the tables where they belonged, then approached Kane's table. "One scotch and soda. That will be five-fifty. You can pay me now or run a tab." She smiled archly. "Perhaps you'd like to buy your lady friend a drink."

"Oh, no. I'm fine right now," the blonde replied. Up close she was older than Cassie had first guessed. The woman laughed, a touch of quiet desperation in the sound. "I was just trying to get him to dance with me."

Cassie knew Kane never danced. "Good luck." She looked back at Kane. "I'll just run a tab for you, sir."

He nodded and she left the table. When she gazed back over about ten minutes later the woman was gone and Kane once again sat alone.

For the next hour Cassie was too busy to think. She served drinks, bantered with customers and fought a growing sense of frustration as Mercer didn't show up.

She'd just taken a fifteen-minute break and when she returned to the floor, she saw that Mercer had arrived. Unfortunately he wasn't seated in her section, but rather in the section next to hers.

Adam Mercer was a handsome man with black hair shot through with silver strands and blue eyes that even in a photo appeared piercing. Impeccably dressed in a gray suit, it was easy to see that he was the king of his immediate surroundings.

He shared the table with a man and a woman at his

right and two men on his left. At either ends of the table were men who couldn't be mistaken for anything but burly bodyguards.

How was she supposed to capture his attention if she wasn't even serving him? It would certainly look suspicious if she asked the waitress in that section to allow her to serve that particular table.

She cast a look of frustration toward Kane, who returned her gaze without expression. She got back to work figuring that tonight was a loss. Tomorrow night, Sunday, the bar was closed. It would be Monday night before she'd have another chance to meet Mercer unless she could come up with something creative tonight.

As she worked her tables, she kept an eye on Mercer at his table. They'd ordered a round of drinks and seemed to be having a good time chatting and laughing among themselves.

Cassie continued to work her tables, but several times she felt Mercer's gaze on her. Once their gazes locked. She smiled, then quickly looked away as she tried to figure out how to make personal contact with the striking man who was her quarry.

Adam Mercer sat up straighter in his chair as he watched the waitress working the tables nearby. She was new. He'd never seen her before and Adam had been coming to Night Life long enough that he knew most of the waitresses by name.

She was stunning with long, shapely legs and a lithe

figure that looked both feminine and athletic. Adam had always had a weakness for blondes.

As she served her customers, she had a pleasant, but distant expression on her face, as if she dreamed of bigger things than a waitress job in a nightclub. There was also a touch of cool disdain there as well.

That intrigued Adam as much as anything…the fact that she looked so cool, so emotionally and intellectually removed from this place and this moment.

Sherry, his ex-wife, had specialized in cool disdain. Her nickname in college had been Ice Queen. But it hadn't taken Adam long to discover that beneath the ice was a passionate, sex-crazed wanton who'd only needed the respectability of marriage to get in touch with her wild side.

Sherry was gone now. She'd divorced him almost two years before, after the death of their daughter by a drug overdose.

The divorce hadn't been particularly friendly, but he and Sherry still shared some business dealings and had reached an uneasy acceptance of one another. But after the divorce Adam had discovered that he was a man who didn't like to be alone. He needed somebody beside him, sharing his dreams, sharing his visions.

He intended to usher in a brave new world, a far better world than the one existing now. He'd like to have a special woman at his side, playing the role of Eve to his Adam.

He'd thought he'd found his Eve with Nicole, another waitress who had worked here at the club. Nicole had been beautiful and sexy. Ultimately he'd been bitterly disillusioned. Nicole had proven herself disappointingly unimaginative and ordinary.

Watching the new waitress, Adam felt the anticipation of possibility. It had been too long since he'd played the courting game. It was time to play again.

By the time closing time came, Cassie's feet were killing her and her frustration level had climbed to massive proportions.

She got her personal items and spare uniform from her locker, then left by way of the elevator.

A sense of failure weighed heavily on her shoulders. She had no idea what the time frame was of this particular job, but knew that with any assignment time was of the essence.

Although her cover was as a waitress, her job wasn't to serve drinks, but rather to get close to Adam Mercer. Tonight she'd been unsuccessful. Maybe the agency had overestimated Mercer's desire for a new girlfriend. Maybe they had overestimated her attractiveness.

She left the elevator and headed for the front door of the building. As she stepped outside she drew a deep breath of the warm night air. Even though it was humid, it was a welcome relief after the smoke-filled club.

She tensed as a sleek black Lincoln pulled up to the curb in front of her. A man got out of the back seat and she recognized him as one of the two bodyguard-types she'd seen with Mercer.

She backed up, wary because of the lateness of the hour and the deserted street. He seemed to sense her wariness and stopped in his tracks. His pale blue eyes raked over her and an Elvis sneer curled his upper lip. It looked better on the King. "My boss, Mr. Mercer, would like to take you out for a late dinner," he said.

A euphoric buzz sounded in her brain. So he had noticed her after all. Her mind raced. She knew her next move was vital. She'd read the files on Mercer, sensed what he liked and didn't like in women.

She took a calculated risk. "I don't know your boss and I don't have dinner with strangers."

Without waiting for any reply, she turned and headed toward the back lot where her car was parked. She listened for the sound of footsteps following her, but heard nothing but the slam of a car door and the car pulling away from the curb.

She hoped she hadn't just made a horrible mistake.

It was three-thirty when Cassie got back into her apartment. She unlocked the door, opened it and jumped in surprise as she found Kane seated on the sofa.

"Haven't you ever heard about the concept of knocking on a front door then waiting for an invitation inside?" she asked.

"I was afraid you wouldn't invite me in. Besides, I don't want anyone seeing me coming and going from this apartment. It's vital we aren't seen together."

Cassie looked at the window and noticed it was open. He'd scaled the side of the building to get inside.

He watched as she threw her purse on the small

kitchen table, then hung her two uniforms in the closet.

She flopped down on the sofa and kicked off her shoes. "I'd forgotten the perils of waitressing," she said and pulled one of her feet up to rub the pad. For a moment she rubbed as he remained silent. "Did you know this place has cockroaches the size of coconuts?" she asked when the silence had stretched too long. "I killed one just before I left for work tonight."

"Maybe it was the only one in the place," he said.

"Yeah, right," she replied dryly. She pulled her other foot up then jumped as he grabbed it and began to knead the soreness away. She closed her eyes at the slightly painful pleasure.

Every muscle in her body relaxed and she wanted his strong hands rubbing her legs, rubbing her back, touching her…she snapped her eyes open and pulled her foot from him.

"I made contact."

"Tell me." He leaned forward and his eyes held the hard glint of all business.

"I was leaving the club when a big black Lincoln pulled up in front of me. One of Mercer's goons got out and told me his boss would like to have a late dinner with me."

"So what are you doing sitting here with me?"

"Playing a hunch," she replied.

Kane frowned, his dark gaze skeptical. "You turned him down?" She nodded. "Do you know what you're doing?"

The question irritated her and she got up from the sofa to pace the floor in front of where he remained seated. "Are you questioning my judgment?"

"No, it's just that timing of all this is important. I thought you understood that you don't have months to get close to Mercer. It seems like the wise thing to do would have been to accept the dinner invitation and get the ball rolling."

She sighed. "Kane, I read the dossier on him. Reading between the lines I'd say Mercer is a man who likes a bit of a challenge with his women. Call it women's intuition. I think I did the right thing. I can't have you questioning my every move. I thought I was trusted to use my own judgment."

"Whoa…take it easy." He rose from the sofa and walked over and placed his hands on her shoulders. "You're overreacting to a simple question. When you overreact that means you're tired."

The heat from his hands warmed her and memories of those hands stroking her intimately streaked through her mind. She was tired…bone weary. She had to be because for just a moment she'd wanted to fall into his arms. She was obviously deliriously tired. "You're right. I'm tired and if you go away, I'll go to bed."

He dropped one of his hands from her shoulder, but the fingers of his other hand trailed down her throat and traced the lines of her breastbones.

The intimate touch seared through her, weakening her knees as the heat from his fingers seeped through her entire body.

"I don't like the uniform," he murmured, his breath warm on her face. "I saw him looking at you."

"I thought that was the general idea," she replied, her voice a mere whisper.

He yanked his hand away as if the feel of her skin burned him, then stepped back, his dark eyes appearing angry. "It is," he said curtly. "I'll get out of here and let you get some sleep." He walked over to the window, but paused as she called his name.

Although she still felt the burn of his fingers on her skin and her heart still beat an accelerated beat from the contact, she needed him to do something for her. "Before you leave could you just do me one little favor? Could you take the cushions off the sofa and check?"

He asked no questions, but moved to the sofa and began to take the cushions out of the frame. If she hadn't seen the roach on the wall earlier, she'd have never asked him the favor.

She didn't have to explain to him. Kane was the only person on earth besides Max who knew about her irrational fear of bugs. She'd once climbed him like a pole in a cellar where the floor had been covered with water bugs. Definitely not one of her prouder moments.

"All clear," he said as he put the cushions back where they belonged. "You have a sheet or a blanket?"

She walked over to the closet and pulled a sheet from the stack inside. She handed it to him and watched as he shook it out, then tucked it into the back of the sofa, leaving enough for her to cover up with.

When he was finished he looked at her and for just

a brief moment she thought she saw a flash of something close to tenderness in his eyes.

It disconcerted her. She could handle almost anything from Kane except tenderness. "Thanks," she said gruffly.

"No problem." He walked over to the window, extended a leg over the sill, then disappeared into the darkness of the night.

Chapter 7

Cassie slept ridiculously late the next morning, getting up after eleven. The first thing she did was go to the window and peer outside where the sun beat relentlessly on the pavement and the city market was in full Sunday morning swing. Good, her first plan of the day was to get some fresh fruit and veggies into the fridge.

Within thirty minutes she was showered and dressed and headed across the street to the market. For the next hour Cassie squeezed melons and picked through vegetables. She bartered with the vendors for the best price, then returned to her apartment arms full of fresh food for the refrigerator.

She fought an edge of impatience as she made herself a big salad for lunch. The club was closed today so nothing would happen. It was the kind of day in the middle of an assignment that agents hated.

When she'd finished her salad, she picked up the cell phone Kane had given her and called Max. "Cupcake," he said the moment he heard her voice. "You okay?"

"I'm fine," she assured him. "Just wanted to call and touch base with you while I have the chance. They've got me in one dump of an apartment."

Max chuckled. "You've lived in worse. Remember that box you slept in when I first met you?"

"Don't remind me," she replied. "You doing all right?"

"Fine...fine. Virginia is cooking dinner for me tonight. She's a sweet woman."

"She cooks for you fairly regularly. Is there a bit of romance in the air?" Cassie asked. There was nothing she'd love more than for Max to find a companion his own age in his life...a permanent companion who adored him as much as she did.

"Don't get your hopes up. Virginia is nice and cooks a mean pot roast, but I could never consider getting serious with a woman who talks about her regularity every time I'm with her."

Cassie laughed. Just hearing Max's gruff voice made her feel more centered, stronger. "You feeling all right?"

"You know me, cupcake. I feel strong as a horse. If I could just trade in this bum back and weak legs of mine, I'd dance with you until dawn."

"Don't mention dancing until dawn," she replied. "I worked last night waitressing tables and dodging dancers' flailing arms and legs."

"How are things going with you and Kane?"

She hesitated a moment. "Fine. Maybe a bit strained."

"You didn't expect anything different, did you? I

mean, you walked away from the man five years ago without any explanations or discussion. Have the two of you had a chance to talk about that?"

"No, and I don't intend to bring it up. He certainly hasn't, so it's obviously a nonissue." She sighed. "I'd better go, but I just wanted to check in with you. I have no idea when I'll be able to call again. It's probably not a good idea for me to call too often." The last thing she'd want to do was bring danger to Max's door.

"Don't you worry about me. I'll be fine. You just take care of yourself. Don't forget everything that I've taught you and if all else fails, tuck and roll."

Tuck and roll. A few minutes later as she cleaned up her lunch mess, she thought about Max's parting words. Tuck and roll was the last-ditch effort made by somebody when a stunt had gone wrong. You tucked your body to hopefully prevent internal damage, then rolled away from danger.

She wondered how well that would work if things got dicey with Adam Mercer. He might think it odd if she curled up like Lara Croft and spun to the nearest exit. But that's exactly what she would do if it meant living another day.

By the time the next evening arrived and it was time for her to go back to work at the club she was more than ready. Tonight would be an earlier night than Saturday. On the weekend nights the place stayed open until three, but during the week closing time was 1:00 a.m. She hoped Mercer would show up again tonight. She also hoped her curbside rejection of the dinner offer Saturday night hadn't messed things up.

The club was a lot less crowded tonight than it had been on Saturday night. Cassie worked her assigned ten tables, four of which were empty, and kept one eye on the door in hopes that Mercer would walk in.

The first two hours went by fairly quickly, although she had a table of rowdy young men, one who was going from rowdy to obnoxious.

She was just coming off her break and ready to head back to her station when the obnoxious drunk appeared in front of her. "There's my sexy waitress. How about a little sex on the beach?" He stood too close to her, invading her personal space.

"I'll get that drink to your table right away," she said and attempted to step past him.

He thwarted her attempt by moving in front of her and placing a hand on her shoulder. "I don't want the drink, honey. I just want sex on the beach with you."

She looked for Jake or Sam, but didn't see either of the bouncers nearby. Cassie grabbed his hand and pulled it from her shoulder. In one smooth move, she spun him around and pulled his arm up behind him. He yelped in surprise.

She leaned close to his ear from behind him. "If you go back to your table and be nice, then I won't serve you a broken arm in a bar. Do we understand one another?" She kept her tone cool and pleasant.

He nodded rapidly and she released his arm. He scurried back to his table and Cassie went back to work. He and his pals left the bar soon after that. She hoped her boss hadn't noticed the incident. Thankfully, none of the other waitresses seemed to have. She didn't want to be seen chasing away customers. But the guy had it coming.

It was just a few minutes after eleven when Cassie saw Mercer and his two bodyguards entering the premises. Her heart stepped up in rhythm as he took a table in her section.

The two men sat on either side of him. As she approached the table Mercer's gaze locked with hers. There was power in those cold blue eyes of his…an awesome power and intelligence that threatened to suck the breath right out of her.

She held the gaze for a long moment and in that breathless space of suspended time she recognized he would be a worthy adversary. The biggest mistake she could make was to forget that fact and underestimate him.

"Good evening, gentlemen. What can I get you?" she asked.

"Two beers and a scotch on the rocks. Tell the bartender to use the top shelf scotch." Mercer's voice was pleasant and deep. "And before you leave, I'd like to introduce myself. My name is Adam Mercer and these are two of my associates." He didn't bother to give the names of the other two.

"Nice to meet you, Mr. Mercer," she said and gestured to her name tag. "I'm Jessica and I'll be right back with your drinks."

"Lucky you," Dana said a moment later as Jessica waited for the bartender to fill her order.

"Lucky me?"

"Mr. Mercer is in your section. He's a terrific tipper."

"That's always good to hear," Cassie replied.

"He's also a very nice man. For a while he was dating one of the other waitresses, Nicole."

"Oh, does she still work here?"

"No. She quit soon after she met Mr. Mercer. I heard she moved in with him, then I heard they broke up, but I don't know whatever happened to her. She didn't come back to work here."

The conversation halted as the bartender gave Cassie her drink order. She went back to the table to serve them. "Here we are," she said. When the drinks were on the table, she smiled at Mercer. "You were in the car Saturday night that stopped, right?"

"Right, and I must apologize for that. I should have known better than to ask you to dinner without even a formal introduction taking place."

A raw power emanated from him. He was a very attractive man. His features were sharply defined, strong nose, chiseled jaw and nice lips.

"I don't have dinner with people I don't know," she replied.

"Ah, but now we've been introduced." His eyes sparkled and his smile was charismatic. She could smell his scent, the odor of money...of expensive cologne and grooming supplies. "Perhaps you would consider having dinner with me after work this evening?"

She allowed her smile to waver with indecision. "But I don't know you and you don't know me."

"Name me a better way of getting to know somebody besides talking over good food?" His voice was softly cajoling. He was obviously a man who didn't take no for an answer easily. "I'm having dinner downstairs when the club closes. I'd love for you to join me. Think about it."

She nodded, then gestured toward the other tables. "I've got to get back to work."

She liked the fact that he didn't intend to take her anyplace in his car, that she could be in control of when she decided to leave. Any woman would be a fool to accept a dinner date with a man she had just met at a place where she would not be in control.

The rest of the night passed quickly. At ten minutes until closing time she saw Adam and his two goons leave. When the club closed, she cashed out as quickly as possible, then hurried to the locker room to change.

Tonight she'd come prepared just in case Mercer showed up again with dinner on his mind. She pulled the overnight bag she'd brought to work with her out from the locker.

The bag contained a simple black dress, the nicest one she'd found in the closet in the apartment. She quickly changed from her waitress uniform into the skimpy—for her taste—black dress and black heels. The finishing touch was a spritz of light perfume and a pair of inexpensive silver hoop earrings.

As she viewed her reflection in the mirror she felt no

nerves, but rather a cool focus on her goal. She had to be charming enough to bewitch Mr. Mercer, engaging enough that he'd find her addictive and smooth enough to figure out a way to find out the information she sought.

She left the dressing room and took the elevator down, mentally preparing herself for the game to come. She waved goodbye to several of the other waitresses who were heading out the door as she walked toward the entrance to the restaurant.

Although the lights were on in the restaurant, the door was locked. Cassie frowned, wondering if perhaps she'd misunderstood the invitation. Before she could turn to leave, a short, middle-aged Italian man appeared at the door to unlock it.

"You must be Jessica," he said. "Welcome to Anthony's. Mr. Mercer is waiting for you."

She had to admit, she was impressed. It was obvious Mercer had made arrangements to eat after the place was closed for the night. She was led to a table in the back where Adam sat at one table and the two bodyguards sat at a nearby table.

Adam rose as they approached. "Jessica, I'm so pleased you decided to join me."

She didn't sit right away. She looked at the two men sitting near them then back at Adam with confusion. "I don't understand…if those men are business associates, shouldn't they be sitting with you?"

Adam smiled. "Please, join me and I'll explain." She slid into the chair opposite him, poised as if to run although she had no intention of going anywhere. "Anthony, we'll have a bottle of Dom."

Anthony nodded and scurried away. Adam turned his attention back to Cassie. "Those men aren't exactly business associates. They're employees of mine...bodyguards to be exact."

"Bodyguards?" Cassie feigned a look of surprise. "Are you some kind of a celebrity or something? I don't watch much television..."

Adam laughed, obviously delighted. "No, nothing like that. However, I am a successful businessman and I find it necessary to protect myself. I depend on Burt and Sebastian for my personal safety."

So the bodyguard with no-neck and the Elvis sneer was Burt, and the bald bulldog was Sebastian. She filed this information away. She'd want Kane to do a full background check on each of the bodyguards.

"I hope you don't mind, I took the liberty of ordering already," Adam said.

Cassie raised an eyebrow. "You ordered even before I'd agreed to have dinner with you? What would you have done if I'd declined your invitation?"

He smiled. "Then Burt and Sebastian and I would have had a big, delicious meal."

It took several minutes for Anthony to serve them wine, leave a basket of warm bread, then serve salads. When they were left alone Adam turned his full attention to her. "So tell me about Jessica Sinclair."

"There isn't a lot to tell," she said and took a sip of her wine. Sitting across from him at the table, with his total attention focused on her, she once again felt the aura of power that surrounded him. Not just power, she thought, but an innate curiosity as well.

She set her glass back down and continued. "I just moved to Kansas City from Des Moines. My plans are to work at the club until I get up enough money to go back to school and get my teaching degree."

"Teaching…a noble profession." He speared a cucumber from his salad and popped it into his mouth.

"I love working with kids. I've always wanted to be a teacher."

"So what made you leave Des Moines for Kansas City?" he asked.

She picked up her wineglass again and broke eye contact with him. "I just needed a new start." She took a drink of the wine, returned the glass to the table, but kept her gaze downward.

"Because of your brother's death."

Her gaze shot up to his face. The sly fox had already checked into her background. "What do you know about my brother?" she asked, her voice radiating a coolness he couldn't mistake for anything but distrust.

He smiled, a charming open smile that showed the perfect row of his white teeth. "I must confess, I did a little check into your background," he said.

"For a simple dinner date? What planet are you from?" She dabbed her mouth with her napkin and started to rise.

"Jessica…please." He placed a hand on her arm in order to stop her escape. He had no idea that she didn't intend to go anywhere. "Please…sit down." Those Paul Newman eyes of his pleaded with her and she eased back down into her chair as she shrugged off his hand.

"I should explain," he said.

"Yeah, that would be nice." She placed her napkin in her lap once again and glared at him.

"I don't know how much you know about me," he began.

"Nothing, except for what one of the other waitresses told me earlier tonight, that you were a nice man and a good tipper. I didn't have a chance to run a background check on you."

"And I apologize for the necessity I felt to do that," he replied smoothly. "I'm a wealthy man, Jessica…extremely wealthy. Through my years as a businessman and a philanthropist I've made friends and, unfortunately, I've made some enemies. So now I live my life with bodyguards and background checks. I assure you it was nothing personal."

Cassie pretended to soften a bit. "It just doesn't seem quite fair. You know all about me, but I really don't know anything about you."

At that moment Anthony appeared at their table once again, bringing with him the dishes Adam had ordered as entrées. There were a total of three…a veal dish, a vegetable and linguini Alfredo and lasagna. He left them with empty plates so they could serve themselves.

When he'd left them alone once again, Adam served her a small portion of all three dishes, then served himself. He settled back in his chair and smiled at her. "What do you want to know about me?"

"I don't know…I guess first things first…are you married?"

"Divorced. What if I was married? Would that make a difference to you?"

"Definitely," she said without hesitation. "It would mean that this was our one and only dinner together."

"So you don't dally with married men?"

"I don't dally at all, unless it's a meaningful dally, emotionally speaking." She could tell she was making points with him. She knew enough about him by reading his background material that the kind of women he liked weren't cheap or loose.

They began to eat and in between bites she asked more questions. "So how long have you been divorced?"

"It will be three years in October. My ex-wife and I are still on civil terms. I'm kind of a silent partner in her business and we speak frequently."

"That's nice. Were you married a long time?"

"Almost twenty years."

"Any children?"

It was as if the question caused a shroud of gray to embrace the space around them. A stark grief stole all the light from his eyes and he suddenly looked every day of his fifty-four years. "I had a daughter. She died."

There was no way he could pretend the depth of emotion that racked his voice with those words, no way he could manufacture the utter despair in his eyes.

Even though Cassie knew this man's sorrow had

crossed the line into a form of madness and his plot for revenge was one of maniacal devastation, she couldn't help but feel sorry for his loss.

And, in true character, she reached across the table and covered one of his hands with hers. "We have this in common…the loss of a beloved one," she said softly.

He turned his hand over and entwined his fingers with hers, the darkness in his eyes lifting like strands of fog burned off by brilliant sunshine. "Yes, we have that in common, but tonight is not the time to dwell on unhappy things." He released her hand and picked up his wineglass. "I'd like to make a toast…to more late dinners shared with you."

She clinked her glass with his, recognizing that she had accomplished what she'd intended…he wanted to see her again and she hoped within a couple more days he'd feel as if he couldn't exist without her.

Adam was enchanted. As they enjoyed their meal and played the courtship game of question and answer, discovery and digest, he felt a hope swell inside him. It was the hope that she was the woman he'd been waiting for…the one who would understand him, accept him and stand beside him as he ushered in a new world.

As he dined with the lovely Jessica he wondered if perhaps fate had brought him to her at this place in his life. He knew about her brother's death in a drive-by shooting, so they both had lost loved ones to the scourge of drugs.

Still, it was too early to tell whether she would have

any part in his life. At the moment she was nothing more than a possibility, a pleasant date and a potential partner.

He'd thought he'd found the right woman in Nicole. He'd groomed her to have a special place in his life, bought her jewelry and clothes befitting her position as his lover. And, when he'd thought the time was right he'd shared with her his vision, his plan and she hadn't understood.

Now Nicole was gone and the lovely Jessica held the allure of shared pain, common anger and hopefully, the promise of understanding and acceptance.

He and Jessica lingered over coffee, sharing tidbits of their pasts. He was reluctant to call an end to the night, but when she stifled a yawn for the third time, he knew it was time for them to say goodbye.

"You're exhausted," he said.

"No...I'm fine," she replied, but instantly was plagued by another yawn. She covered her mouth, then laughed. "Well, okay, maybe I am tired. But it's been such a lovely night."

"It has." As Adam rose from the table, he was aware of Burt and Sebastian doing the same from their table. They were good bodyguards, loyal to him for monetary gain, partnered with him by criminal intent and greed.

Jessica rose as well. He'd already made arrangements with Anthony regarding their bill for the night. Anthony unlocked the door and he led Jessica outside.

Hot, humid air greeted them despite the early-morning hour. "I keep hoping this hot spell will snap," he said as they stood on the sidewalk in front of the restaurant.

"It will only get worse," she replied. "We haven't even hit July or the dog days of August yet."

"Don't remind me." He took her by the arm. "Come on, I'll walk you to your car."

"That isn't necessary," she protested. "It's just around back. I'll be fine." She stepped away from him.

"Then Burt will see to it that you get to your car safely." He looked at the big man.

"I'd be happy to," Burt said as he stepped closer. But there was nothing in his tone to indicate he'd be happy with anything. That was Burt. He was a loyal body-guard, but a lowlife grunt with a mean streak and a bad attitude.

Although under other circumstances Adam wouldn't have been caught dead in the same room as Burt Weath-erby, Adam had been forced to forgo some of his own personal integrity to fulfill his dreams.

"No, really, I'm fine," Jessica protested again, then smiled at him. "Thank you, for a lovely meal and great conversation. I had a wonderful time."

He took her hand in his. "I had a wonderful time. I'd like to see you again."

Her green eyes sparkled with pleasure. "I'd like that."

"Why don't I pick you up tomorrow around four and we'll plan something fun, something exciting."

"That sounds wonderful, but I have to be here to work at eight."

"I'll make sure you're back in time for work."

Her eyes narrowed just a bit. "I guess I don't have to give you my address."

He winced. "I apologize for the background check."

"You're forgiven. Thank you again and I'll be ready at four." She turned and he watched her walk off. With a lift of his finger he sent Burt to follow behind her. He liked to take care of his women as long as they behaved themselves, and when they didn't behave, he let Burt take care of them for him.

The burly bodyguard followed Cassie too closely, invading her personal space in a way that felt slightly threatening. Cassie pulled her keys from her purse, then halted and twirled around. "Do you mind? You're invading my space," she exclaimed.

He snorted with derision but backed off a bit. "I'm just telling you right now, Blondie, don't even think about taking advantage of Mr. Mercer."

"What's your problem? All I've done is have dinner with the man," Cassie replied.

"I don't like you." His gaze held a malevolence that surprised her.

"Well, that seals it. You're off my Christmas card list." Cassie turned and advanced toward her car.

She unlocked her door and slid in behind the wheel. As she pulled away she looked in her rearview mirror and saw Burt scowling at her.

Once again she reminded herself to tell Kane she wanted a full background check done on the two bodyguards. She had a feeling no-neck Burt was going to be trouble.

Chapter 8

There were many things Cassie missed from her house…like the air conditioner that didn't moan like a cat in heat, her favorite mug with the chipped handle and the queen-size bed among other things. But the item she missed more than anything was her punching bag.

She enjoyed her workouts at the gym and when she couldn't get to the gym she liked to work up a sweat by punching and kicking the bag in her spare room.

When she got up the next morning she decided to transform her little studio apartment into a mini gym. She had a feeling she was going to have to be in top physical shape for things to come.

The long sofa cushion leaned against one wall made a perfect target for fists and feet. With the coffee table moved aside, the center area of the living room provided enough room for stretching and strengthening exercises.

She worked out for an hour and a half, until sweat

oozed from her pores and her muscles ached with a good kind of hurt. Then she took a long, lukewarm shower and threw on a robe.

It took her only minutes to put the room back the way it had been, then she glanced at her watch and frowned. She had almost two hours to cool her heels before Adam would arrive to pick her up. She wondered what he had planned for the late afternoon date.

As far as Cassie was concerned, the date couldn't come too quickly. There was nothing she hated more than having to cool her heels and wait for things to happen.

She wandered the tiny apartment restlessly, then jumped when the telephone rang. She hadn't even realized there was a phone in the apartment. She followed the jarring noise and discovered the cheap instrument on the bookcase. She grabbed it and answered.

"Jessica?" Adam's smooth voice was instantly recognizable.

"Hi, Adam." She thought about sitting down on the floor next to the bookcase. But with the sunshine beating through the nearby window and emphasizing the dreary condition of the carpeting, she decided to remain standing. She hadn't minded the dirty carpet during her workout but now she was nice and clean.

"Did I wake you?"

"No, I've been up for hours."

"Good, I wouldn't have wanted to interrupt your beauty sleep, although you certainly don't need sleep for beauty."

"And you are one charming man, Adam Mercer," she replied.

He laughed. "I'm only charming to those I want to charm. Now, the reason I called is to tell you to dress cool and casual. There's a concert in the park this evening and I thought it might be fun to picnic first, then enjoy as much as we can of the concert before it's time for you to go to work."

"Sounds wonderful," she agreed. Good food, live music and the company of a charming psychopath. She supposed it could be worse, the psychopath could be distinctly uncharming. "I'll be ready at four."

"I'm counting the minutes," he replied, then hung up.

Cassie hung up as well then walked over and sank down on the sofa. Wealth and charm…it was a potent combination. She could understand how easily a young, vulnerable woman might fall for his line.

Yes, Adam Mercer could be viewed by many as a chance at something better. She wondered if his last girlfriend, the missing Nicole, had found what she was looking for with Adam. Apparently not, since as far as Cassie knew from what Kane had told her the young woman was still missing.

Cassie was ready by quarter to four. Dressing for dates with Adam would quickly become challenging since Jessica didn't boast a great wardrobe.

She found a pink sundress in the closet that had enough ruffles on it to choke a Girl Scout. But the dress would be cool and comfortable for a warm evening in the park and the girlish ruffles certainly characterized Jessica's small-town innocent girl persona.

Beneath the dress she strapped on a thigh belt with

a knife sheath and put in her favorite switchblade. Funny, she never felt fully dressed unless she could feel the presence of a knife somewhere on her body.

At precisely four o'clock, a knock sounded at her door. Apparently Adam Mercer was a punctual psychopath. She opened the door to greet him and again was struck by his lethal attractiveness.

Clad in a pair of beige slacks and a mint-green and beige short-sleeved dress shirt, he looked casually elegant. He filled the room as he entered it, making Cassie's nerve endings jangle discordantly as his restless energy seemed to shrink the dimensions of the small apartment.

"My dear, you look ravishing," he said as he took her hand. His gaze swept the room. "But it pains me to think of you living in these kind of conditions."

"It's not too bad," she protested. "At least it's all mine and I'm not beholden to anyone."

He dropped her hand and walked over to the bookcase.

Cassie tensed, hoping the items there shored up her life as Jessica Sinclair.

"Is this your brother?" he asked and gestured to the picture of the young man in the center of the top shelf.

She nodded. "Yes…that's Jimmy." Her voice held just a hint of grief.

"He was a fine-looking young man," Adam said and turned back to face her, his expression one of empathy.

"He was a good boy, bright and loving. He would have been a great man." She caught her bottom lip between her teeth and blinked rapidly a couple of times as if fighting back tears.

Adam took two long steps to stand before her. He touched her cheek with the pad of his index finger. "I'm sorry. I didn't mean to bring up bad memories." He sounded sincere, but there was a calculation in his vivid eyes that made Cassie wonder.

He took her hand and squeezed it. "The bad times are behind you, Jessica. As long as you're with me I promise nothing bad will ever happen to you again."

A master of manipulation, Cassie thought. How smooth, to bring up a tragedy, evoke emotional responses of grief and sorrow, then promise to make it all better. No wonder Mercer was a hit with young women. He knew exactly what buttons to push.

"I'm ready if you are," she said. He nodded and together they left the apartment. Burt awaited them just outside her apartment door. His harsh features were expressionless, although she thought she saw a spark of malevolence in his eyes when his gaze met hers.

Tonight if Kane didn't show up, she'd call him about that background check. Forewarned was forearmed and she had a feeling before this was all over Burt intended to make trouble for her.

"Where's Jeff?" she asked as they stepped into the elevator.

"Jeff?" Adam looked puzzled.

She pointed to Burt and smiled impishly at Adam. "There's Mutt…where's Jeff?"

Adam laughed, obviously appreciating her sense of

humor. Burt didn't. "Sebastian is at the park holding a table for us. With the concert tonight people get to the park early and the picnic tables are the choice spots."

It took them only fifteen minutes to arrive at the Northland park where the concert was scheduled to begin at five. Sebastian sat at the table beneath a large oak tree that provided welcome shade and a perfect view of the stage where the musicians would perform.

A bright red linen tablecloth covered the rough wooden table and in the center a silver ice bucket held melting cubes and a bottle of Dom Perignon. A large picnic basket set nearby and Cassie had a feeling that Adam picnicked differently than most folks.

Sebastian jumped up from the table as they approached, coming to attention like a private in front of his general. "Wonderful, Sebastian," Adam said and the big man visibly relaxed. "Thank you."

The words were obviously a dismissal, for Burt and Sebastian walked over to a couple of lawn chairs set up nearby and sat.

"Won't they get too warm in the sun?" she asked with feigned sympathy.

Adam waved his hand as it to dismiss the topic. "They're tough. I pay them more than enough to compensate them for a little time in the sun."

He gestured her to the bench, then grabbed two champagne glasses from the picnic basket and poured them each a glass of Dom.

"To good music, good food and better company," he said.

"Hear, hear." They clinked glasses and drank. He set his glass down and got the picnic basket and placed it on the side of the table, then joined her on the bench, sitting close enough that she could smell the scent of him, but not so close that she could be in any way offended.

"Are you hungry?" he asked.

She smiled. "I'm always hungry."

"Wonderful. I like a woman with a healthy appetite." He opened up the picnic basket and began to pull out the contents.

Whoever had packed the basket had thought of everything. There was fresh fruit, cheese and crackers, two kinds of breads, chicken and ham slices, cold pasta salad, and chocolate cake for dessert.

It wasn't a picnic…it was a feast fit for a king and as they ate, Cassie encouraged Adam to talk about himself and his work. "So what is it exactly that you do?" she asked.

"I was lucky in birth and was born into money," he said. "When my parents died and I found myself more wealthy than I'd ever dreamed possible, I knew I wanted to do something to give back to the community. So I began an organization to fight against drug abuse… MAD…Men Against Drugs."

"But why drugs?" Cassie asked. "What made you decide to help people with drug problems?"

"When I first started, nobody was really crying out about the problems of drugs, but I'd seen enough of my friends go down to know that the drug problem in this country was going to be huge. My drug programs here in Kansas City were some of the first in the nation."

There was no denying the pride in his voice, a pride coupled with more than a hint of arrogance. "I saw the problems before anyone else did and within five years had shelters and rehabilitation centers in all the major cities around the country. That was over fifteen years ago."

"Gosh, I'll bet you've helped thousands of people by now," Cassie said, wide-eyed with admiration.

He nodded. "I maintain a list of all the people who have passed though the doors of my centers. I send them updates on new centers and shelters. I also keep in touch with some of them."

Cassie's heartbeat raced just a touch. Had he helped her mother at some point in time? Was it possible that he had her name in his computer…her current address? Was Billy with her?

For the next hour he explained to her about the shelters, the treatment programs and the private facilities of his organization.

She was glad that he was one of those men who liked the sound of his own voice, that all he required from her was an appropriate amount of admiration to shine from her eyes and words of praise for him to fall from her lips.

He didn't mention a word about his maniacal plan to solve the drug problem of the country, but she hadn't expected him to. It was too early in their relationship for that kind of confession from him.

Cassie wondered what it would take from her to get

into his house, get access to his computer. She knew he worked from home often, so his computer there most likely contained the contact list and information about his deadly plan. Would she have to sleep with him and indulge in a little pillow talk for him to tell her what he had in store?

Kane hadn't been Cassie's first lover. Although she'd managed to survive on the streets without being raped, she'd had a brief affair with a stuntman when working on her first movie.

She'd sleep with Adam only as a last resort. She wouldn't like it, but she'd do it. It certainly wouldn't mean anything to her. It never did…except with one man. Then making love had mattered, it had mattered so much that Kane had almost lost his life and she had nearly lost her mind.

By the time the music began, the bottle of champagne was half gone and Adam suggested they move from the table to a blanket in the grass.

They sat side by side, Adam close enough to her that his thigh was pressed against hers. They leaned back against the trunk of the tree as the sound of Bach filled the air.

Adam went quiet once the music started, allowing her to immerse herself in Bach's Toccata and Fugue in d minor. As she listened to the music she thought of Max, who had insisted that a decent education should include classical music appreciation.

How many times had she worked on a particular stunt while the sounds of Beethoven or Mozart rang in her ears? While listening to the masters of music she'd strained muscles, pulled tendons, and twisted her body into positions the body was not meant to make, all beneath the watchful eye of mentor Max.

God, she'd only been undercover for less than a week and she realized she was homesick for the old man.

"Are you all right?" Adam leaned down and whispered in her ear. His breath was warm and scented with the faint odor of a breath mint.

"I'm fine…why?"

He caressed a strand of her hair, as if needy to make some sort of physical contact with her. "You looked sad for just a moment."

"Music affects me on an emotional level," she explained. "I can get sad even listening to oldies music, and country and western songs kill me."

He smiled. "Ah, Jessica, you are such a delight," he said. He pulled her into his arms so that she was leaning back against his chest rather than using the tree trunk as a back brace.

She could feel the muscles of his chest through the thin material of his shirt. Adam might be an older man, but he had the physique of a much younger man. He wrapped his arms around her as if to keep her captive.

She leaned back and pretended to relax as dusk began to steal over the park, shading everything with a soft golden light. Everything except Burt, who divided his attention between the stage and Jessica. Whenever their gazes met she felt the man's animosity like a wild, living entity.

Was it just her personally, or did he always have problems with all his boss's girlfriends? Whatever the case might be, his dislike for her was palpable in the air whenever he was around.

At seven-thirty Adam motioned for Sebastian to pack up the picnic items and he and Jessica headed toward the car. The concert was still going strong. "I'm sorry we have to leave early," she said as they made their way across the park to the lot where the car was parked.

"I'm sorry you have to go to work," he replied.

"Me, too. But the rent has to get paid and the utilities. However, if you keep feeding me like you have been I won't have to worry too much about my grocery bills."

They reached the car and Sebastian got behind the wheel as Burt opened the rear door. Adam slid through the back, then she started to get in next to him.

As she began to enter the car she felt the hot press of a hand on her bottom. She jumped and nearly fell into the back seat.

"Are you all right?" Adam asked in alarm.

"Fine. I'm fine. I just caught my foot as I started in." She turned to look at Burt, who showed no emotion as he shut the back door. The slime ball. He didn't like her but that didn't stop him from copping a quick feel.

"I spent the entire evening talking about me," Adam said once they were on their way to the club. "Now, let's talk about you."

She laughed. "This is going to be a short, boring conversation."

"I doubt that," he replied. His gaze held hers. Those intense blue eyes of his seemed to seek everything that might be found in her thoughts, memories and dreams. "So tell me, Jessica Sinclair...what are your plans... your long-term goals?"

"My long-term goal certainly doesn't include working long term at Night Life," she replied. "I only intend to work there long enough to get together enough money to go back to college for my teaching degree. I mentioned to you the other night that teaching was my real love."

"Go back to college? You already have some college under your belt?" he asked.

If he'd done a background check into her life as Jessica Sinclair, then he probably already knew the answer to his question. She wondered if he was testing her or just trying to make conversation.

"I had just finished my first year at a community college when my parents were killed in a car accident," she replied. "I quit school to get a full-time job and take care of Jimmy."

"Your parents didn't have life insurance?"

She smiled ruefully. "My parents were lucky if they could make the rent on time. They both worked minimum-wage jobs. We always had a lot of love and food to eat, but there were never any extras. Life insurance would have been a luxury they couldn't afford."

"But surely you could have gotten help from the state," he replied.

Cassie stiffened her shoulders. "I didn't want help. I handled it on my own. Jimmy got social security as an underage dependent with both parents dead, and even though it wasn't much, it helped."

"Ah, I sense a strong streak of pride," Adam observed.

Cassie laughed and nodded. "Along with more than my share of stubbornness."

Adam leaned forward. "I like that in a woman."

Cassie worked at allowing a blush to steal over her features. Sure, he liked stubborn women, but she had a feeling he didn't like them if they were butting heads with him.

There was no doubt in her mind that Adam was a control freak, that there would be no such thing as a fifty-fifty kind of relationship with him. He would be the boss and he wouldn't tolerate insubordination.

Still she felt the power of his subtle seduction.

His gaze never wavered from her and he seemed to hang on her every word as if she were imparting pearls of great wisdom instead of telling him about growing up poor in Des Moines, Iowa.

He touched her frequently, reaching out to grasp her hand or rub her arm as if unable to help himself. "Are you coming into the club tonight?" she asked as Sebastian pulled up at the curb in front of the Night Life building.

"Not tonight. I've got some work to do."

Cassie tamped down a wave of frustration as she grabbed her bag and together she and Adam got out of the back seat. He walked with her to the door of the building.

"I had a wonderful time, Adam," she said.

"I did, too." She knew he was going to kiss her. She saw his intention in his eyes before he leaned forward and covered her mouth with his. The kiss was neither particularly pleasant nor unpleasant. His lips were a bit hard against hers, as if trying to establish some form of dominance.

It wasn't until she placed her hand on his arm that he took it as encouragement and wrapped his arms around her as he opened his mouth to deepen the kiss.

Cassie pretended to melt against him, as if overwhelmed with the mastery of the kiss. Men were so easy to manipulate when it came to matters of sex and their egos.

Reluctantly he ended the kiss and released her. "Can I call you tomorrow?"

She nodded. "I'd like that."

He opened the door. "Good night, Jessica."

"Good night." She slid through the door and headed for the elevator. She went into the club and directly into the locker room to change into her uniform. Finding herself alone in the room, she took the opportunity to pull her cell phone from her purse and call Kane. She got a machine and left a message that she wanted the background on Mercer's bodyguards.

For the next five hours she waited tables, bantered with customers and thought about Mercer. Although she knew she couldn't rush things with him, she also knew that each moment that passed brought him closer to his plan.

She was exhausted by the time she got back to her apartment. She threw her keys and purse on the tiny kitchen table, then went into the bathroom. She popped her colored contacts out, then started the shower to wash off the smoke smell that lingered on her after time in the club.

Freshly showered, she pulled on a pair of clean panties and a long T-shirt, then left the bathroom. She'd taken only one step out of the bathroom when a hand touched her on her back.

Her reaction was purely instinctive. Adrenaline spiked through her, she grabbed the hand, stepped back and threw the body that was attached to the hand over her shoulder and to the floor in front of her.

She leapt down, straddling the body before she realized it was Kane.

He stared up at her, his face expressionless. "Isn't there a nicer way for you to say hello?"

"That's what you get for sneaking up behind me." She grinned. "I'm good."

He didn't even blink, but in one smooth movement he flipped her on her back so he straddled her. His hands held her wrists above her head and his face was mere inches from hers. "You're good, but I'm better."

She was aware of every point of contact...his hands holding tight to her wrists, the strength of his thighs on either side of hers and the hot intimacy of their positions. Her heart was racing at a full gallop in the space of a second.

Their gaze remained locked and in his eyes she saw a flicker of burning hunger. He felt good...and right...and terribly dangerous. "Kane." His name whispered from her and she wasn't sure if it was a plea or a protest.

He was on his feet in an instant, his eyes darkly shuttered and not displaying any of the hunger she'd thought she'd seen in the dark depths. He held out a hand to help her up off the floor, then moved across the room.

"Sebastian Smith and Burt Weatherby," he said matter-of-factly. "Both ex-cons, although they've both kept their noses clean since coming to work for Mercer a little over a year ago."

"I guess you got my message," she said, hoping her heart would quickly find a more normal rate of speed. "What did they do time for?" She tried to keep her thoughts focused on the conversation even though she was suddenly remembering the way Kane kissed.

Kane's mouthwatering lips had always been soft against hers and he'd never seemed to need to establish some kind of weird dominance through a kiss. Kane was so comfortable with himself that he didn't need to play macho games with the woman in his life.

She frowned. She shouldn't be thinking about Kane's kisses when she should be thinking about getting closer to Mercer. She shouldn't be thinking about Kane at all.

"Smith did time for possession with intent to distribute, robbery and assault. Weatherby is another animal altogether. Aren't you going to offer me something to drink?"

"You aren't staying that long," she replied, grateful that her voice betrayed nothing of her emotional turmoil. "Tell me about Weatherby."

"Bad news. He's been in and out of prison since the age of eighteen on a variety of charges. Was arrested four years ago for the beating death of a young woman."

"So why isn't he in prison now?"

"The arresting officers screwed up, made so many mistakes the judge had to declare a mistrial. The prosecution was so fractured by the errors, they couldn't go forward with another trial. Why are you asking? Problems?"

"No…no problems. Just wondering, that's all." She'd known it would be something like this, that Burt with his wicked dark eyes and malevolent aura had more than a little bit of the devil in him.

"I watched the two of you in the park. You looked pretty chummy." There was just a hint of something—anger?—in his voice.

Cassie sank onto the sofa, momentarily overwhelmed.

She was surprised to learn that he'd been in the park watching her and Mercer and the anger she thought she'd heard in his voice only added to her confusion. "Kane, I have to get chummy with him. It's the only way we can find out what we need. It's why you brought me back."

There was a moment of silence. His gaze was suddenly dark, brooding as it lingered on her. "Why'd you leave, Cassie?"

It was the question she'd hoped he wouldn't ask, the question she'd hoped she'd never have to answer. She didn't know whether he was asking her why she'd left the agency or why she'd left him. In any case, it was a question she didn't want to answer. "It's complicated," she finally said.

"Then uncomplicate it for me." Although he didn't raise his voice, there was a hard edge to it that demanded an answer.

However, Cassie refused to be bullied, no matter how subtly, into talking about something she wasn't ready to speak of. She stood. "Kane, I've got enough on my mind with the here and now. I'm not going to have a discussion about my actions five years ago. Now, do you have any other useful information for me about Weatherby and Smith?"

"Yeah, stay away from Weatherby. He's bad news. He liked to hurt people."

"I'll do my best. Anything else?" She followed him as he walked toward the window.

"Don't underestimate Mercer and his minions," he said. "Don't take unnecessary chances."

"You know me better than that," she replied.

Again his gaze held hers. "I know you, and that's why I'm telling you, don't take risks. It's important to me." Without warning he pulled her up against him and captured her lips with his.

Kane's kiss had all the spark that Adam's had lacked. Fiery heat swept through her as his tongue parted her lips and slid sensually against hers.

Before she could come to her senses, he released her and swung one of his legs over the windowsill. "You need to stay healthy and well because I'm not finished with you yet, Cassie Newton." With these words he disappeared outside.

Chapter 9

"Oh, my gosh, I had no idea," Cassie exclaimed as Adam Mercer's estate came into view.

It was once again a Monday evening. She and Adam had talked on the phone every day for the past week and three of those nights after her work they'd shared a late dinner. Finally he'd invited her to his home for dinner and drinks.

Mercer's home was on the south side of town and set behind a ten-foot-high stone wall that made it look more like a fortress than a home.

As the car pulled up to the gates, they swung open and the car pulled around the circular driveway to the front door.

The house itself was a three-story monstrosity, bigger than any single dwelling she'd ever seen in her life.

"Between my inheritance, my own earnings and the fact that I'm a silent partner in my ex-wife's import-export business I do fairly well," Adam explained. "And then there are my investments. Using my business acumen, I've managed to make a considerable amount of money."

Cassie made a mental note to have Kane check into Adam's ex-wife and their business dealings, if the agency hadn't already. "I'm so pleased to be able to show you my home," Adam said and squeezed her hand.

"I had no idea," she replied as the car came to a halt. "It's rather intimidating."

Adam laughed and squeezed her hand once again. "It's just a house, Jessica. Just bricks and stones and wood."

"A lot of bricks and stones and wood."

He laughed again and together they got out of the back seat of the car. Burt followed them to the front door while Sebastian drove the car toward the unattached four-car garage.

They entered a foyer bigger than Cassie's apartment. A carved glass table sat in the center, topped with a huge bouquet of fresh flowers. To the right was a grand staircase leading up to regions unknown. But it was to the left that Adam led her, through French doors and into a living room that stole her breath away with its casual elegance.

"See, a television, a sofa, coffee tables…just like any other living room," he said, although there was obvious pride in his voice.

"Yeah, right." She followed him through a doorway that entered a formal dining room with a table big enough to seat at least twelve. The table was set for two, with elegant candles burning in the center and the chandelier overhead emitting a faint glow.

"If you'll have a seat, I'll just let the cook know that we're here." He gestured her toward one end of the table, then disappeared out of the room.

While he was gone Cassie moved her place setting from the end of the long table to the chair right next to his.

There was no way she was going to sit ten feet away from Adam and try to carry on a conversation. As she waited for his return to the room, she tried to contain the thrum of excitement that swept through her. Finally she was in his home. Finally their relationship had gone a step further, hopefully a step closer to getting her into his confidence.

She only hoped he didn't push for any kind of physical intimacy or contact. Even the most casual touch from him had started to give her the creeps. Suddenly she wasn't sure she could sleep with the man, if need be.

Adam looked at her in surprise when he returned, then smiled with obvious pleasure as he sat next to her.

"I like this much better," he said, his gaze filled with a heat she hadn't seen before.

"I don't want to have to shout to talk to you over dinner," she explained. "Besides—" she looked down at her plate as if struck by intense shyness "—I like sitting next to you."

"And I like having you with me," he replied, his voice filled with the heat that his eyes had held moments before.

At that moment a thin dark-haired woman entered

the dining room carrying a large bowl of salad and a basket of yeast-scented rolls.

"Jessica, this is Ramona, my chief cook. Ramona, this is Jessica."

"Nice to meet you, Ramona." Cassie smiled at the woman, who didn't return the gesture. Silently she served them each a helping of salad, placed the bowl between them, then disappeared back where she had come from.

Adam smiled ruefully. "Forgive Ramona. She's short on social skills but is one hell of a cook."

"Has she been with you long?" Cassie took one of the rolls from the basket.

"About a year."

"What did you do? Hire a bunch of new staff a year ago? Burt and Sebastian and Ramona…" Instantly she realized her mistake. Adam hadn't told her that Burt and Sebastian had only been working for him about a year, Kane had told her that information.

"How did you know Burt and Sebastian had only been with me a year?" he asked, his eyes taking on a pale, frosty light.

"That first night that we had dinner and Burt walked me to my car behind the club, I asked him how long he and Sebastian had been working for you." She mentally kicked herself for such a stupid mistake. It was those kinds of mental errors that could blow the entire operation and maybe get her killed in the process.

He visibly relaxed and picked up his fork. "Actually I did do some staff housecleaning about a year ago. My ex-wife had always been in charge of hiring the household help and when she left, some of the help went with her. I decided it was time to downsize. I know the few people I hired now work for me without any torn loyalty to my ex-wife."

"It must take a huge staff to keep a house like this running smoothly," she said.

"Actually not as many as you would think. I prefer to have a small staff of people I trust than a lot of relative strangers running around."

"I guess that's one of the drawbacks about being wealthy, that you don't know who you can trust."

"It's not just a matter of my wealth," he explained. "I have political enemies and of course my work with drug addicts hasn't exactly make me beloved by the drug lords and street thugs."

"It must be awful, to always have to look over your shoulder," she observed.

"You get used to it after a while."

Dinner was served and was not surprisingly another feast, consisting of roast duckling in a mint sauce with new potatoes on the side. Their conversation flowed, a mixture of small talk combined with a hint of sexual innuendo and teasing.

When dinner was finished, Adam offered to take her on a tour of the house. She eagerly agreed, hoping she would spy where his home office was located in the house.

He led her upstairs to the second floor first. "The third floor is strictly for staff," he said. "But this floor is where my bedroom and all the guest suites are located."

He showed her the master suite first, a huge bedroom with a king-size bed covered in a rich, black-and-gold brocade spread.

An oversize walnut dresser and highboy stood against the walls and the nightstands were equally impressive with large lamps on each one. There was no computer visible anywhere in the room.

The connecting bath featured a marble, three-head shower and gold faucets and a hot tub big enough to swim in.

He showed her five guests suites, one more beautifully decorated than the last, then paused in front of a closed door.

"This is just another suite," he said, not offering to show it to her.

Instantly she knew whose room it had been. She placed a hand on his arm, giving him a soulful look of sympathy. "This is her room, isn't it? Your daughter's?"

He nodded. "Yes, this is…was Miranda's room." He hesitated a moment, then opened the door. "Go on," he said and gestured for her to enter the room.

It was more a shrine than a room. It was apparent that nothing had been touched in here since the young woman's death. The canopied bed was all pink ruffles and lace and a dressing table nearby still held the remnants of makeup and perfume.

A huge corkboard hung on one wall and caught Cassie's attention. She walked over to it and studied the pictures and notes and mementos stuck to the board. "This is Miranda?" she asked, pointing to the center photo of a beautiful brunette with big blue eyes.

Adam nodded, but in his eyes she saw no sorrow…only a festering, burning rage and a hint of madness she'd never seen there before. "They killed her…those druggie friends of hers. I told her, I warned her about drugs from the time she was a little girl, but the minute she went to college they got to her."

He punched a fist into the center of the corkboard, the madness in his eyes full-blown and black as night. "Sons of bitches, they'll pay. You wait and see, every last one of them will pay dearly."

"Adam!"

He drew a ragged breath, as if to regain the control he'd momentarily lost. He looked at her as if surprised to see her standing next to him. "I'm sorry," he said. "It just makes me so damned mad. She was so beautiful, so filled with life and with such a bright future ahead of her."

"I know," she replied softly. She stepped close to him, so close her breasts lightly touched his chest. "I know about that anger…that rage. I feel it every time I think about Jimmy."

He grabbed her to him. "Come on, let's get the hell out of here." His gruff voice let her know the anger still had control of him.

They left the room and he closed the door behind them. "Maybe it's time for an after dinner drink," he said as he led her back down the staircase.

"I apologize for my outburst," he said a moment later as he poured himself a healthy shot of scotch and a glass of wine for her. He handed her the glass, then joined her on the sofa.

"Please, don't apologize," she replied. She stared down into her wineglass. "After Jimmy's death I still had to go by the corner where he'd been shot on my way to and from work.

"It was a corner known for drug dealing and I'd see the dealers standing around and I'd want to scratch their eyes out."

She gasped, as if appalled by her own outburst. "I can't believe I just told you that."

"Please, don't apologize. It's so refreshing to find a woman who isn't afraid of her own emotions, even if those emotions aren't always socially acceptable," he said.

"That's why I had to leave Des Moines...because I was so filled with hatred, and afraid that eventually that hatred would drive me to do something terrible in revenge."

"Is revenge such a bad thing?" His eyes glittered intensely as if her answer were the most important thing she'd ever say to him.

She smiled ruefully. "It is if it will put you in prison for the rest of your life. Even if I killed those creeps selling drugs, I'd still face murder charges."

"And that is the injustice of our justice system." He gestured to her nearly empty wineglass. "Would you like some more?"

"No, thank you. I'm fine. Are you going to show me the rest of your home? It's just so beautiful." She had to find his computer.

She hoped she didn't sound too eager to invade his personal space. He didn't seem to take offense. "Yes, of course," he said. He stood and reached for her hand. "I always enjoy showing off my home."

He showed her the rest of the main floor, a huge kitchen that could easily fulfill the needs of a busy restaurant, a glassed-in sunroom with a killer view of the lush gardens. "I often enjoy my morning coffee here," he said.

"So where do you work from? Do you have an elegant office downtown?"

"No, there's nothing elegant about my work space and I work such odd hours that I have my office right here." He led her from the sunroom down a hallway and into a large study.

Bingo! Cassie thought as she saw the state-of-the-art computer that was on and humming on the beautiful, massive walnut desk.

"Now when you call me and tell me you're working I'll be able to picture you sitting in this room," she said.

He walked over to her and drew her into his arms. "I hate talking to you on the phone and envisioning you in your home surroundings," he murmured close to her ear.

"Not everyone can live like a king, Adam," she chided. "My apartment might not be The Ritz, but at the moment it's home and I'm not beholden to anyone for it."

He stroked a strand of her hair, hunger evident in his eyes. "I want you, Jessica." He dropped his hand from her hair and instead grabbed her by the waist and pulled her closer against him.

She hesitated, unsure what her response should be. All her research had indicated that Adam Mercer liked a challenge, but when it came to women and sex what exactly constituted a challenge?

"I'm sorry...I'm rushing things," he said, taking away the need for any definitive response from her. He leaned forward and kissed her forehead.

"Adam, I'm very attracted to you and I love spending time with you. I just don't want to move too fast and make a mistake."

"I agree," he replied. "But, I can tell you this, I don't feel as if I'm making a mistake with you."

She smiled shyly. "I feel the same way."

"Good." A smug smile curved his lips. "And now, how about a walk through the gardens?"

The June sun had fallen just enough to transform the light of day with shades of pink and gold. The gardens were a sight to behold. The air was filled with the scent of flowers in a variety of colors and shapes.

Even though Cassie oohed and aahed over the floral wonderland, her mind cataloged far more than the display of planned nature. She saw that the stone wall encircled the entire compound. There were outbuildings on the back left side of the house and the swimming pool and a large treed area to the right.

She saw no guards, although she spied video cameras mounted atop the stone wall at regular intervals. If anything went wrong it was vital that she know the surroundings, where the best escape route might be, how to flee the area in the most expeditious way.

As they walked through the garden, Adam held her hand and told her about the variety of flowers contained in the different beds. There was a patronizing quality to his voice and that, along with the thoughts of his earlier outburst made him climb higher up her personal "ick" meter.

In the past week she'd gotten a better handle on what kind of a man he was and she found his character sadly lacking in decent human qualities. He was rude and arrogant to his employees, impatient with people in general and she suspected he might be having some cash flow problems.

There was nothing specific she could put her finger on to back up her suspicions, just a lot of little things that added up to the possibility. She'd overheard a terse phone call between Adam and his personal banker when they'd been out to dinner, and the fact that he'd fired most of his household help hinted at some financial problems.

By the time they had finished their walk of the grounds and he'd shown her his pool and pool house, night had erased the last of the day's light.

"Stay the night," Adam said when they were once again in the living room. "You can have any of the guest bedrooms you like. I'd love to have my coffee in the morning with you sitting opposite me."

"But I didn't bring any nightclothes," she protested weakly. Nothing served her purpose better than spending the night in his home.

"I took the liberty of buying some things in case you'd ever want to spend a night here with me."

"You are a very presumptuous man," she teased, then sighed with a touch of wistfulness. "I did like that bedroom with the white-and-gold bedspread."

"Then tonight it will be yours," he said firmly. "I promise I'll have you back to your apartment before noon tomorrow."

She hesitated another moment. "All right, then I'd love to stay the night and have coffee with you in the morning."

"Wonderful."

The rest of the evening passed quickly. Adam put music onto the stereo system and they sat in the living room and talked.

The longer she spent in Adam's company, the less she liked him. She could certainly understand how a young, impressionable woman might find his arrogance attractive, his ostentatious display of wealth seductive and his aura of power magnetic.

But Cassie saw beneath the polished smooth facade of Adam Mercer, and what she saw there was a megalomaniac who had a warped conscience and sense of morality, and a burning rage over the death of his daughter.

She wondered about his marriage, if it had really been Miranda's death that had destroyed the union or if maybe his wife had used that tragedy to escape from a man who had probably mentally abused and controlled her.

The fact that she didn't particularly like him made her job both easier and more difficult. It was easier because she could take him down without losing a wink of sleep, more difficult because before she brought him down she had to make him believe she was smitten with him.

It was a relief when they decided to call it a night. He escorted her up the stairs and to the doorway of the room she'd seen earlier.

"Sweet dreams, Jessica," he murmured and gathered her into his arms. His hard lips captured hers in a searing kiss she guessed was supposed to spin her senses and make her gasp with desire. It did neither.

But as he released her she stumbled backward and heaved a sigh of what she hoped sounded like sensual pleasure. Apparently he was satisfied that he'd overwhelmed her with passion. "Why don't we plan on breakfast about seven-thirty in the morning in the sunroom? Is that all right with you?"

"Fine as long as there's an alarm clock in the room. Without an alarm, I'd sleep until noon."

"I think you'll find everything you need."

"Thank you, Adam. I'll see you in the morning." She entered the bedroom and closed the door behind her. She turned the lock on the door, then checked to make sure there were no hidden cameras or surveillance devices in the room.

She knew it was crazy to even think of such a thing, but she wouldn't put anything past Mercer. She didn't relax until she'd assured herself the room was clean.

She'd specifically chosen this particular bedroom not because of the decorating style, but because it was nearest to the stairs and furthest away from his master suite.

Somebody had been in the room to prepare it for her. Not only was the bed turned down, but a pink silk night-gown and matching robe was laid out on the bed.

In the adjoining bathroom a basket filled with sham-poos and soaps and perfumed moisturizers awaited her use. She knew it would be hours before she could get to what she wanted to do, so she indulged herself in a long, steamy, sweet-scented bath in a tub that was sin-fully large.

Although it had been years since she had lived on the streets, she'd never taken for granted the luxuries like hot water and soap and the exquisite pleasure of a lei-surely soak in a tub. And tonight she would sleep in a bed where she didn't have to worry about creepy crawl-ers…if she managed to sleep at all.

She soaked in the tub for a long time, her thoughts drifting back in time, back to Los Angeles, back to the moment when she had first realized her mother wasn't coming back for her.

She'd sat near the curb for hours, watching for her mother's boyfriend's truck to come back, for her mom to laugh and tell her it had all been a horrible joke.

She could still remember the smells of that day…the

hot odor of oil and tar from the nearby street, the stench of garbage rotting in the heat, the horrifying smell of fear that emanated from her own body and overpowered every other scent.

Hope had been her only companion for that first long afternoon and night. She'd clung to it like a security blanket, certain that when her mother came to her senses she'd remember to come back for her.

But the afternoon passed, the evening came and went and the frightening darkness of night fell. Cassie had spent that first night in the alcove of a storefront, terror keeping her eyes open and her heart pounding.

By the time Cassie was ten, she'd known her mother had a problem, that she took pills that made her stay up for days, then she'd take more pills and would sleep for an entire day. She'd grown accustomed to the smell of grass that clung to her mother's clothes and hair, although at that time she didn't know what to call the rolled cigarettes her mother liked to smoke.

It was only as she grew older that she realized her mother's real weakness was not so much the pills or the marijuana, but rather a character flaw that made her mother weak, afraid to be alone and easily abused by the men who rolled in and out of her life.

She ran the sponge across her shoulders then leaned forward to add more hot water into the tub. When she stretched back out once again, she thought of the man who had been with her mother when she'd been left on the streets.

His name had been Rick. She didn't remember his

last name, but she remembered in the four months her mother was with him the way his small dark eyes had followed her, how he'd find ways to put his hot, sweaty hands on her. He'd rub her shoulders, or pat her butt, all seemingly innocent, but there was something in his touch that made Cassie afraid.

Still, she couldn't believe that her mother had left her on a strange street in a strange city in the middle of the afternoon with no intention of ever coming back for her.

What kind of a mother did something like that? And what had Cassie done that had made her mother throw her away? By the afternoon of the third day, Cassie realized desperately nobody was coming back for her. She was on her own.

She stirred, pulling herself from the past, surprised to discover tears wetting her cheeks. She grabbed a washcloth and scrubbed her face, irritated that thoughts of that long ago betrayal still had the power to move her emotionally.

As she dried off she wondered why she even cared about seeing her mother again. Why did she want to find the woman who had dumped her out of a truck and never looked back?

She told herself she just wanted to find Billy. She wanted to find the little brother she'd loved and lost. But it was more than that. She needed to look her mother in the face and ask one simple question…why?

She wanted her family. The hunger inside her for family never completely went away. It shouted at her in quiet moments and whispered to her during busy ones.

The hunger was a constant companion and she knew the only way she could get relief from the pain was to find them.

She pulled the silk nightgown over her head, glad that it was knee-length rather than floor-length. If she was going to skulk around the house in the dark, she didn't want to be tripping over her hemline.

An alarm clock on the nightstand next to the bed read almost eleven. It would be several hours before she attempted a foray outside the bedroom.

She set the alarm for six-thirty the next morning, then shut off the lights in the room and moved to the window. From this vantage point she had a view of the back grounds. The three-quarter moon overhead spilled down a silvery illumination that made visibility good.

She remained at the window for an hour but during that time saw no patrols, no guards of any kind. Apparently Adam depended solely on the video cameras for security.

After thoroughly assessing the situation, she left the window and crawled into bed. She wasn't afraid she'd fall asleep. Adrenaline pumped through her, chasing away any thought of sleep.

Adam had indicated that he did everything on his computer. She was hoping his plans for his future annihilation were there.

He couldn't be doing it all alone. The plot was too big for one man to accomplish. Someplace, somewhere somebody had to be manufacturing the tainted drugs, somebody had to be arranging for shipment. Adam was enough of a control freak that he'd need to be in touch with those people on a daily basis. The easiest way to maintain contact would be either through cell phone or e-mail.

She needed to get to his computer.

When the clock read one forty-five, she pulled herself out of bed. She didn't bother to pull on the long robe, afraid that she'd get tangled in the silky material should she have to move fast.

With her room still dark except for the moonlight that crept in, she made her way to the door. She unlocked it, then turned the knob and opened it, grateful that it didn't creak.

She stood in the threshold, listening for any sound that would indicate anyone in the household was still awake. Nothing.

She peeked down the hallway, toward the end where Adam's room was located. The door was closed. She hoped he was lost in sweet dreams of murder and mayhem.

Leaving her doorway, she crept toward the stairs, still listening intently for any noise that might indicate another human presence.

One stair at a time. She moved with the stealth of a cat down the long staircase, hearing only the knock of her heart against her rib cage.

At the bottom of the stairs she paused, her gaze finding reassurance in the darkness that greeted her on the bottom level.

She padded lightly across the foyer floor and into the living room where the moonlight sliced through the darkness and cast shadows across the walls.

She wasn't afraid of shadows. What she feared was a living, breathing person like Adam or worse, Burt. Even the taciturn Ramona could cause problems if she caught Cassie sneaking through the house in the dark.

A faint illumination coming from Adam's office stopped her in her tracks. Was Adam working? The illumination in the room was too strong to be moonlight, but too weak to be a desk lamp.

Drawing a deep breath, she peered into the room and relaxed as she saw that the light shone from his computer screen and there was nobody in the room.

Apparently Adam's arrogance was so huge, he felt assured that nobody in the house would betray him, nobody in the house would enter his study and access his files.

He hadn't counted on her. She crept into the office and peered at the computer screen. A screen saver was up and running, sending tropical fish swimming across the flat screen monitor.

She punched the enter button and the screen saver disappeared. "Damn," she breathed under her breath as she saw the amount of files contained in the system. It would take her a year to go through the content of all the files he had stored.

Instead of trying to look at each one, she quickly entered the Windows program and read the title of the files. She looked for any that might point to a file containing the information she sought, any entitled Blue, or Miranda, or some key word that made sense.

On her first cursory glance, there was nothing… nothing that caught her eye. Quickly, aware of the minutes passing, she closed down the program and accessed his e-mail.

Again she mentally cursed at the number of e-mails contained in folders. Did the man save everything? Didn't he know what the delete button was for?

Again she scanned subject lines to see if anything sounded an alarm in her head. One subject line caught her attention. It read: Enter Drawing to Win Blue Explorer.

Although on the face of it, it sounded like one of the thousands of unsolicited advertisements users had to put up with on a daily basis. But she wasn't leaving anything up to chance.

It wasn't an advertisement and her heartbeat quickened to an almost painful pace. The e-mail was from a sender named Whitegirl. Cassie knew White Girl was a nickname for cocaine. She was able to click on the e-mail so that it showed in the frame below. She could read the message that way without actually opening the e-mail and alerting Adam that it had been used. The note said: Expect delivery of your shiny blue vehicle at the arranged location on July 4th.

The Fourth of July, that was less than three weeks away. She closed the message, then froze. A noise…the distant sound of somebody coughing.

With frantic, trembling fingers she pulled up the

screensaver, then raced out of the study. She'd just stepped into the kitchen and taken two steps toward the large refrigerator when the overhead light clicked on.

"What in the hell are you doing?" Burt demanded.

Chapter 10

Cassie threw a hand over her mouth in a gesture of surprise. "You scared me to death," she exclaimed.

"What the hell are you doing down here?" Burt eyed
her suspiciously, then looked across the doorway toward the study.

"I got thirsty." She dropped her hand from her mouth
and instead crossed her arms over her breasts as Burt's
beady eyes swept the length of her.

"Mr. Mercer doesn't like people sneaking around
the house in the middle of the night."

"Then he should have a refrigerator in every room."
Aware of his gaze still burning into her with distrust,
she walked over to the refrigerator and opened it. She
spied a carton of orange juice and pulled it out, figuring she'd better find a glass instead of drinking from the
carton.

"I could have shot you as a prowler," Burt said. "I
could beat you to death right now and tell Mr. Mercer
I mistook you for a robber." There was a depravity in

the gleam in his beady eyes, as if he'd thoroughly enjoy beating the heck out of her.

"What is your problem, Burt?" she asked impatiently. "You've been a jerk to me every since we met." She opened first one cabinet door, then another seeking a glass for the orange juice.

"I don't like you." The Elvis snarl was back, curling one corner of his upper lip in a gesture that did nothing for him. He walked over to a cabinet, pulled a glass out and slammed it on the counter.

"Is it something personal or do you just hate women in general?" She poured the juice into the glass and returned the carton to the refrigerator. She was grateful to see the suspiciousness gone from his eyes. Apparently he believed her story about wanting something to drink.

"I don't hate all women." Once again his gaze swept over her, lingering on her scantily clad breasts, then down to the long length of her bare legs.

She didn't try to cover up. Let him look, the creep. Even though his gaze made her skin threaten to crawl off her body, she wouldn't give him the satisfaction of letting him know it.

"I don't like women with attitudes...smart asses, and I think you're a smart ass," he said.

She smiled cheerfully. "And I think you're a dumb ass."

He glared as she quickly drank her glass of juice, then placed the glass in the sink. "And on that note, I think I'll say good-night."

She started to walk past him but he stepped in front

of her, impeding her exit through the door. "You'd better sleep with one eye open."

Cassie sighed, weary of his macho posturing. "I just want to go back to bed, Burt. I'll try to stay out of your way if you stay out of mine. Deal?"

He stepped aside. "I'm watching you, Blondie."

Cassie passed by him, smelling the rank odor of stale sweat that emanated from him. She was aware of him following her out of the kitchen and felt the burn of his gaze on her as she climbed the stairs back toward her bedroom.

It wasn't until she'd reached the privacy of her room and had locked the door that she began to tremble. She sank on the bed and allowed the tremors to sweep through her.

If she'd taken one second longer in the study, she would have been busted. And there was no doubt in her mind that Burt would have killed her.

She got in bed and pulled the sheets up to her chin, her mind racing. She believed she'd gotten one important detail…the date of the delivery of the tainted drugs.

The buzz of the alarm awakened her at six-thirty. She wished she could just get dressed and take off, find Kane and tell him what she'd learned. But her game wasn't over yet. She had the when, but she didn't have the where and the how.

A long hot shower erased any lingering sleep and by seven-thirty she went down the staircase and headed for the sunroom where Adam had told her he'd meet her for breakfast.

The sunroom was empty, but she heard Adam's voice

coming from his study. She crept toward the office hoping to overhear something that might fill in the blanks.

"I don't give a damn what kind of problem you've run into," Adam's voice held a cold fury she'd never heard before. "Fix it or I'll find somebody who can. Nobody in this operation is irreplaceable. Don't call me again with problems. Call me with results."

Cassie crept backward, back toward the sunroom. She'd just sunk into one of the wicker chairs at the table when he appeared.

Clad in a crisp white pair of slacks and a turquoise and white short-sleeved shirt, he looked elegantly cool and completely collected. There was no hint of the intense fury she'd just heard in his voice apparent on his features.

"Good morning, my dear." He kissed her on the forehead, then took the seat opposite her at the glass-topped wicker table. "I trust you slept well."

"Like a baby, although I did get up at one point and came down here for a glass of something to drink." She figured she'd better mention it in case Burt had already told his employee about it.

"I hope you found what you needed?" he asked.

She smiled. "Orange juice. I'm an orange juice addict."

"Now that's a healthy addiction to have. I instructed Ramona to fix a big, country-style breakfast this morning."

"You shouldn't have her go to all that trouble," she protested. "I would have been satisfied with coffee and toast."

"Nonsense. What's the use of having a cook if she doesn't cook? Besides, I was in the mood for a big breakfast." Ramona entered the room carrying a tray with a silver coffeepot, two cups and saucers and cream and sugar.

As with the dinner the night before, she served them silently, but efficiently, then disappeared back toward the kitchen.

Adam served the coffee from the pot and chatted about his household help, explaining to her who was in charge of what and how smoothly things ran.

Cassie nodded when it was appropriate, but her mind was busy trying to figure out a way of sneaking into Adam's computer one last time before he took her home. But it was looking like there would be no more opportunities on this particular visit.

Breakfast was huge, in typical fashion—eggs and thick slabs of ham, hashed browns and biscuits and gravy. Cassie ate with gusto and when they'd finished breakfast she told Adam she really needed to get back home.

"I just didn't plan on spending the night anywhere and I made lunch arrangements with one of the waitresses from the club," she lied.

"Of course," he agreed smoothly. "Actually I have some work to attend to this morning as well. If you don't mind I'll have Sebastian drive you home."

"Thank you, that will be fine."

Within minutes after the meal, Cassie was ensconced in the back of Adam's Lincoln being driven back to her apartment. He'd sent her off with a passionate kiss and the promise to see her that evening at the club.

The moment Cassie entered her apartment she made two phone calls. The first call was to Dana, who had given Cassie her phone number the second night that the two had worked together.

She set up a lunch date at exactly noon at the small café across the street in the city market. If by some strange chance Adam was having her watched, then he would see she hadn't lied about the lunch date.

The second call she made was to Kane. She told him to meet her at the city market at eleven-forty. With the most urgent details taken care of, she spent the next hour working out.

At eleven she took a quick shower, pulled on a yellow sundress, then headed out of the apartment and across the street to the market place. Even though it was a Tuesday morning, the place was packed with people.

Cassie walked up and down the aisles, chatting with vendors and buying more fruit and vegetables. Although she appeared intent on her buying, her gaze never stopped scanning the area, looking for a familiar face who might be tailing her for Adam. She knew Adam probably had hundreds of people on his payroll and wouldn't be stupid enough to use somebody she might recognize.

She was checking out a display of huge green peppers when she became aware of somebody standing a bit too close to her.

"Two for a dollar," the eager vendor said to her.

"Nothing better than stuffed peppers," a familiar male voice observed.

She cast a glance sideways and swallowed a chuckle of surprise. Clad in a pair of worn jeans and a short-sleeved plaid shirt, a straw hat on his head and a piece of straw dangling from his lips, Kane looked every inch the Missouri farm boy. A handsome…sexy farmer.

"Personally I like them cut up in salads."

"If you like salad they got a nice display of lettuce over there," he gestured to a more congested area of the market.

"Three," the vendor exclaimed. "Three for a dollar and you pick the biggest ones I've got."

"Done." Cassie picked out three peppers and paid the vendor, aware that Kane had moved away from her side. She took the sack from the vendor then moved toward the display where Kane awaited her.

She moved next to him, not so close that they would be mistaken as acquaintances, but close enough that they could converse without shouting.

"Got news." She grabbed a head of lettuce and pretended to examine it.

"You spent the night with him." Kane's voice was flat, displaying no emotion at all.

She shot him a quick glance. "We slept in separate rooms." She put the head of lettuce down and picked up another one. "Which gave me a chance to sneak into his study and access his computer."

Kane walked to the next vendor who had bushels of corn on the cob spilling out of baskets. She waited a minute, then followed.

"So what did you find out?"

"A date," she replied. "Fourth of July."

"What a sick lunatic to turn a national holiday into a day of death. What else?"

"That's it. I had to stop. Burt almost caught me at the computer." She motioned for the seller to give her six ears of corn. When she glanced at Kane she saw alarm in his eyes.

"Cover intact?"

"Fine."

"Are you sure? Maybe we should pull you out."

"Don't even think of such a thing," she hissed beneath her breath. "I'm in and I'm fine and it would be stupid to pull me out now. Don't go soft on me, McNabb."

There was a long pause. "Don't worry, I did that once and didn't like the consequences."

She felt the flush that swept over her as again the ghosts of their shared past rose up between them. "I need to stay in long enough to get the rest of the information we need. Just the date doesn't help us a bit." She grabbed the corn from the vendor and when she turned to look at Kane he was gone.

She cursed under her breath, not because he'd disappeared but rather because he'd made her remember vividly the last time she'd seen him when she'd quit the agency five years before.

During the time they had worked together Kane had always seemed bigger than life to her. His passion and drive and energy lit her up inside. His determination and commitment to the job encouraged her to be the best that she could be.

The last time she'd seen him he'd been without passion, without drive or energy. He'd been clinging to life by a thread, lost in a hospital bed hooked up to a bevy of machines working overtime to keep him alive.

She'd stared at him from the hospital room doorway in horror, knowing she was responsible for his condition. He'd gone soft on her and she'd allowed it, encouraged it.

Assured by the doctors that he would survive, she'd left his room and had never looked back. Until now. And she'd never questioned her decision. Until now.

She and Kane had shared something and when she'd left, she'd walked away with a hole in her heart. Never had that hole been as apparent as it was now, with him back in her life even on a strictly business level.

She consciously shoved these disturbing thoughts aside and checked her wristwatch. It was time to meet Dana.

Dana made an entertaining lunch date. She was smart and savvy, but also had a sweetness of spirit that intrigued Cassie. Under different circumstances they might have been friends. Other than Asia's wife, Cassie really had no other female friends.

She found most females difficult…game players or vapid or murderously competitive. Maybe it was because she'd had no real female influence in her early life except for eleven years with her drug-addicted mother.

Cassie enjoyed talking with Dana about clothes and men and the other waitresses at the club, even if she had to lie about the men part and let Dana chatter most about fashion. They both ordered sinfully chocolate desserts and lingered over coffee.

Afterward Cassie went back to her apartment and took a nap, knowing she would need to be mentally and physically rested for the night to come.

Adam stood at his office window and stared out at the manicured grounds of his home.

"I don't like her."

Adam turned around and smiled with amusement at Burt. "You never like any of them. If I didn't know better, I'd swear you were a misogynist at heart."

"I don't hate women. I just don't like her," Burt replied with a mulish expression. "I was right about Nicole, wasn't I?"

Adam walked across the floor and sat at his desk chair and stared up at the ceiling, thinking about the lovely Nicole. She'd been beautiful, with a lush body and an eagerness to please he'd found attractive.

Adam had been quite smitten with her. He'd even moved her into his house for a month, and for a while he'd believed she was perfect for him and his future plans.

He sighed and looked at Burt, who was seated in the chair opposite his desk. "Nicole was a real disappointment," he agreed. "But Jessica is different. She's much brighter than Nicole was, yet more innocent."

"I just don't want to see anything get screwed up," Burt said. "We're too close to success." He rubbed his hands together as if already feeling the money that would flow into his palms.

Adam smiled. "Nothing is going to screw things up. Trust me, Burt. I have everything under control. Now, I've got work to do here and you're keeping me from it."

Burt stood, a hulk that darkened the opening of the room. "I hope you've got everything under control because I've got a lot of men who are going to be pissed off if this thing doesn't come off as planned."

"I told you it's under control."

Burt nodded and left the office. Adam turned to his computer and retrieved his e-mail messages.

Burt was getting nervous, as he should be. Burt was betraying a lot of important drug lords and street gang members. If any word leaked of their plan to distribute tainted drugs, Burt's life wouldn't be worth anything. It was no wonder the man was starting to get nervous.

Adam had no idea what Burt's plans were immediately following the distribution process, but Adam intended to be long gone by the time the dopers and dealers realized what was going on.

The Fourth of July would usher in death and destruction, which would wreak havoc for days, weeks and months afterward. He had no doubt that there would be anarchy in the streets as people died. Fear would reign, then anger would follow.

Adam was a patient man. It would be years before anyone would smoke a joint or snort some coke and not be afraid of instant death. It would be a kind of justice for Miranda.

It would be nice if he had a beautiful blonde to share his triumph…a beautiful blonde named Jessica.

Chapter 11

"I want you to move in with me."

Cassie looked at Adam in surprise. It was Thursday evening and for the past three nights she and Adam had shared late night dinners after she finished working at the club. Tonight they were once again in Anthony's.

"I know it's a big step," he continued. "And you could have your own bedroom until you felt ready to take the next step and move into mine." His voice was smooth seduction, but it had zero effect on her.

She pretended to contemplate his offer. If she were living there, then surely she'd be able to find time to access the rest of his files and e-mails and get the rest of the details of his plan.

"Look, I know you're an independent woman and don't want to be beholden to anyone, but this would mean so much to me," he continued.

"It's a big step," she said softly. She picked up her wineglass and took a drink, her expression thoughtful. She placed the glass back on the table and twisted the stem between two fingers. "We've had lovely times together so far. But living together is quite different than dating. You might find me utterly irritating."

He laughed. "I doubt that very seriously. It's quite possible you'll find me a bore."

"Never." She frowned. "We really haven't known each other that long, Adam." She hesitated a long moment and felt his tension building. "What about a kind of trial run…maybe we try it for a week and see how things work out?"

"Sounds like a good plan," he agreed, obviously pleased. "I feel confident you're going to see that we are meant for each other."

"At the moment the only thing I'm confident about is the fact that it's past my bedtime and I need to get home."

"And pack," he said. "If I had my way, we'd take you home right now, pack you up and get you settled into my place."

"Tomorrow," she said. "I'll pack up after a good night's sleep and be at your place tomorrow."

He reached across the table and captured her hand with his. "I guess that will have to do, although I confess I've never been a patient man. I want what I want when I want it and I want you in my life, in my home, right beside me right now."

She squeezed his hand. "Good things come to those who wait." She placed her napkin on the table and stood, eager to get home, take a shower and wash away the stress and strain of acting the smitten girlfriend with Adam always produced.

Within minutes she was in her car heading for her apartment. Tomorrow she would be living in Adam's house and surely at some point or another she would be able to either access the files on his computer to find the information she needed, or overhear a conversation that would clue her in about his Fourth of July massacre.

In return he'd have access to her, running his hands over her shoulders with that smug, proprietary smile on his face. During the last several days she'd had to endure more and more of his touches, his love pats and strokes and always with ice-blue eyes gleaming with the pride of possession. It made her skin crawl.

As she drove her thoughts turned to Max. She wondered how he was doing. Before this assignment she'd spoken with him almost every day. She missed him, missed his wit and frank advice, his ability to cheer her up and keep her honest with herself.

But even though she'd like nothing better than to hear his voice, she didn't want to risk calling him. She had no idea if Adam had tapped her calls, how far-reaching his power might be.

Beyond exhaustion, she parked her car and got out. Even though it was late and she was tired, she needed to contact Kane and let him know her plans to move in with Mercer.

As soon as she was in her apartment, she used the cell phone to call Kane. He didn't answer and she left only a four-word message. "We need to talk." She clicked off, opened the window, then sat to wait, knowing that he would arrive soon.

Ten minutes later she watched as first one long leg, then Kane's head appeared inside the windowsill. As always she was amazed by his agility. Even though she'd been expecting him, she'd heard no scrape or bump to herald his arrival. He'd managed to climb the building facade without making a single sound.

"Got your message," he said, once he was fully inside the apartment. "What's going on?" He sank down next to her on the sofa.

"I'm moving in with Adam tomorrow."

Kane stood and stared down at her, his eyes darker than she'd ever seen them before. He looked like a vampire ready to bite in his black get-up as he loomed over her. "Is that really necessary?"

She could tell from his cool tone he didn't like the idea. "I have to have access to his computer and living there will hopefully give me that access. Yes, it's necessary."

"I don't like it."

"I'm not jumping with joy over the prospect myself," she replied dryly. "Please, sit down. You're making me nervous." In truth, she felt unusually fragile, worried about moving in with Adam and vulnerable to Kane's nearness.

He returned to the sofa and sat, a frown tugging at his handsome features. "How long do you think it will take to get the rest of the information for us? The Fourth of July isn't that far away."

"I can't make any promises, but I'd hope I can get

something over the next day or two…if he leaves me alone long enough. What's happening on your end?"

Kane ran a hand across his lower jaw, a gesture she knew spoke of frustration. "Nothing. We're trying to find out who is manufacturing the drugs, where it might be coming from. But none of our sources have come up with any information on this particular deal."

"So nobody on the street is talking about this?"

"On the contrary, everyone on the street is talking about a big deal going down in the near future, but nobody seems to have any substantial information."

"All the more reason why it's necessary for me to move into Adam's house."

Kane stood once again and shoved his hands in his pockets. "I guess I figured it would come to this, but I was hoping it wouldn't. You know this is the most dangerous part of your assignment."

She nodded, then tried on a small smile. "It can't be any more dangerous than carrying a tray of drinks through a crowded bar."

"You spill a drink, no big deal. You screw up with Mercer you get dead." He drew a deep breath and pulled his hands out of his pockets. "Mercer's old girlfriend showed up last night."

"Really? Where?"

"The morgue." He paused a moment to let his words sink in.

They sunk in all right…digging deep into her bones and injecting her blood with an icy chill. "I don't suppose she died of natural causes?"

"Only if you consider being strangled and having the hell beaten out of you natural."

Cassie sank back onto the sofa. "Where was she found?"

"Some distance off one of the walking paths in Riverfront Park. Apparently a couple of kids playing in the park stumbled across her."

Cassie was silent for a long moment. Poor Nicole. From everything she'd heard from the other waitresses at Night Life the young woman had been genuinely nice.

All she'd wanted was a better life than the one she'd been dealt, and she'd thought Adam Mercer was the ticket to that better life. Instead she was dead, beaten and strangled and left in a park to be discovered by kids.

"How long had she been there?"

"Hard to say for sure, but my sources told me that the park was just the dump site and she'd been there for several weeks."

"Forensic evidence?"

"Nothing so far and nothing expected to turn up. Unfortunately in the last couple of weeks we've had typical Missouri weather…high winds, rain and heat. Whatever trace evidence might have been there has probably blown or washed away by now."

Cassie swept a hand through her hair and leaned her head against the back of the sofa. "Will they question Adam?"

"Certainly." Kane leaned with his back against the wall next to the window. "He was questioned initially when she was reported missing but there's no evidence tying him to the murder except that he once dated Nicole. They'll question him again now that her body has been found."

"He was probably the last person to see her alive."

"True. But you have to remember nobody knows what we know about Mercer. To most of the world, to most of the cops in this city, he's a wealthy man doing good works for this community and others."

"You know he killed her…or he had her killed," she said. Probably Burt, if she had to make an educated guess. He already had a history of violence.

"We're coordinating with the authorities to go easy in their investigation of the murder where Mercer is concerned. We don't want to put unnecessary heat under him and screw up the drug deal."

"Yeah, the last thing we need is to scare him off and have him set up another time in the future that we might not get wind of," she replied.

"Cassie, it's important you understand that these men play for keeps. When Mercer breaks up with a woman, apparently he breaks up forever."

"I appreciate you telling me, but of course Nicole's death changes nothing. If I don't get in and get the information to stop the distribution of the drugs, then Nicole's death will only be the first of thousands."

Cassie leaned her head against the back of the sofa and closed her eyes. If her mother still used drugs, then it was quite possible she could be one of Adam's victims. If Billy had followed in their mother's footsteps, then he, too, could get hold of the poisoned drug and die. "We have to stop him," she said.

She jumped and opened her eyes as Kane's hands fell on her shoulders. She hadn't heard him move behind the sofa. As his hands gently kneaded her shoulders, she closed her eyes once again.

For just a moment she allowed herself to feel only the pleasure of his touch. She wanted him. Even though she'd left him years ago, even though she knew wanting him was the last thing she needed in her life, she couldn't help the raw emotions that roared through her as he rubbed her shoulders.

His familiar scent eddied in the air. She could feel his warm breath on her neck and a responding heat swept over her. "Don't be a hero, Cassie," he said softly. "If things get too dangerous, then get out."

"I've got to get the information."

He dropped his hands from her shoulders and walked back to stand in front of her. "It's too late to save them, Cassie." His voice was soft, gentle. "They were lost a long time ago."

She didn't pretend not to understand who he was talking about. He knew her too well. He knew the hole inside that had been created when her family had left her on the street and driven away. Max was the only other person who knew her hunger to find her mother and brother.

"They're my family, Kane. I have to find them. And even if I can't find out anything about their whereabouts, we've still got to stop this shipment. Too many lives are at risk."

"I wish we could trade places."

She stood and walked with him toward the window. She forced a smile to her lips. "I'm afraid you aren't Adam's type."

Those dark eyes of his gazed at her intently. "I wish you weren't."

She frowned, not liking the way the conversation was going. She didn't want Kane to care. His personal feelings for her was what had almost gotten him killed on the last job they had worked together.

"Be grateful I am," she said sharply. "Somebody has to get in and get that information. It was what I was brought back to do, remember?"

A muscle ticked in his jaw. "Yeah, right. The White Rose is back on the job. I just don't want to see you getting yourself killed by taking unnecessary chances."

"You'd know all about that, wouldn't you, Kane?" Her words hit the mark. His features tightened and his hands fisted at his sides. Instantly she wanted to call the words back. An apology formed in her head, but before it could reach her lips, he backed her up against the wall.

"You picking a fight with me, Cassie?" His voice was dangerously low as he pressed his body close to hers. She put her hands up against his chest to push him away, but it was like pushing against a rock-solid wall. Or maybe it was because she didn't push all that hard.

"I don't want to fight." Her voice was slightly husky and her heartbeat raced.

"Neither do I." His mouth crashed down on hers…possessing…demanding her to give in to the desire reeling through her. He shoved her hands away from his chest and pulled her tight against him, so tight she could feel every muscle of his taut body.

His tongue battled with hers and instead of pushing against him, she found herself grasping his shoulders to pull him closer, closer still.

She had no thought of consequences, no ability to think of anything but the heat of Kane's mouth on hers, the frantic need that rose up inside of her and the crazy feeling of homecoming that filled her as she stood in his arms.

With an abruptness that made her gasp, he dropped his hands and backed away from her and toward the window. His eyes glittered with something that looked like anger.

"Just don't take any unnecessary chances, Cassie. Get in, get the information and get out."

Then he was gone.

She stared at the open window for a long time, waiting for the strength to return to her legs, for her heartbeat to find a more normal rhythm. She finally managed to close the window and stumble back to the sofa where she sank down and drew a deep breath.

She hadn't realized how difficult it would be to deal with Kane again. She hadn't expected the memories or the unwanted renewed burst of desire for him that knocked her flat every time he was near.

There had been other men in Cassie's life, not many but a few. But none of them had affected her on all the levels that Kane had, none of them had touched her both physically and emotionally the way he had managed to do.

Max was right. She apparently had unresolved issues where Kane was concerned. The problem was she didn't know how to resolve them. So she did what always served her best…she stuffed them deep inside and ignored them.

Besides, she had more important things to think about…like how to get what they needed and stay alive.

"Where are you?" Adam's voice drifted across the phone line.

"Here. Packing," Cassie replied. It was just before noon and she'd spent the last hour gathering the things she needed to make the move to Adam's house.

"I've been expecting you all morning." There was a slight petulance in his voice.

"I'm sorry. I slept later than usual and I've been moving slow this morning."

"Having doubts?"

"Absolutely not…what about you?"

"Never." The petulance disappeared and his deep laugh filled the line. "In fact, I feel like a schoolboy getting ready for a date with the popular cheerleader of my dreams."

"I'm no cheerleader," Cassie said with a laugh.

"And I'm no schoolboy, but that's how you make me feel…young and excited about life. How long will it be before you are here with me? Do you need help? I can send one of my men over to help you."

"That's not necessary," she protested quickly. The last thing she wanted was one of Adam's goons in her apartment. "I shouldn't be too much longer here. I imagine I'll be at your house by one."

"Then I'll instruct Ramona to have lunch waiting for when you arrive."

"That would be nice. You know me, I'm always starving."

"And I'm starving for your nearness, the scent of your perfume and your laughter."

As she finished her packing she thought of the days to come. They were going to be difficult days and nights, spent with a man not only capable of murder, but planning the murder of many. She didn't even want to think about the possibility of having to sleep with him.

It was just a few minutes before one when she pulled her car in front of Adam's house. Apparently security had been alerted of her arrival, for when she pulled up in front of the gates, they automatically opened to allow her entry.

Adam greeted her in the driveway, flanked by Burt and Sebastian. He instructed the two men to unload the car and drive it to the garage, and then led Cassie inside for lunch.

"So how do you like to spend your spare time?" he asked while they were eating lunch. "I don't know what you do when you aren't working or aren't spending time with me."

"Not a lot," she replied. "I don't have a lot of hobbies, although I like to read." She lowered her voice and continued, "When Jimmy was alive I didn't have time for hobbies. I was so busy working and taking care of him."

"Now you'll have time to pursue whatever hobby strikes your fancy," he said. "In fact, I'd really like it if you would consider not working at the club anymore."

Cassie set down her fork and frowned. "But I have to work, Adam." It would definitely work to her advantage not to have to worry about working at the club. The more time she spent in this house, the more opportunities she'd have to sneak into his study.

"Why? Why do you need to work? I'm a wealthy man, Jessica. I can provide you with everything you need. I can give you everything you want. I like taking care of my women."

Control. That's what it boiled down to. He liked being in complete control and a woman with her own job, with her own financial means was too independent for his taste.

"It's not in my nature to just take, Adam," she said softly, hoping she wasn't overplaying her hand. "That's just not the kind of woman I am. I like to work for my keep." She frowned thoughtfully. "I could help with the housework. I'm sure there's plenty to do in a place this size."

"Nonsense," he exclaimed, obviously appalled by her suggestion. "I will not have you working like a common laborer."

His protest was exactly what she'd hoped for. "Then maybe I could do some secretarial work for you…you know, type up letters and things like that. I worked as a secretary when I was supporting myself and Jimmy."

She reached across the table and covered his hand with her own. "Please…let me do something. I'd love to quit the club, but I won't unless you let me do something to earn my keep."

He curled his fingers around hers and squeezed. "You are something else, Jessica Sinclair. I'll take you up on your offer of secretarial services. I always have correspondence and business letters that need to be typed."

Yes, she thought with excitement. This was better than she could have hoped for…real access to his computer. "Thank you," she said fervently.

"No, thank you," he replied. "After lunch I'll give Jackson a call and tell him you won't be coming to work for him anymore."

No more waitressing and access to the computer without fear. Getting the information she needed should be a piece of cake. There was nothing more she wanted than to get that information and get the hell away from Adam Mercer.

Chapter 12

She'd hoped their arrangement would give her unlimited access to Adam's files, but she'd been mistaken. Over the next eight days she typed up letters for him, filed paperwork and did a couple of hours of secretarial work a day for him, but he was always present. He never left her alone in the study.

By the time those eight days had passed frantic despair raced through her. If the date in the e-mail she'd read was correct, they had just over a week to stop the shipment. She had just over a week to get the rest of the information they needed.

Not only was the time bomb ticking louder in Cassie's brain concerning the drug shipment, but she wasn't sure how much longer Adam would be willing to allow her the privacy of her own bedroom.

With each passing day, each passing night, his amorous intentions grew more pronounced and she knew it was only a matter of time before he'd insist she move into his bedroom.

With these concerns eating her alive, in the middle of the night of her eighth night beneath Adam's roof she crept down the stairs and headed for the study.

In the past eight days in the house she'd gotten a handle not only on Adam's daily routine, but of the household help as well. The only wild card in the mix was Burt, who seemed to have free access to roam the halls and rooms of the house whenever he felt like it.

The rest of the household staff usually retired to their rooms on the third floor around 10:00 p.m. and were rarely seen downstairs or around the house after that time.

She was hoping Burt was in bed, sleeping the sleep of the damned. As she slithered through the darkness toward the study, her head was filled with thoughts of Adam.

Several times she'd thought he was on the verge of spilling everything to her. She'd held her breath in anticipation of him telling her all about his plot, but in the end he'd clammed up.

She'd been right about him suffering a cash flow problem. She'd overheard more than one conversation between him and bankers indicating that he was late on payments of business loans.

She'd also heard that he'd closed down one of his shelters. He'd mentioned it at dinner one night and she'd probed him on why. He'd said that the building was a large structure with few patients and he'd decided to transfer the patients and close it for cost efficiency reasons.

During the past eight days with him, she'd learned more about his character…or lack thereof. She realized Adam didn't want a lover or a partner as much as he wanted an adoring audience.

She had the distinct feeling that what he wanted was somebody he could confide in and who would tell him how brilliant, how wonderful, how powerful he was. He wanted somebody to worship at the feet of his brilliance, encourage his sick plot for revenge.

There were moments when he let his guard down just enough to see the sick soul that shone from those ice-blue eyes of his.

She had begun to wonder if his plot was less about revenge and the loss of his only daughter and more about the power and money it would bring to him.

As the sole supplier of the desired drug, Adam would make millions in the initial distribution. He was a man who liked wealth, a man who liked buying and selling people. And at the moment he thought he'd bought sweet little Jessica Sinclair.

She breathed a sigh of relief as she reached the study. Before she touched the computer she listened to make sure there were no sounds coming from any other place in the house. Nothing. No sound except the normal noise that a house made.

At the computer she quickly accessed the program she needed and spent several minutes typing. She closed that window then pulled up his e-mail, quickly reading through the latest batch of messages he'd received.

Damn. There was nothing in the most recent spate

of e-mail messages that indicated anything about Adam's plot. Of course, he'd already read this batch of e-mail. If there had been a message sent, he would have read it then possibly deleted it. There was no way she could download new e-mail without him knowing that the program had been tampered with.

She moved from the e-mail program to his regular files, once again scanning file names for one that would ring an alarm in her head.

She paused as she saw one that indicated it was a database of names and addresses. Was this the record of people who had passed through Adam's drug shelters and treatment centers?

She had to know. This might be her only opportunity to find any information at all about her mother and her brother. Fingers trembling, she pulled up the database and began to scan the names.

Thankfully they were listed in alphabetical order, so she keyed down to the N's. Newport. Newsom. Newson. Newstead. Her heart hammered faster. Newstrum. Newswadder. Newton.

Rebecca Newton.

The shock of seeing her mother's name made her knees weak as she looked for the latest entry. There…an address update as of five years earlier: 1327 Paseo Drive. Right here in Kansas City.

With the address burned into her brain, she got out of the database. The overhead light burst on and made her blink blindly as her heart crashed against her rib cage. She looked up to see Burt glaring at her from the doorway.

"You are in a load of trouble, Blondie," he said. He held a gun in his hand. "Don't you move. You hear me?" He walked over to the wall where there was an intercom and pushed a button. "Mr. Mercer. I'm sorry to bother you but we have a situation in the study."

Adam's disembodied voice filled the room. "I'll be right down."

Cassie's heart had been pounding before. Now it threatened to burst out of her chest as she saw the dark glee in Burt's eyes. "You're going back to slinging drinks in a club quicker than you can say spit," he said. "And that's the best that you can hope for."

She said nothing. He held the gun. He held the power and she knew all she had to do was utter one word he didn't like and he'd shoot her and deal with the consequences later.

"What's going on here?" Adam appeared in the doorway. Clad in a navy silk dressing gown, hair tousled from sleep, he glared at first Burt, then Cassie.

Cassie promptly burst into tears. "I couldn't sleep…and I can down here…I was making you something…" The words escaped her on deep, wrenching sobs. "And he's going to shoot me…and I just wanted to do something nice…"

"Nobody is going to shoot anyone. Put that gun away," he instructed Burt. Irritation rang not only in his tone but in his gaze as well.

Burt narrowed his eyes and slid the gun into his waistband. The look he gave Cassie was filled with such venomous hatred it almost stole her breath.

Adam moved closer to Cassie. "Now, tell me again, what are you doing down here in the middle of the night?" His voice held a cool edge of suspicion.

She released another round of sobs and motioned him to the computer screen. There, in colorful display, was the beginning of the poem she'd typed in when she'd first accessed the computer.

"I…I was going to give it to you at breakfast. I'm sorry…I never thought…I didn't dream…"

"Hush." He pulled her into his arms and patted her back like she was a small child who'd fallen off a tee-ter-totter. She buried her head in his chest, fighting the impulse to stick her tongue out at Burt.

"Go back to your room, Burt. You've caused enough problems for one night." Adam's voice held cold fury.

Cassie wailed louder, her shoulders shaking as if sobs threatened to rip her in half.

"Shh, it's okay. I'm sorry if he frightened you," Adam stroked her hair and hugged her tight.

"I thought he was going to shoot me. He doesn't like me anyway and I've never done anything to him." She sniffed audibly and raised her head to look at him. "I just wanted to surprise you."

He smiled teasingly and swiped at her tears with his thumbs. "I guess we both got a surprise."

She buried her head against his chest once again and shuddered. "I don't like those kinds of surprises."

"Come on, let's get you tucked back into bed," he said. "It's quite late and I have an early morning meet-ing to go to."

Together they left the office and Cassie mentally congratulated herself for having the foresight to prepare an alibi.

He led her back up the stairs, his arm around her shoulder and she continued to shake as if the entire experience had scared her to death.

"Maybe it would be a good idea if you don't wander the house in the middle of the night," he suggested. "At least not in the area of my study. I'm afraid Burt is a bit overzealous in his guard duties. He meant no harm."

Meant no harm, my ass, Cassie thought. He'd probably been waiting for her to make a misstep of some kind.

They stopped in front of Cassie's bedroom door. "Maybe you'd feel better sleeping the rest of the night with me?" His voice was husky, as if seeing her at the business end of the gun had stirred his libido.

She looked up at him. "Oh, Adam, you know if I go to your room we won't sleep and I don't want our first night together to be like this." She shuddered. "At the moment I feel a bit traumatized by having a gun pointed at me."

"You're right, of course." Disappointment tugged his eyebrows closer together. He leaned forward and kissed her forehead. "You sure you'll be all right?"

She nodded. "I'll be fine as long as Burt doesn't sneak into my room and try to finish the job."

"Don't you worry about Burt. I'll take care of him."

Murmuring a good-night, Cassie slid into her bedroom, closed the door and stumbled to her bed, afraid that her trembling legs might buckle beneath her.

That had been too close. If she'd have breathed wrong, Burt would have put a bullet through her brain. She got beneath the covers on the bed and willed her breathing to slow to a more normal pace.

She wouldn't get another opportunity at the computer, not unless Adam left her alone in his study for any length of time.

At least he'd bought her story tonight, otherwise she wouldn't be lying in bed but would be fighting for her life. That had been way too close.

As her breathing slowed and she began to relax, her thoughts turned to another matter: 1327 Paseo Drive. Five years ago her mother had lived at that address. She must have rented the place, for none of Cassie's searches in the past had pulled up her name at this address. Was she still there? Was it possible Cassie could walk up to the front porch, knock on the door and face the woman who had thrown her away so many years ago?

She squeezed her eyes shut and dug in her mind for memories of that woman. Laughter. That's what first came to Cassie's mind…the sound of her mother's laughter.

Rebecca Newton had been gifted with the true, tinkling melodic laugh of an angel. And she'd laughed often, especially after toking on a couple of joints.

The distinctive scent of marijuana filled Cassie's head as she searched her mind for memory concrete enough to hang on to. Billy could be dirty and sobbing with hunger in the corner and her mother and her latest paramour would laugh as if the entire world was nothing more than a big joke.

Cassie turned from her back to her side, staring at the darkened wall of the bedroom. Her mother hadn't laughed as much with Rick. He'd had a mean streak in him that had frightened Rebecca, but apparently not enough to kick him out and be alone.

Cassie sighed. This wasn't what she wanted, what she needed to remember. She didn't want to remember Billy's cries and her mother's laughter. She didn't want to remember overdue bills and moving in the middle of the night. She didn't want to remember the men who appeared and disappeared in their lives like magicians vanishing in a poof of her mother's tears.

She needed to remember one moment of love, one memory that whispered of gentleness or caring, one single reason to walk up to the door at 1327 Paseo Drive and knock.

Hard as she tried, nothing came to her mind.

"Mr. Mercer won't be home until sometime later this afternoon," Ramona explained as she poured Cassie a cup of coffee the next morning. "He told me to tell you to spend the day relaxing…go out by the pool or take a nap. No work today for you." The words were delivered in a resentful tone that let Cassie know Ramona had no use for her. "Will you be wanting breakfast?"

"No, thanks. Just coffee is fine. Thank you, Ramona," she said to the woman's back as she left the sunroom.

Cassie sipped her coffee and stared out the window at the lush gardens. She wondered what kind of a meeting had called Adam away. Was he finalizing his plans for destruction? Meeting with drug lords to stir a frenzy for his drug? And she hoped wherever Adam was, Burt was with him.

If Adam had believed her story last night, which she thought he had, then it was possible he'd given Burt some sort of dressing down. Burt had been dangerous before last night. If Cassie had created tension between him and Adam, then he'd be even more dangerous now.

She needed to get out of here. But she couldn't leave until she knew more. She couldn't allow Adam's plot to play out.

She finished her coffee, then before going back upstairs to her bedroom walked down the hall toward the study. The door was shut. Not a good sign. This was the first time in the week she'd been in the house that the study door was closed.

With Adam gone for the day, it would have been a perfect opportunity to access the files she hadn't had time to access the night before. But that closed door worried her.

Looking around, hearing sounds of Ramona busy in the kitchen, she crept closer to the door and placed her hand on the doorknob. She slowly tried to twist the knob.

Locked.

She could easily pick the lock, but she knew the room was equipped with an alarm. If she'd had enough time to explore the room, she might have been able to disarm the alarm, but she hadn't had the opportunity to study the alarm system. She couldn't risk it.

She turned and hurried back down the hall and toward the staircase to her room. If Adam had bought her story last night completely, then why had he locked his office door? Maybe she hadn't completely convinced him after all?

In her bedroom she walked over to the window and stood staring outside, her thoughts whirling with supposition. Last night she'd felt relatively secure of her place here and her position with Adam. A locked door had shattered that illusion.

From this vantage point, beyond the extensive gardens she could see the bright blue water of the swimming pool and the roof of the pool house.

Uncertainty and a sudden case of nerves forced restless energy through her. Maybe this afternoon she would use the pool. Swimming laps would be good for working off both the nerves and the useless energy.

There was nothing she could do to figure out Adam's frame of mind until he returned from wherever he'd gone. It was important that she was mentally and physically prepared for anything.

It was after lunch when she walked through the garden to reach the pool, which was Olympic-size and the water crystal clear. Ramona had indicated to her that she'd find whatever she needed in the pool house for an afternoon of lounging in the sun.

There were brand-new bathing suits in a variety of sizes, huge fluffy towels, a number of different types of suntan oil and a wet bar with both alcoholic and non-alcoholic drinks.

She chose a conservative two-piece tankini and even though she considered goggles goofy, she grabbed a pair of those as well. She had no idea how chlorine worked with contacts so figured the goggles were probably a good idea. Armed with everything she thought she might need, she settled into a lounge chair to sun for a few minutes. The pressure of her concerns weighed heavily on her.

That locked door.

She wished she would have gotten up early enough to have a conversation with Adam before he'd left that morning. She would have been able to read his mood and know whether she truly needed to be worried or not. At the moment there was nothing she could do but wait and see what the mood was when he finally returned home.

The afternoon passed quickly. Cassie loved to swim although she hadn't learned until she was fourteen and Max had insisted. His apartment complex in L.A. had had a pool and Max, still functioning under the delusion that he was training the world's greatest stunt woman, had made sure that swimming was part of her education.

She dove into the water, pleased to find it the perfect

temperature with just enough chill to be invigorating. There was nothing worse than swimming in water warm as a bath.

She swam twenty laps before coming up for air, then rolled over on her back and floated for several minutes. The time bomb in her head ticked loudly this afternoon. While she was back floating in a swimming pool, Adam's plans moved forward minute by minute.

Had he given her clues she hadn't picked up on in the conversations they'd shared? She racked her brain, trying to replay every word of every conversation they'd shared in the past eight days.

A shipment of drugs as big as what Kane had implied would have to be arriving by truck, but they didn't even know if the drug had been manufactured here or in another country. She wondered if Kane and the agency had had any luck in finding out where the drugs were being manufactured.

It was possible Adam had a lab right here in town, transforming ordinary marijuana and cocaine into the magical Blue drug.

Who was working with him? He couldn't be doing this all alone. The people who were putting the poisonous ingredients into the drugs had to be aware that they were involved in a huge murder plot.

Certainly drug dealers wouldn't be a part of that process. They weren't about to be part of something that would halt their livelihood and cut down on the number of gold chains they could wear.

It had to be his cohorts from MAD. She thought sar-

donically how Men Against Drugs had somehow become Men Arranging Death. A good thing taken to such
extreme that it had gone bad. Extremists were always
dangerous.

She did another twenty laps, then got out of the pool
and dropped into one of the sinfully comfortable loung-
ers. She removed the goggles, slathered on some suntan lotion, then stretched out on her belly and let the sun
bake her backside.

She snoozed off and on. In the moments of awakeness her thoughts whirled with her assignment and how
she was going to get what she needed. In the landscape
of dreams she suffered visions of a sneering Burt with
his gun, memories of Rick, her mother's boyfriend's hot
hands stroking her back, the vision of the pickup truck
as it pulled away from her. Finally the vision of Kane
lying in a hospital bed and her inability to accept the fact
that she was responsible for putting him there—even if
inadvertently—tormented her dreams.

She wasn't sure how long she'd been lying there, half
asleep, when she heard his footsteps. She had come to
recognize Adam's walk…long strides, determined and
confident, unlike Kane who never made a sound when
he walked.

Pretending to be asleep, she kept her eyes closed
even as every muscle in her body tensed.

"Now that's a lovely sight," he said.

"Adam!" Her eyes flew open in mock surprise and
she started to sit up.

"No, no, don't get up," he said and sat next to her on

the lounger. "I see you took my advice and decided to have a nice leisurely day."

There was nothing in his voice to indicate anything had changed between them and a touch of relief fluttered through her. He gestured her to lie back down, then grabbed the bottle of suntan oil and squirted some into his hand.

Cassie fought a flinch as he applied the lotion to her back, stroking her skin with long, languid strokes. "Beautiful," he murmured. "You are so beautiful." His hands pressed harder, feeling feverish even against her sun-baked skin.

"I find myself thinking of nothing but you, thinking about making love to you all the time." He leaned forward and kissed the skin in the center of her back. "Don't you think I've waited long enough, my love? I think it's time you moved into my bedroom. I'll have somebody move your things there this evening during dinner."

He left her no room to wiggle. As far as he was concerned it was a done deal and it was obvious from his voice that he would brook no argument from her.

Dread ripped through her. Tonight she would be in his bed. She raised up just enough to turn and catch his eye. She smiled. "I'd like that," she said simply.

"Good, then it's settled." He continued to rub her back for several minutes, then stood. "I'm going to go back inside and shower and work a bit in my study. You just enjoy the rest of the afternoon and I'll see you at dinner."

As he walked away, Cassie got up and dove back into the pool, needing to erase the feel of his hot hands, his wet kiss off her back.

She'd hoped to be out of here before this moment came. The last thing she wanted was anything intimate with Mercer. But he was right. He'd been more patient than she'd thought he would be.

Still, it was bad enough that she hated even looking at slimy bugs, it made her positively ill to think that before the night was over she'd be sleeping with one.

Chapter 13

There was no denying the expectancy in the air, the simmering energy of anticipation as Cassie and Adam ate dinner that evening. The air of expectation only served to plump up the ball of anxiety in Cassie's stomach.

Adam spent the meal telling her about his day. He told her nothing specific, but talked in generalities, sharing with her the lunch he'd had with a business associate and an irritating two hours spent at a passport office to renew his passport.

"I don't suppose you have a passport?" he asked.

Cassie laughed. "I didn't exactly need one to move from Des Moines to Kansas City."

"We'll need to see about getting you one. I think we'll be doing a lot of traveling in the near future."

So he intended to leave the country. She certainly wasn't surprised. In the weeks and months following Blue hitting the streets, Adam would be a likely target for every drug czar in the world. He probably had a hideout all ready for him, a place where he could claim himself king. He definitely showed signs of suffering from delusions of grandeur.

"I've never been out of the country before," she replied. "I've never even been out of the Midwest."

"Then you are in for a treat. There are places on this earth so beautiful it brings tears to your eyes. Of course, before we do any traveling, we're going to have to see to your wardrobe."

Cassie frowned and ran a hand down the front of the sundress she wore. It was another cotton dress, worn and faded from too many washings and obviously cheap. She feigned a look of hurt.

Adam laughed. "Don't feel bad, my dear. I know such materialistic things don't mean a lot to you, that's what makes you so dear to me."

His eyes gleamed with a light she'd never seen before…it wasn't the possessiveness she'd come to expect. It wasn't desire or tenderness, it was something she couldn't quite define. "Unfortunately I'm a bit more materialistic than you are and it's important to me that the woman I'm with look good."

Cassie worked a blush to her cheeks. "I'm sorry if I embarrass you."

"Darling, of course you aren't an embarrassment to me. I'd just like to buy you a new wardrobe. We'll go shopping tomorrow in celebration of our first night truly together."

"That sounds nice," she agreed.

"Good, then it's settled." He smiled, the gesture not

directed at her, but rather inward, as if he were immensely pleased with himself.

Maybe the excitement that simmered in the air wasn't just the fact that tonight he intended to sleep with her, but also because his plot was mere days away and things were on track.

When dinner was over they moved to the living room, as had become their custom in the time she'd spent in the house. There Adam turned on soft music and poured them each an after-dinner drink.

As usual, Adam talked. He liked to talk about himself and his work. The man who had briefly courted her, hanging on her every word, gazing lovingly into her eyes, had disappeared over the last couple of days. She knew she was seeing the real man now…a smug, arrogant egomaniac.

As she listened to him explain the workings of his rehabilitation centers, she tried to keep her mind off the night to come. But it was difficult to avoid thinking that within hours she'd be beside him in his bed.

Maybe then he'd bare his soul to her. Maybe then he'd tell her of his plot to avenge his daughter's death. If she got the information she needed to take back to Kane and the agency, if in the afterglow of sex he spilled his guts to her, then it would be worth it. Saving others would make it all worthwhile.

She thought of the drug users she'd be saving. It wasn't just the street addicts who would suffer if Adam's tainted drug hit the marketplace. It would be businessmen who took a cocaine break at noon to get them through the rest of a long day. It would be young people experimenting for the very first time. It would be housewives and doctors, college kids and lawyers. And just maybe it would be her mother.

Drug use crossed economic, ethnic and age lines. Almost everyone had a friend or a family member who suffered from some form of drug addiction or another. She might save her mother or her brother.

As always thoughts of her family shot warring emotions through her. Deep need mingled with anger, hunger battled with pain. All she'd ever wanted was to find her family.

The address that was burned into her brain was a bonus of the job. But it was the death cries of all those people who would die that had driven her to this place and this time. Adam had to be stopped.

All too soon, Adam sat next to her on the sofa and placed an arm around her shoulder. "I think it's time to retire to our bedroom, don't you?" His blue eyes looked more arctic than usual, as if the fire of desire didn't burn hot in him, but rather cold.

"All right," she replied.

He stood, grabbed her hand and pulled her to her feet. "I can't tell you how much I'm looking forward to this." He ran a hand down her back, his hand hot, almost feverish even through the material of her dress.

They climbed the stairs together, trepidation beating through her with each step climbed. She glanced into her bedroom as they passed it and saw that it looked as if she'd never been in there.

When they reached Adam's room and stepped into the door, she saw that all her possessions were stacked in a pile near the foot of the massive king-size bed. Cassie was vaguely surprised by the careless assemblage of her things. She'd assumed her clothing would have been hung in Adam's closet, her toiletries placed in the master bath.

Burt stood nearby. Although no expression played on his blunt features, a glint of something ugly shown from his eyes.

"What's he doing in here?" she asked.

"Is that everything?" Adam asked Burt as he gestured to the pile of her belongings.

"Right down to her toothbrush," Burt replied.

"Good." Adam turned to Cassie and smiled. "There's been a small change of plans in the night's activities."

In those words, an invisible gust of danger blew cold through her. Danger snapped and crackled in the air, like lightning portending a particularly damaging storm.

"What do you mean? What's going on here?" she asked. Every muscle in her body tensed.

"It seems you have a bit of a problem, Ms. Newton," Adam said.

If Cassie's blood had been cold before, it froze solid now. He knew. She looked at Burt and for the first time a smile curled his lips, like the rictus of a skeleton as he pulled out his gun and pointed it at her.

"I don't understand…why did you call me that?" she tried to bluff. "What's going on here? Adam, you're frightening me. Why does he have a gun?"

"Don't waste my time with your feeble protests," Adam snapped. "Cassandra Newton, member of the Kansas City Police Department and snake in my grass."

Adam stepped closer to her, so close she could feel the chill emanating from his eyes. "There's a mouse in your house, Ms. Newton, and the mouse has whispered in my ear that you aren't just a cop, but a SPACE invader as well."

Cassie stepped backward from him, shock making her knees momentarily weak. A mole. There was a mole in the agency and whoever it was had sold her out.

Her switchblade burned the skin inside her bra, but there was no way she could get to it before Burt could pull the trigger of the gun that was pointed at her midsection. From this distance, she couldn't hope that he would miss her.

"Sit down, Cassandra." Adam pointed to the bed and a new fear shot through Cassie. She would force Burt to shoot her before she'd allow the two men to rape her. "Don't make me tell you again," Adam said when she didn't move.

She weighed her options and decided compliance was the best one to take at this moment. She moved to the edge of the bed and sat.

Adam paced the floor nearby, careful not to step between Burt's gun and her. "I must say, I was quite disappointed when I learned your real identity this morning. I had high hopes for us. But now the cat is out of the bag so to speak."

He stopped pacing and looked at her with a touch of

amusement. "I must confess, you were quite good. If it hadn't been for my source, and the nagging suspicions of Burt, I would have swallowed your act hook, line and sinker."

He paused and looked at her as if expecting her to say something witty or charming. She said nothing. "I know what you want, and I'm going to tell you all about it. I've been eager to share it with you anyway." He began to pace once again, pride radiating from every pore in his body. "You must admit, the plan is pure genius. I paid top dollar to produce a product so pure every user would want a piece of it. I flooded the market with it and created a demand the drug market has never seen before."

He seemed to grow in stature as he spoke, as if his self-important words pumped him full of air. "And I've paid top dollar for the new, improved product that is set to hit the marketplace on Independence Day."

"Does Burt know the new drug is poison? Does he know he's not dealing a good high, but instead is dealing death?" she replied. All she could hope for is that Burt didn't know and she could create dissention in the ranks.

Her hope died bitterly in the sound of Burt's unpleasant burst of laughter. "I don't give a damn if the dope turns everyone into aliens or instantly stops their heart. I get my cut the moment the stuff is distributed and I don't intend to hang around to see what happens after that."

"This morning a shipment of furniture from Central

America arrived in San Francisco. The furniture isn't stuffed with foam. It's stuffed with Blue." It was as if Adam felt compelled to tell her everything, as if he wanted her to hear and recognize his genius.

"What about inspectors? How do you expect to get that kind of shipment by the inspectors on the docks?" she asked.

Adam looked at her as if she were an imbecile. "I've bought all the people I need to make this a successful operation. Tomorrow the shipment will leave San Francisco by truck and will arrive at the point of distribution on the morning of the Fourth of July. From there it will be distributed to top dealers in the country and the rest, as they say, will be history."

As he told her the details she knew she was hearing her death sentence. Now that she knew the plan there was no way he intended her to leave this room alive.

"I guess now we get to the part where you kill me," she said, a strange calm descending upon her. There was no way she could take out both of them with her knife, no way she could do much of anything as long as Burt had the gun.

"Don't be ridiculous," Adam scoffed. "I don't dirty my hands with such jobs. I leave that for Burt. He seems to enjoy this kind of thing." Adam walked to the bedroom door and opened it. "Goodbye Cassandra, it's a real shame that you weren't who you pretended to be. I was quite fond of Jessica." He turned his attention to Burt. "Try not to make a mess like you did with Nicole. Blood is so difficult to get out of a bedspread and carpeting."

He walked out of the bedroom and closed the door behind him, leaving her to face Burt and his gun.

Cassie certainly wasn't surprised to have confirmed the fact that poor Nicole had met her death at the hands of the burly, bald Burt.

But she didn't have time to grieve for the woman she'd never known. The moment Adam had left the room he'd bettered the odds for Cassie. All she had to do was get the gun away from Burt and the odds would be even.

"You aren't so full of smart talk now, are you," Burt said, his Elvis sneer returning to his lips.

"Adam said not to make a mess," she replied. "If you shoot me I promise you I'll bleed all over the room."

Burt walked over to the door and locked it, his gaze and the aim of the gun never leaving her. "I'm not into death by gunshot…not intimate enough." He lowered the gun and her muscles bunched, growing taut in anticipation of what was to come.

There was one final piece of information Adam hadn't given to her. "Just tell me one thing, Burt. Where is the distribution to take place? If you're going to kill me, I'd like to die with all the answers."

He shrugged. "You mean Adam's ex-wife? She has a warehouse on the north side of town. The bitch doesn't have a clue about it, but that's where it's going down."

If she just lived long enough to get the information to Kane. The feel of her knife in her bra was reassuring, but she didn't want to get it out yet. If she got it into her hand too quickly there was a possibility he might take it away from her. She had to wait until the right moment to take it out and use it to save herself.

"Besides, I don't want to kill you until I've had a little fun with you." There was no mistaking the excitement that lit his eyes, the sexual excitement of a predator.

To her surprise he emptied his gun, turning the barrel to allow the bullets to spill to the floor. He then set the gun itself on top of the walnut highboy.

The moment his fingers released the gun, Cassie stood. She didn't intend to sit passively and wait for his attack. She wasn't going to allow him to rape and beat her without a fight. If she went down, she'd go down like a wildcat, fighting and kicking, scratching and stabbing until the last breath left her body.

Burt apparently read her intent and his sneer turned into a full-blown grin as he approached her. "You going to rumble with me, Blondie?"

"I'm going to beat the hell out of you, Burt. You're going to wish you'd kept that gun loaded and used it on me before I'm finished with you."

He laughed. "This is going to be fun," he said, then rushed her like a bull charging a rodeo clown.

Just before he reached her, she leapt from the floor to center of the bed, landing there on her feet while he crashed with his knees into the bed and his upper body fell forward. She jumped on his back, then onto the floor behind him as he bellowed.

He whirled to face her, his beefy face red. He rushed her again. She tried to evade him, but he anticipated her move and caught her midsection, driving her backward into the dresser.

Slammed into the piece of furniture, her breath whooshed out of her. Pinned between the dresser and his thick body she was momentarily rendered helpless.

Before she got her breath back his right fist slammed into her jaw. Pain seared through her as her mouth filled with the tangy taste of blood. Stars floated in the air and she closed her eyes and flailed her arms.

The stars faded and she opened her eyes, still churning her arms like a windmill. He leaned back to avoid getting hit and in that instant she brought her knee up and connected solidly where it counted.

He stumbled backward in a crouch, his hands cupping himself as if to keep the injured body parts connected to his body.

Cassie took the opportunity to move away from the dresser, not wanting to get pinned there again. "Are you having fun yet, Burt?" she asked, the words coming from her in half-breathless pants.

She didn't want to display her switchblade until she was certain he was too weak to take it away from her. She was no fool, Burt was big enough, brawny enough that with a little bit of luck the weapon she was depending on might be used to kill her. She needed to wear him down physically before going in for the kill.

He straightened. His eyes gleamed with not only anger, but with a new challenge. "I'm not going to make your death a fast and painless one. I'm going to make sure you die slow."

He leapt toward her and managed to grab her by the legs before she could jump aside to avoid his assault.

She fell to the floor, her legs trapped by the grip of his arms. While he held tight to her legs, she reached to grab his ears. Sweaty hands made it impossible for her to get a good grip.

She went for his eyes.

Poking.

Gouging.

Scratching.

He let go of her legs. She kicked out, hitting nothing but air as he once again rose to his feet.

She jumped up from the floor and spat a mouthful of blood on the carpet. She hoped it took Mercer months to wash away the nasty stain.

There was no time to catch her breath. His fist caught her again, this time square in the stomach. Her lungs expelled all their air. He hit her again.

Tuck and roll. Max's voice sounded in her head and she obeyed. She tucked herself and somersaulted across the floor away from Burt.

He chased after her and tried to kick her, but missed. But by the time she'd executed several somersaults her breath was back and she felt more solid.

She stood once again and reached into the V-neck of her dress and pulled out her switchblade. She couldn't wait any longer. She just hoped she could remain strong enough to make sure that he didn't get hold of the weapon.

With a whispered *whittt,* the blade opened and she faced Burt.

He laughed. "What do you think you're going to do with that little pig-sticker?" he asked.

"I'm going to stick a pig." She jabbed it toward him, keeping him distant enough that he couldn't swing at her and connect.

Her jaw ached from where he'd connected before. It pissed her off that he'd managed to get in such a solid blow. Although she could throw the knife and knew she could hit him, what worried her was his bulk.

He was over six feet tall and solid muscle covered with a layer of fat. Even if she threw the knife and hit him, there was no guarantee it would be a killing blow.

The best she could hope for was that the knife would be a distraction. He had little respect for the switch-blade. He advanced with surprising speed, as if she held nothing more than a feather in her hand.

Cassie slashed, a grunt of satisfaction leaving her as the knife caught his cheek and opened up a gaping wound. Blood welled up, then began to pour down Burt's jaw, but that didn't stop him as he tried to grab her hand to halt the slashing of her knife.

Unable to grab her hand, he stepped back and open hand slapped her, the blow catching her nose just enough to make it start to bleed.

Again stars appeared and with an enraged cry of her own, Cassie kicked. It was a high, powerful kick and even though she was momentarily blinded by the stars, she felt it connect. The sound of a body falling to the floor was preceded by a deep, low groan.

As her vision cleared she saw Burt lying on his back

on the floor. He was breathing, but unconscious. Cassie wasted no time indulging in relief. She raced to the nightstand and used her knife to cut the cord of the pretty lamp. She pulled the cord out of the socket and returned to Burt.

Using the cord as rope, she tied the big man's hands together. She used the cord from the lamp on the other side of the bed to tie his feet. She then ripped off a long strip of the brocade bedspread and used it to bind his mouth closed.

Then, aware that she might only have minutes to escape, she pawed through the pile of her belongings, found the cell phone Kane had given her, then moved to the window and pulled it open.

Tucking both the cell phone and the switchblade back into her bra, she stuck her head out the window. Nobody.

She was two stories up and directly below her was a brick patio surrounded by flower beds. If she dropped from this height the odds were good that she'd possibly break her legs on the brick surface. She was good, but she wasn't good enough to get up on two broken legs and run away from pursuers.

Thankfully the facade of the house was stone and part of Max's education when she'd been younger had consisted of climbing up walls with few finger and toe purchases. As she swung a leg over the sill she hoped this stone structure would be a piece of cake to descend.

Knowing time was of the essence, unsure how long

she'd have before an alarm would be sounded, she eased out of the window and to the ledge just outside. She reached out to her right and found a firm fingerhold, then found a similar hold for her left hand and hung for a moment as her feet scrambled to find a hold.

Shoulder muscles burned and her arms trembled until finally her feet found enough of a ledge to release some of the pressure of her arms. Thankfully the stones were set out a bit and she managed to scale down the wall with relative ease.

When she hit the patio she took off running. Heart racing, she sprinted like a deer, running through a field, aware that a gun might go off at any moment and she'd fall to the ground in death.

She kept her eyes focused on the stone wall in the distance. All she had to do was get up and over it before somebody found Burt, before they came hunting for her.

Her mouth still tasted of blood and blood still seeped from her nose, but she was alive and she intended to stay that way.

She hit the wall and didn't waste time contemplating how exactly to get over it. She just began to climb. Inch by inch she made her way up as sweat trickled down the small of her back and her heartbeat crashed against her ribs.

At any moment she expected a shout to pierce the air, a bullet to rip through her back. When she reached the top of the wall one of the cameras turned to point at her.

She wasn't sure whether it was the fact that she was

scared or angry, but she smashed the camera with her fist, then dropped from the top of the wall to the ground below.

It was a long drop and as she hit the ground she bent her knees to absorb the shock of the drop. Then she ran. She didn't look back but ran as fast as her legs would carry her away from the Mercer mansion.

It was only then she realized she should have grabbed Burt's gun.

Chapter 14

Kane sat on the back deck of the safe house and popped open a beer. Around him the sounds of a neighborhood settling in for the night rode on the warm night breeze.

A dog barked, a woman's voice called for children to get into the house and the neighbor's television drifting from an open window next door all combined to create the noise of the normal lives of normal people.

Kane had never had a normal life. As the only son of a high-ranking military general and a respected FBI agent, most of his childhood had been spent being raised by housekeepers and military schools around the country.

There had been very little normal family bonding as the demands of his parents' careers kept them away from the family home for long periods of time. He'd often wondered why his parents had decided to have a child. As much as he loved his parents, he'd always recognized that he was often a complication in their busy lives.

Still, it had been his family connections that had brought him to the attention of SPACE. He'd been twenty-one, trained in all forms of combat and trying to decide a direction for his life. SPACE had given him that direction.

During the times he found himself in places like this, immersed in the center of a neighborhood and surrounded by people who went to regular jobs every day and ate dinner together every night, he wondered what it would be like to be just a regular Joe.

What would it be like to come home each evening and eat dinner, watch television or go for a walk, then make love to the same woman every night? The contemplation usually only lasted a minute, then he'd mentally laugh because he knew he would never, could never be a regular Joe.

There had only been one time in his life that he'd seriously considered leaving the agency behind. That had been when he'd been lying in a hospital bed recuperating from a bullet that had nearly taken his life. But, ultimately when faced with his own mortality, he'd decided he'd rather die by the sword as an agent for SPACE than die an easy death as a regular Joe.

He took a deep swallow of the beer and leaned back in the deck chair, his thoughts on the woman who had never been far from his mind in the last five years.

From the moment he'd first been assigned to work with her, he'd wanted her. Even then she had been exasperating and independent, stubborn and amazing in her abilities. He'd both admired and respected her even thought she drove him half crazy most of the time.

He took another drink and stared up at the darkened sky where hundreds of stars blanketed the dark night sky. He hadn't heard from her in almost a week, wondered what was happening. How long would it take before she'd get the information they needed? The Fourth of July was approaching too quickly and they didn't have the details they needed.

The thought of her in Mercer's house, the thought of the man's hands on her body, his mouth tasting her lush lips made him more than half-crazy. Guilt consumed him as he thought of what Cassie might have to do to get the information they needed.

He should have insisted the agency leave her alone, leave her to her new life, but ultimately it hadn't been his decision to make. But the guilt couldn't compete with the sheer torture he'd been experiencing at the thought of her having to have sex with Mercer.

His cell phone vibrated against his hip and he grabbed it and punched in to connect. "Kane."

"There's a mole in the agency," Cassie's voice, wild and breathless filled the line.

Kane stood, adrenaline pumping through him as he heard the dangerous edge in her voice. "Where are you?"

"I'm out. They knew who I was. I got out."

"Cassie, where are you right now?" he asked again. "I'll pick you up."

"No…no…I need some time. I need to think."

"Come here. Get to the safe house."

"There is no safe house." The words screamed from

her. "Didn't you hear what I said? Somebody told them about me, and if they knew about me they'll know about the safe house."

"Then tell me where you are and I'll come and get you." Kane gripped the phone more tightly against his ear. "Cassie, for God's sake, tell me where you are."

"I…I can't. I need some time. I don't know who to trust."

The line went dead.

"Dammit!" Instantly Kane punched the numbers that would reconnect him to Cassie, but the phone rang and rang and there was no answer. She'd either shut it off or was ignoring it.

"Dammit," he repeated and raked a hand through his hair in distraction. Her cover was blown and he'd heard the paranoia in her voice. He didn't blame her for that, but he wondered if she had any idea of the danger she was in.

Not only would all of Mercer's goons be after her, but it wouldn't take long before every street dealer in the city would be looking for her as well. There was no doubt in his mind that Mercer would put the word out that she could screw up the dope deal of a lifetime.

At the moment Cassie's life wasn't worth a plug nickel. She was out there on her own and she hadn't even trusted him enough to tell him where she was.

He didn't have time to think about anything but what had to be done. He stared at his phone, knowing he should make calls to Greg Cole, their immediate supervisor and to John Etheridge, head of Homeland Security for the United States, and the single most powerful man in the SPACE agency.

But he wasn't sure who to trust. A phone call to the wrong person might put Cassie in more danger. Five minutes ago he wouldn't have questioned Greg Cole's integrity, but with Cassie's life on the line, he wasn't taking any chances.

He punched in the number that would connect him to John Etheridge, head of SPACE. Kane had trusted Etheridge with his own life many times in the past. He had to trust him with Cassie's. He had to tell the man that there was a traitor among them. Then he needed to get out on the streets and find Cassie.

Cassie had stopped running only long enough to make the call to Kane and the moment she disconnected from him she began to run again.

She needed a plan. She had nothing but her knife and her phone and the knowledge that she was marked for death. She couldn't go back to her apartment. It wouldn't be safe.

Nor could she go to Asia's or Max's. If they knew who she was, then they'd know the people she was close to, the people she trusted.

The one thing she had to do at the moment was to get as far away from the Mercer compound as possible. With this thought in mind, she ran down a residential street, looking for a car she could boost.

There was no way she could hitch a ride out of the area. She was covered in blood, both her own and

Burt's, and nobody in their right mind would pick her up and not ask questions.

She couldn't chance ripping off a car parked close to the house in somebody's driveway. She was afraid the sound of the car being started would be heard by the house occupants who would then call the police.

At this point Cassie didn't trust anyone…not even the local authorities. She raced up the street, looking for an appropriate car. She stayed away from late models, knowing most of them were equipped with either alarm systems or antitheft devices.

It was in the third block that she found what she needed, a 1982 Honda parked out by the curb. It apparently belonged to a teenager. Multicolored feathers and fuzzy things hung from the rearview mirror and a stack of CDs were loose in the passenger seat. Apparently in this upscale neighborhood people didn't worry too much about theft.

The car was unlocked. Cassie slid into the driver's seat, then playing a hunch she checked the glove box and under the seat. Nothing. She'd hoped to find a spare set of keys. She couldn't even rely on her hunches at the moment.

It took her only minutes to hot-wire the car and pull away from the curb. Even though panic roared through her, she kept her speed at the limit, not wanting to get pulled over in a stolen car.

It had been years since she'd hot-wired a car. There had been a winter when she'd been thirteen that the temperatures had gotten unusually cold. Cassie had spent some of those cold nights in cars she'd hot-wired not to steal, but rather for the blessed heat that flowed from the vents.

She'd start the engines and huddle in front of those vents. She'd never stay in any one car for too long, just long enough to take the chill from her body. No amount of heat could take away the chill that now possessed her body.

She drove north, toward the downtown area, but before she got downtown she pulled to a curb on another residential street. She didn't want to leave the car near where she intended to end up for the night.

She cut the engine, but before leaving the car she checked the back seat to see if there was anything she might be able to use.

A rumpled blue T-shirt and a breakfast bar were the only things she found worth taking. She grabbed them both. She changed from her bloody white blouse into the T-shirt and stuffed the breakfast bar into her pocket, then left the car behind.

As she walked her mind whirled. Somebody had betrayed her. Somebody in the secretive, covert agency had sold her out. She wondered what the price had been. Surely as much as thirty pieces of gold.

She had the information to stop the drug plot, but didn't know who to tell, didn't know who to trust. She trusted Kane, but was afraid of who he might choose to tell.

She felt more alone now than she had all those years ago when she'd watched her mother and her mother's boyfriend drive away from her.

Staying away from busy thoroughfares, keeping off main roads and interstates, Cassie clung to the shadows of the night. She had a specific destination in mind, knew there was a Catholic Church soup kitchen downtown and where there was a soup kitchen there would be a population of homeless people nearby. She would be able to get lost there, at least temporarily, until she figured out what to do.

When she was almost to her destination, she stopped to take a breather.

She sank down on the back side of a storage shed in somebody's yard. If anyone looked out the house window they wouldn't be able to see her. Besides, she didn't intend to be here long, only for a few minutes.

A hand to her face let her know that her nose was crusty with dried blood and a simple touch to her jaw shot pain through the entire side of her face. Burt had been a worthy opponent.

She had to warn Max. There was a strong possibility that some of Mercer's men would try to get to him, use him as leverage to get at her.

She grabbed the cell phone and punched in Max's number, relief flooding through her when his strong, gruff voice answered.

"There's trouble," she whispered into the phone.

"Tell me," Max's voice was instantly alert.

"My cover is blown, I'm on the run. I just wanted to let you know they might come after you."

"Let 'em come. I'll be waiting for them. Me and Mr. Smith & Wesson."

"Max, you got a lady friend you could move in with for a couple of days?"

"I'm not leaving my apartment for anyone," he said with obvious exasperation.

"For me, Max. Please. These are not nice people. It's important that I know you're safe. Just for a couple of days, Max. That's all I'm asking."

There was a long pause. "I suppose I could arrange something with one of my lady friends. What about you? What are you going to do?"

"I'll think of something. You know me, Max. I'm a survivor."

"Cupcake…you know I love you."

Cassie squeezed her eyes tightly closed against a wave of unexpected emotion. "Back at you," she said, then disconnected.

She wasted no time, but instantly stood and took off again. She not only had to worry about one of Mercer's men spotting her, but anyone else seeing her as well.

Nobody would think twice about calling the authorities concerning a woman wandering through their neighborhood with a bloodied face.

She had no watch, no way to tell what time it was, but it seemed as if it had been hours since she'd climbed over the stone wall at Adam's place.

The night shadows grew deeper, more profound as the night hours crept by. She finally came to the place where she would spend some time thinking about what next to do. She crawled up and sat beneath the concrete overpass where two Interstates met.

She leaned her head back and closed her eyes, for a moment doing nothing more than listening to the traffic roaring by overhead and the beating of her heart.

Exhaustion burned her muscles and threatened to muddy her thoughts, but she couldn't rest, at least not mentally, until she figured out what she intended to do.

A mouse in the house, that's what Adam had told her about the agency. A rat was more like it. There was only one person she trusted implicitly and that was Kane.

She didn't trust him because they'd once been lovers, but rather because she'd been his partner and his friend. During those years they had shared together, she knew what made Kane tick, and it wasn't money. Nobody would ever be able to buy him.

Besides, she knew what kind of a man he was, knew how much he believed in the work he did, knew the integrity that flowed in his veins. Kane would never betray her.

After all, he'd taken a bullet for her.

Rubbing her jaw thoughtfully, she felt the first stir of emotion building inside her. She'd had no time to react emotionally to all that had happened and now fear battled with anger inside her.

She was on the street alone, a marked woman because somebody had a big mouth. Somebody had sold her out and if she got through this and when it was all over, she hoped she had five minutes alone in a room with the person who had given her up.

The concrete beneath her was warm, retaining the day's heat and feeding the fevered anger that coursed through her. She had sworn years ago that she would never again spend the night on the streets. She had vowed when she bought her home that she would always have the security of her own bed, her own safe space.

Yet here she was again, with the stench of the street in her nose and nowhere to feel safe or secure. She felt as if she'd come full-circle. She was once again alone, afraid and settling into the street life she'd thought she'd left behind.

She couldn't help but think of her mother. Where was she at the moment? Was she at the address Cassie had found in Mercer's computer? Was she snuggled into a warm bed without thoughts of the daughter she'd dumped so many years before? Had she ever entertained a thought of what had happened to the child she'd abandoned in California?

For months after she'd been left Cassie had remained near the place where her mother and Rick had dropped her off at the curb. She'd been certain that it was just a matter of time before her mother would return for her. She'd been afraid to get too far away from that particular place on the street in case her mother came back.

Eventually Cassie had realized she wasn't coming back and Cassie wasn't going home. Her mother was gone from her life, as was her baby brother.

A deep loneliness now swept over her and angrily she swiped at a tear that fell down her cheek. Self-pity served no purpose, she told herself. What's done is done. That trauma of long ago was finished and she had a new drama to get through. She had to figure out how to stay alive and stop that shipment.

With the rumble of cars and trucks passing overhead and with her switchblade ready in her hand, she closed her eyes and allowed herself to sleep.

Mercer stood at the window in his study and stared out at the darkness of the night. It was almost two and he was awaiting a report from Burt.

He couldn't believe that Cassie had managed to escape, although he felt confident that any threat Cassandra Newton posed to his plans would be neutralized before dawn.

The alarm had gone out on the street hours ago and there was no rock Newton could crawl beneath that wouldn't be upturned and looked under. He'd told his contacts that she was trying to screw up the deal to get Blue back on the streets.

He would know if she managed to get word to the agency about the details of his plan. He had no doubt that his source within the agency would contact him the moment Newton made contact.

He turned away from the window, a deep frown creasing the center of his forehead. If she managed to escape them and get word to the agency then he'd have to change the location of the distribution and the timeline he'd developed so meticulously would be blown to bits.

He slammed a hand down on his desk. If she screwed things up for him he'd personally hunt her down and extract his own form of revenge.

* * *

She awoke in the throes of a nightmare, flailing her arms and legs against an attacker from her distant past. Within seconds she realized she was fighting phantoms and, with her heart racing, she waited for the last of the nightmare to pass.

When it did she took stock of her surroundings. She had no idea how long she'd slept, but had a feeling it was longer than she had intended. Although it was still dark outside she thought she saw a hint of pale illumination crawling out of the eastern sky.

Her eyes burned and she realized she still had in the color contacts that had been part of her disguise. She popped them out and threw them into the nearby grass.

What she needed more than anything was a cleanup. She needed to find a gas station where she could use the ladies' room to clean the blood off her face. There was a gas station not far and she took off in that direction.

She finally reached the gas station, and was grateful to discover the ladies' room unlocked. She went inside and stared at herself in the slightly distorted, dirty mirror above the sink.

She looked like the loser in a prize fight. Her jaw was slightly swollen and discolored and her nose was crusty with dried blood. She grabbed a handful of paper towels and ran them under cold water, then applied the towels to her aching jaw.

A sigh of pleasure escaped her as the cool compress eased the ache. At least she was relatively certain that nothing had been broken.

She scrubbed her face, removing all the dried blood. A long hot shower would have been heaven-sent. Her muscles ached both from the fight with Burt and from the hours spent on the hard concrete beneath the overpass.

When she left the ladies' room, she felt more alert and, for the first time since she'd climbed over the wall at Adam's place, she realized how deeply she was in trouble.

She had the information the agency needed to stop Adam, but didn't know who to share that information with. By now Adam would have summoned his forces to be looking for her. It wouldn't be just street punks out to find her, it would be everyone who had any kind of connection to the drug deal who would be out trying to kill her.

She had to lie low, she thought as she headed toward the downtown area where she knew she could get lost among the other lost souls.

By noon she'd managed to snag a baseball cap and a pair of sunglasses from a parked vehicle. With her hair tucked up beneath it and with the blue T-shirt she'd gotten from the back seat of the first car, at least she felt she looked different enough that she wouldn't immediately be recognized.

She found an electronics shop nearby with televisions facing the front glass window. She stood and watched the news, the voices of the newscasters drifting out of the open front door.

The heat wave would continue, there had been two

robberies overnight and a body had washed up at Smithville Lake. As she watched the noon report, her mind whirled. She had to call Kane and tell him what she knew. She had to trust that he would know who to give the information to.

A picture of herself in her police uniform yanked her attention to the televisions in the window. "Again, this report just in…a deadly fight for a Kansas City policewoman overnight."

Cassie moved closer to the open door to better hear the female newscaster. "Our sources indicate that Officer Cassandra Newton attempted to arrest a felon, Burt Weatherby, and witnesses say a fight ensued between the two. Weatherby was killed by a single gunshot wound but not before he shot Officer Newton, who died later from her injuries."

It was a surreal experience, to be standing on a street and watching a newscaster report your own death.

Dead. Officially she was dead. Somehow, someway, somebody had arranged her death. She wondered if Burt was really dead or if somebody from the agency had managed to pick him up and get him out of the way.

She hurried away from the store window and at the same time pulled her cell phone from her pocket. Kane was about to get a phone call from a dead woman.

She walked until she found an alley between two boarded up buildings, then with a single punch of a number, she dialed Kane.

He answered on the first ring.

"Saw the news a few minutes ago."

"Cassie! Where the hell have you been?" His voice held an edge of panic in it. "I went all over the city looking for you last night. Where are you now?"

"How did you manage it? Is Weatherby really dead?" She wanted her questions answered before she answered any of his.

"We got to your apartment in time to see Weatherby heading upstairs. We had intended to get him into custody but we had to shoot him. He's dead. Cassie, where are you?" he asked again.

"That's not important. What is important is that Mercer had planned to use one of his ex-wife's warehouses as the distribution point, a warehouse in the north area. I'd say we have to assume that he'll change the plans since he won't know who I might have contacted after escaping his house. I screwed up, Kane."

"Don't say that," he replied, a trace of anger still in his voice. "You've got him scrambling, and that can only work to our benefit. Any ideas what a new location might be?

"The shelter. He just closed down a shelter. I don't know where it is, but he mentioned it being on the north side of town and that it was a large building."

"We'll get men on those locations as soon as possible. If he thinks you talked, then he might move up the timeline."

"The shipment is coming by truck. I don't think he can move the timeline up by more than a day or so," she said.

"That gives us two days."

"Kane, be careful who you're talking to."

"I'm not talking to anyone in the agency except John Etheridge. I've filled him in on everything. He's hunting down the source of our leak and at this point in time he's the only one I trust," Kane said. "I'll pass this information along to him. Now, tell me where you are. I'll come and get you."

"Kane, if they knew about me, there's a strong possibility that they know about you. We shouldn't be seen together. I'm better off on the streets for the next two days."

"It's still dangerous," he protested sternly. "Somebody could recognize you. Come in, Cassie. I'll make sure you're safe."

She closed her eyes against the promise of his words. She was never safe when she was with Kane. He was a menace to her mental health.

She opened her eyes once again. "I know how to be invisible on the streets. I'll be fine. But, Kane, I want to be there when Mercer is brought down."

"Okay," he said.

"You figure out the details and let's set up a meet two nights from now."

"Just tell me when and where."

"There's a soup kitchen run by a Catholic Church downtown. It's in the basement of the Holy Family Church. They serve dinner to the homeless there every night from six to eight. I'll be there in two nights at around six-thirty."

"Then I'll be there. Cassie…" There was a long

pause, as if he wanted to say something more but was afraid of how she might react.

"Goodbye, Kane." She disconnected.

There had been something in the way he had said her name…a softness…a tenderness that had made her decide she didn't want to hear what he might say.

Two days. She had two days to live on the streets and stay alive. Right now the report of her death had been greatly exaggerated. She needed to keep it that way.

Chapter 15

The streets of Kansas City were just as unkind to her now as the streets of Los Angeles had been almost twenty years ago.

Cassie spent her two days in the downtown area of the city, in the shadows of the tall old buildings that had once comprised a thriving shopping district boasting some of the finest stores in the country.

Now the storefronts were mostly empty, business murdered by the birth of suburban malls. There were still companies conducting business from downtown offices and during the daylight hours those workers gave the place an aura of hustle-bustle.

However, by seven in the evenings, the streets became deserted, traffic became sparse and the homeless claimed the area as their own.

At twilight the homeless men and women drifted out from the shadows of the buildings and alleys, foraging in the public trash cans for food or anything that might come in handy. Whenever an occasional patrol car drove by they scattered like seeds to the wind.

During her two days and nights on the street, Cassie had plenty of time to think. An alcove doorway of one of the abandoned stores became her "crib" and she spent those two days sitting against the boarded up doorway, her mind racing as her body rested.

The heat and humidity made any kind of comfort impossible. Any kind of breeze felt as if it came from a blast furnace and only served to stir up a cloud of dust.

It was impossible to be out on the streets once again and not think about those days so long ago when survival had depended on how smart, how fast and how strong she could be.

Even though the first eleven years of her life with her mother had been difficult ones, nothing had prepared her for being thrown out into the streets to survive on her own.

But Cassie had been a fast study. After the first initial days she'd learned survival of the fittest. She'd fought for food and to protect herself. She'd beaten and got beaten more times than she could remember. She'd learned street scams and thievery, pickpocketing and shoplifting.

She wasn't proud of what she had done, but she'd survived in the only way she'd known. Until Max had entered her life and had taught her a way to live within the law, a way to live with pride and dignity.

Now she was back on the streets and she guarded her space with the ferocity of a territorial junkyard dog. She slept with one eye open, as she had done all those years ago when she'd been prey to people bigger than her. She kept her switchblade in her hand, ready to use in self-defense, but thankfully didn't need to use it.

The address burned in her head: 1327 Paseo Drive. When this was all over she'd go there and confront the woman who had given her birth then had dumped her out of a car like a box full of unwanted puppies.

These thoughts played in her head while she cooled her heels waiting for her meeting with Kane. She also wondered what was happening. Had SPACE covered all the bases? Had they managed to discover the definite location for the distribution? Had John Etheridge identified the mole in the secret organization?

She felt so disconnected from everything that was happening, so isolated from everything she held dear. She not only missed her home and Max, she was surprised to realize she even missed her cantankerous neighbor.

However, before she could go back to her real life, she needed to see this assignment through. She personally wanted to be there when Adam was arrested. She wanted to be there at the distribution site to see his face when he realized it had all fallen apart.

She'd spent enough time around Adam to suspect that what had begun as some sort of twisted need to punish those responsible for his daughter's death had become something less complicated, as in greed.

Ironically, he was just like any other dope dealer looking for a big payday. By the time her meeting with Kane came, she was more than ready to get back into the game, to find out what was happening and how they were going to shut Adam down.

At six-fifteen on the evening she was to meet Kane, she entered the basement of the Holy Family Catholic Church.

The basement was dismal. Old stone walls bore the ancient age of the church. What wasn't stone was painted an institutional gray. A large cross hung high on one wall, the only ornamentation in the room.

Along one wall, members of the congregation served up helpings of chicken and noodles, green beans and canned fruit cocktail. The rest of the room was filled with picnic tables and benches.

Even the savory scent of cooked chicken couldn't override the smell of poverty, the odor of the streets that clung to the people seated at the tables. It was the scent of stale sweat and vomit, of unwashed bodies and oily hair. It was the odor of hopelessness and mental illness, of despair and loneliness.

Cassie got in line with the other lost souls, her stomach rumbling with hunger. She'd eaten dinner here every night for the past two nights, sitting alone and not speaking to anyone.

Thankfully the people who worked here didn't pretend to be social workers. Their goal wasn't to change things, or provide counsel. They were here only to feed the hungry.

On this night she took her tray and settled in as she had the previous two nights, at a table facing the door with her back to the wall. From this vantage point she could see everyone who entered the basement.

Kane would be here soon and hopefully he would

have news about what the agency had learned about distribution and a plan to get her inside when the action took place.

She wanted to see Mercer's face when he realized she wasn't dead, when he realized all was lost. She needed to see his defeat stamped on his arrogant, handsome features.

She was tense. The past two days had been difficult ones, stirring up old, unwanted memories at the same time making her worry about who on the street might recognize her.

She was aware that it would only take one sighting by a street punk or dope dealer to negate the story of her death.

Cassie noticed the soup kitchen was unusually busy. It would be closed in two days for the holiday. Apparently nobody realized the homeless got hungry on holidays, too. So tonight and tomorrow night the homeless would come to eat enough to last through the Fourth of July. It wasn't long before the basement was congested.

An old woman sat down on Cassie's right. Despite the heat of the evening, the woman wore layers of clothing. The homeless traveled light, usually wearing or carrying all they owned in the world.

A man eased down on her left. Cassie glanced at him long enough to note the gray scraggly beard and the dirty fishing cap on top of his head.

She ate the chicken slowly, her gaze focused on the door, expecting Kane to walk in at any moment. It had to be six-thirty by now. Where was he? He was never late.

What if something had happened? What if the mole in the agency had given him up and Mercer had gone after him? A hollow ache pierced through her stomach. She refused to even contemplate such a scenario.

"Your disguise isn't as good as mine." The low, familiar voice came from her left and she turned her head to look at the man seated next to her, the man she had dismissed earlier.

Beneath the rim of the fishing hat she saw the rich luster of dark hair. The sensual lips above the disgusting beard turned upward in a smile she'd recognize anywhere. And those eyes, those gorgeous dark gray eyes were impossible to disguise.

Thank God. Relief coursed through her at the sight of him. "I didn't have access to developing much of a disguise," she replied softly. "And yours isn't that good. If I'd really looked at you, I'd have recognized you."

"It's good enough that I've been sitting here next to you for the past ten minutes and you didn't notice me." He paused a moment. "You okay?"

"I'm dirty and cranky and ready for action. So what's up?"

"We have a plan, but we can't talk here. I'm going to get up and leave. You wait a few minutes then follow me. I'm parked down the street to the right on the north side. It's a navy-blue sedan. I'll meet you there."

He returned his attention to his plate, eating like a man who had been too long without food. When his plate was empty he carried the tray to the bin where dirty dishes were collected, then shuffled, shoulders stooped, out of the basement.

Cassie took several minutes to finish eating, then disposed of her tray and stepped outside. Even though it had to be just after seven, the sun still ruled with the humidity and heat indicative of midsummer weather in the Midwest.

By the time she found the blue sedan, Kane had removed the ugly beard and his hat. She slid into the passenger seat and breathed in the soothing coolness coming from the air conditioner.

She took off her sunglasses and eyed him. "So tell me the plan."

He reached out and touched her chin. "Looks like you caught a right cross."

"Courtesy of Weatherby." She leaned back, away from the touch of his gentle fingers.

He put the car into gear and pulled away from the curb. "The first step in the plan is to get to my motel room and let you take a shower. Not for nothing, honey, but you smell terrible."

She nodded, knowing he was right. Two days in the elements without benefit of a bathtub had definitely taken a toll on her personal hygiene. "Have you pinpointed where the drugs are going to be distributed?"

"Not specifically, but we've got men covering Mercer's house, his ex-wife's three warehouses and the shelter that he closed down. We think it's probably going to be the shelter. It's a huge building with a loading dock in the back. It's a perfect place to bring the drugs."

"Any activity at any of the places?" she asked.

"Nothing so far. However, there's been some rumors on the street that the dry spell is just about over and Blue will come in with the fireworks display."

"So that implies the date hasn't changed," she said.

"We have to function on the possibility that the moment you left his house he changed the location and time." He paused a beat, then cast her a sideways glance. "We got the mole."

"Who?" She sat up straighter in the seat.

"Carolyn."

Cassie gasped in surprise. "Ms. Clean Pores herself? The makeup magician?"

Kane's expression was dark. "She won't be putting makeup on anyone for a very long time. She'll certainly never get a chance to spend the money she re ceived for betraying you and the agency."

Cassie stared out the passenger window and thought of Carolyn. She wondered vaguely how much the woman had thought Cassie's life to be worth, but decided not to ask. It didn't matter now. "How did they discover it was her?"

"She made a foolish mistake and deposited a large sum of money into her bank account. When she was questioned about the source of that money, she fell apart and confessed."

Within minutes they were at the motel where Kane had rented a room. "Help yourself to the bathroom," he said as they entered. "I took the liberty of getting you some clean clothes. They're on the counter in there. We'll talk after you're finished."

Cassie bee-lined for the bathroom. As the shower sluiced away the grime of the past two days, she mentally prepared herself for what was to come.

The game was on. Sometime tomorrow or the next day those drugs would pull into the city and Mercer would attempt to distribute them for his holiday of death.

She had no idea what the plan was, but knew Kane would be in the thick of it. And she intended to be at his side. There was no way she was going to sit out the finale after coming so far.

The clothes he'd chosen for her indicated he, too, expected her to be at his side. Black jeans, a black T-shirt and a black stocking cap awaited her when she got out of the shower. She dressed in the jeans and T-shirt, then carried the hat out of the bathroom with her.

Freshly showered and clothed, she was pumped with adrenaline and ready for whatever came next. Kane sat on the end of the bed and for just a moment she thought of what it would be like to move into his arms and make love with him.

She knew the taste of his mouth, the touch of his hands on her body. She loved the scent of his skin, and realized that despite the years that had passed he was still in her heart, still deep in her soul.

It would be wonderful to take an hour, forget about a plot to kill people, forget about tainted drugs and just be with Kane.

But that's what had happened before. They'd made love mere hours before going into the last assignment they'd worked together and Kane had nearly died because he'd sacrificed himself for her.

"Cassie?"

"Let's get down to business," she said briskly. Business, that's what she needed to focus on. "So fill me in." She didn't join him on the bed but rather leaned with her back against one wall.

"My gut instinct is that this is probably going to go down in that shelter Mercer closed down. There has been no news coverage of the place shutting its doors, no publicity whatsoever. We know the original plan was to use one of his ex-wife's warehouses, but he'd be a fool not to change that the minute you escaped from his house."

She nodded and he continued. "We've had the shelter under surveillance for the past forty-eight hours. There are no guards posted, no security whatsoever. Apparently Mercer is confident that the shelter is safe and maybe he thinks that posting guards around the area would draw unwanted attention. So, as soon as it gets dark, you and I are going inside."

"How?"

He stood and began to pace the small space in front of the bed. "I checked out the place last night. There's a small basement window that we can crawl in. We're taking a three-man team in with us."

"Then what?" Raw energy pumped through her. The thrill of the game, the chill of impending danger.

She couldn't remember the last time she'd felt so alive. She hated to realize that she'd missed it…and had missed Kane.

"Then we find someplace inside to hide and we wait. John has assured me that when it's time for more backup, backup will be there."

Cassie said nothing, although she hoped he was right. She hoped John Etheridge could be trusted. She hoped Carolyn the mole didn't have rat friends that went all the way to the very top of the agency hierarchy.

"Backup or not, we have to see to it that those drugs don't leave that warehouse," Kane said, his jaw clenched with determination. He walked over to the closet door and pulled out a thick, long rope.

"We need to check this and make sure it's ready to go."

Cassie got up and grabbed one end. "What's the rope for?"

"The shelter is a four-story building. The rope is in case we find ourselves on the roof with nowhere to go but down."

Together, him starting from one end and her working from the other, they checked the rope for frays or cuts that might prove deadly to one or both of them.

When they'd assured themselves that the rope was in good shape, he moved to one of the nightstands and withdrew two guns. He tossed one of them across the bed toward her. "I'm assuming you're weaponless."

She reached into her T-shirt and pulled out her switchblade. "Not entirely."

He grinned at her. "Some girls have a favorite purse or pair of shoes. My girl has a favorite knife."

She wanted to vehemently protest his use of the term "my girl," but decided now was not the time to create undue tension. He followed the gun with a box of ammo and for the next several minutes they each loaded the weapons.

When the guns were loaded, he handed her an ammo belt. She strapped it on and filled it with additional ammo. With each bullet that clicked into place in the belt, her adrenaline spiked higher.

The weapon and bullets did nothing to give her a false sense of security. She knew it was quite possible the bad guys would have bigger, more effective firepower. But the guns might buy them time, or make life a temporary hell for several of the bad guys.

When they were ready, they got back into Kane's car and headed for the shelter on the north side of town. Night shadows chased the last of the daylight from the sky and it was to their benefit that it looked like it was going to be a cloudy night.

The city skyscrapers disappeared in the rearview mirror as they continued north. "The shelter is near the North Kansas City Hospital," Kane said as he took an exit off the Interstate. "Years ago the building belonged to a small potato chip company. The company went out of business and since then the building has changed hands several times. Mercer has leased it for the past ten years."

Cassie wondered if her mother had ever been in the

shelter. Had she sought help in this particular facility? Once again she was struck by the fact that the people she was saving were the very people who were often responsible for misery in the lives of the people who loved them.

Kane pulled into the hospital parking lot. "We're going to meet the rest of the team here. The shelter is about a mile from here, across those railroad tracks. We'll leave the car here and go in on foot." He pointed to a white panel van parked nearby. "And that's our team."

Together he and Cassie got out of his car and walked to the panel truck. As they approached, the side door swung open and three men got out. Cassie had never seen any of the three men before.

"This is Hawk, Falco and Tiny," Kane made the introductions, using what Cassie knew were code names. "And this is White Rose." All three of them had earphones in, indicating to Cassie that they were in constant communication with the surveillance team.

They exchanged quick greetings, then with the darkness of night cloaking them, they took off walking. "So far the surveillance team reports there has been no suspicious activity around the shelter," Falco said as they crossed the railroad tracks.

"Mercer is smart, he won't do anything to attract unwanted attention until the deal is imminent," Cassie said.

They slowed as they approached a group of four buildings. The grass and brush around the area was high, and they crouched down in the grass behind the third building, a four-story brick structure.

"The basement window is the best way to access the building," Kane said. "It's unlocked and big enough for us to crawl in. Unfortunately, I don't know what the access might be from the basement to the rest of the building."

"We'll figure it all out once we get inside," Hawk said. He handed Cassie and Kane earphones hooked to small transmitter boxes. "This will keep us all in touch with one another."

Cassie placed the earphone into her ear, then clipped the transmitter box on the front of her shirt.

"We go into the basement, then we'll do a general sweep of the building and decide final positions," Kane said.

"Let's go."

Together the five of them ran through the brush and overgrown grass. Hawk led the way, a nimble black shadow. When they reached the basement window, Hawk, Falco and Tiny went in first.

Cassie was about to go in next when Kane grabbed her by the arm and twirled her around to face him. "Just in case I don't get a chance to do this again," he whispered, then pulled her into his arms and captured her mouth with his.

The kiss was devastating. Hungrily his mouth claimed hers. She raised a hand to his chest with the intention of pushing him away, but before she could summon the strength he released her.

For a long breathless moment he held her gaze, then turned and slid through the window.

Cassie felt scalded, not only by the heat in his eyes, but also by the lingering fire of his kiss. She'd tasted all that she'd turned her back on, all that she'd walked away from in his lips. For the first time in those five years, she wondered if perhaps she'd made a mistake. And she wondered, if she lived long enough, if she intended to do anything about it.

Chapter 16

Cassie followed Kane through the window, still shaken by the kiss and by that moment when their gazes had locked. Don't think about it, she told herself. They had a job to do and she couldn't let thoughts of Kane and his kiss distract her.

The basement of the shelter was nothing more than a concrete room filled with a few boxes of nonperishable supplies. As the three other men went up the stairs to check out the rest of the building, Kane and Cassie checked the contents of the boxes. She was grateful for any activity to keep her mind from replaying that kiss.

The boxes contained toilet tissue and paper towels, napkins and a variety of other paper products. No drugs. Nothing suspicious whatsoever.

From the basement Kane and Cassie moved to the first floor of the building where Hawk awaited them. "There's bed frames in some of the rooms and a couple of old desks in what looks to have been an office, but other than that the place is pretty much empty."

"Where are Falco and Tiny?" Kane asked.

Hawk pointed up. "They're setting up on the roof. From that vantage point they'll be able to see anyone coming. I was hoping that the three of us could hole up in the loading dock area, but there isn't much cover."

"Let's check it out," Cassie said.

In a large storage room a huge aluminum garage door took up half of the back of the building. It was easy to imagine a truck backing up to the dock and being unloaded into the huge room.

"There's not any cover," Kane said. The room was completely empty, making hiding places impossible.

"There's a bathroom there." Hawk pointed to a door.

Kane frowned. "We'll be sitting ducks in there."

"We've got agents ready to move in at the first sign of an approaching truck," Hawk said. "Our backup should be able to burst in before any of the men decide to visit the bathroom." He didn't sound overly confident with his own plan.

Cassie stepped toward the bathroom and shone her light in the small, windowless room. She frowned. She didn't like it. She couldn't help but worry about backup she hadn't seen. She couldn't forget that she'd been sold down the river and they had no idea what additional information Carolyn might have told Mercer while she was selling Cassie's soul.

"I don't like the idea of being in a room with no escape route. If you two want to hole up in there, that's your choice. But not me."

"Not me, either," Kane said.

Cassie stepped out of the room and into the hallway. The two men followed. "We could just sit here for the night. From here we should be able to hear if the garage door opens."

"Hopefully our surveillance team will let us know somebody is around long before that garage door opens," Kane replied.

For the next thirty minutes they thoroughly explored the building. Each room they entered that held bed frames or had obviously been used as patient rooms, Cassie wondered if her mother had been there.

Had she slept on one of the beds? Had she come here in an effort to finally get clean, to get a handle on the drug abuse that had plagued her since she was young?

Had she slept in one of these beds and dreamed of the little girl she'd left behind? Had thoughts of Cassie ever entered her mind after she'd driven off on that day so long ago?

Cassie shoved these thoughts away from her mind, knowing she needed to stay focused on the here and now. Distraction could lead to disaster.

After they'd familiarized themselves with their surroundings, they hunkered down for a long night in the hallway just outside the loading dock area. The darkness in the hall was profound.

"What if we guessed wrong?" Cassie said softly to Kane, who sat next to her. "What if the deal has already gone down?"

"We'd know if that was the case. Within an hour of

those drugs hitting the streets we're going to know by the dead bodies that show up."

If her mother hadn't gotten help, if her mother hadn't gotten clean, then one of those bodies that showed up might be hers. Cassie leaned her head back against the wall, wondering how she would feel if she discovered her mother was dead.

Then there would never be any explanations, no closure. She knew much of what had driven her to stay alive and to work as a cop was the need to find her mother and reunite with her family. She'd thought that a job in law enforcement might give her access to records that would lead to her mom, but that hadn't happened.

For the first time in her life as she sat in the dark and waited for Mercer and his shipment to arrive, she faced the realization that she might never gain closure. She may never find her mother or the brother she'd so loved. She may never have the answers to the questions that had burned inside her for so many years.

Her earphone crackled and a male voice spoke. "We've got a semi approaching."

Anticipation shot through Cassie and she felt the tension that rolled off the men on either side of her as well. "Maybe this is it," Hawk murmured.

The three of them waited as seconds ticked by.

"False alarm," the sentry said through their headsets. "The truck drove on by."

The night passed minute by agonizing minute. They remained awake and alert, occasionally pumped up by a sighting of an approaching truck. As they waited, they exchanged war stories of various assignments they had worked in the past.

As Kane told Hawk about several of his and Cassie's past assignments, Cassie found herself remembering other things about working with Kane.

She remembered the laughter they had shared, the fact that they had been sharply attuned to each other's moods and desires. For the first time since leaving him, she allowed herself to remember how safe she'd always felt with him, how warm and loved.

It was easy to entertain those kinds of memories in the shelter of the darkness, but when morning broke and the building began to fill with light, those memories faded.

Instead she felt a bitter disappointment that nothing had happened through the night, that they hadn't been at the right place at the right time to stop Mercer's shipment.

They remained in the shelter until noon, then left through the basement window where they'd entered. A surveillance team would remain in place, along with another team ready to move in, but Kane insisted that they all needed to get some sleep if they intended to be alert and ready when the deal went down.

Cassie didn't want to leave, she wasn't ready to give up yet, but Kane insisted she'd do nobody any good without some sleep.

"Somebody will call us as soon as they see something going down?" she asked.

"We have teams on every structure he might use.

Trust me, I can have you anywhere in this city before they place the cuffs on Mercer's wrists," he replied.

"Good. I don't want to miss it." She couldn't forget that it was Adam who had demanded her death at Burt's hands. There was no way she wanted to miss seeing him handcuffed and led away like a common criminal.

She didn't realize how tired she was until Kane pulled up in the parking lot of the motel, then exhaustion hit her in waves. Kane looked exhausted as well and when they got into the room they stripped off their weapons and ammo and fell onto the bed without a word spoken.

Kane seemed to fall asleep instantly, but for Cassie sleep came slowly, with more difficulty. Part of the problem was Kane's nearness. So much of the night had been spent in memories of intimate times with him. She now found lying next to him on a king-size bed both comforting and disturbing. It also irritated her more than a little bit that he didn't seem at all disturbed by her nearness.

She finally fell asleep with the scent of him surrounding her and his nearness warming her.

Warm lips worked their way across her nape, coming to rest at the sensitive skin just behind her ear. A moan escaped her lips as arms enfolded her and a familiar body molded itself against her back.

Kane. Before full awakeness had completely claimed her, her sleep-fogged mind identified the sweet embrace and yielded to it.

It was wrong, so wrong to want him as badly as she

did. But five years of wanting burned inside her. Five years of wanting ached inside her. Making love to him here…now, was a mistake but it was a mistake she was going to make in spite of all the reasons why she shouldn't.

She turned over to face him and any protest she might have vaguely entertained died instantly in the fiery flames of his eyes.

Those sexy gray eyes of his spoke of five years of want, of need. His mouth took hers in utter possession as he tangled his hands in her hair.

She wrapped her arms around his bare back, in the back of her mind wondering when he had taken off his shirt. His skin was warm and she loved the feel of his sinewy muscles beneath her fingertips.

The kiss left her breathless and when he finally pulled his mouth from hers, he gazed down at her with such hunger, such need that it consumed her. "Cassie." Her name sounded as if it had been torn from someplace deep inside him.

Any restraint that might have existed between them snapped. They undressed in a flurry of frantic movement, then came together like people starved for each other.

His mouth once again captured hers as his hands covered her breasts. Her heartbeat crashed against her ribs as she reveled in his kiss and his touch.

They caressed each other like old familiar lovers who knew each secret place to touch to produce the sweetest sensations, yet there was the excitement of new lovers eager to please, eager to discover all the mysteries of lovemaking.

Kane stroked her body like a master, using his thumbs across her nipples, then gliding his hands down the flat of her abdomen and to her hips. He trailed his fingers across the sensitive skin of her inner thighs and she moaned.

As he kissed her once again he touched her where she most wanted, needed his touch. She arched her hips up to meet the intimate caress as a wave of intense pleasure built inside her.

His fingers moved faster and Cassie grabbed his shoulders and clung to him as the wave overtook her. While she still rode the crest of the wave, he entered her.

For a moment he remained unmoving, buried inside her. He cupped her face with his hands as his gaze burned into hers. "I've missed you, Cassie." He moved his hips against her. She didn't answer, not with words. She wrapped her legs around his hips and pulled him deeper into her.

He hissed his pleasure and moved faster. Cassie closed her eyes and gave herself, mind and body, to him. Rational thought was impossible as he took utter possession of her.

Faster and faster they moved and once again Cassie felt the coil of rising tension in the depths of her, a coil of tension that wound tighter and tighter until it snapped, sending cascades of fire through her. At the same time he stiffened and cried out her name as his release came.

They remained entwined for long minutes afterward,

not speaking as they waited for heartbeats to slow. Immediately regrets filled Cassie.

She felt his gaze on her and turned her head to the side and kept her eyes closed. She didn't want to look at him, didn't want to see whatever emotion his eyes might hold.

"Too late to take it back," he said softly. He untangled himself from her and sat up. Reluctantly she opened her eyes and looked at him. For the first time she saw the deep scar that puckered his chest.

Her scar. It should have been her body that bullet had ripped into, her body in that hospital bed. "It didn't mean enough to want to take it back," she lied. She got up and padded to the bathroom door.

"Cassie." She turned back toward him. "Sooner or later we're going to talk about it."

She went into the bathroom and locked the door behind her. As she stood beneath a hot spray of water, washing away the scent of Kane from her skin, the sight of that scar haunted her.

It had happened on the very last assignment they had worked together. Five years ago she and Kane had made love hours before they'd gone into a dangerous situation.

They had been posing as members of a militant group and were in the mountains of Colorado working a weapons buy. The man they were dealing with was a member of Congress supposedly on vacation with his family in Aspen.

Cassie remembered that day in vivid detail. The

scent of pine laced the cold air and a blanket of snow covered the earth. She and Kane had arrived at the place of exchange on snowmobiles. A member of their team had driven a pickup.

It should have gone down without a hitch. They had backup hidden behind the trees and the negotiations had taken place without any problems. All they had to do was hand the man his money, accept the cache of weapons, then backup would move in and make the arrests.

Congressman Steward had shown up in a paneled van with several armed goons. Cassie hung back as Kane met the men. She would never know exactly what went wrong. She'd never know what gave them away. She only knew that one minute things seemed to be going well and the next moment Kane was backing up and the men were shooting.

In the next instant everything seemed to go in slow motion. She saw the Congressman pull a gun, heard the crack of the shot aimed at her. She had been vaguely aware of Kane's roar as he threw himself in front of her at the same time Cassie hit the ground.

The next moments were a haze, except for the sight of Kane lying motionless against the snow, the front of his white parka a blossom of blood.

Their backup had moved in, the bad guys were arrested and the cache of deadly weapons was taken into custody. But what she remembered more than anything was the cold of the snow as she knelt at Kane's side, crying for him to open his eyes and look at her.

She realized the water in the shower had gone cold

and she turned it off and reached for a towel. She would go to her grave believing that the fact she and Kane were lovers was what had prompted him to jump in front of her, to sacrifice himself for her.

What terrified her at the moment was that they'd just made love again. She hoped, she prayed that history didn't repeat itself.

As Kane showered, Cassie wandered the confines of the small motel room, surprised to have discovered that they'd slept through the afternoon and part of the evening.

There had been no communication from any of the teams at any of the locations. Nervous energy ripped through her as she paced the room and tried to anticipate Mercer's plans.

The Fourth of July was tomorrow. Had Mercer decided to stay with the same date and simply change the location? He had to have known that when Cassie escaped his house she'd tell somebody about his plans. Even though they'd arranged for the report of Cassie's death, Mercer couldn't have been sure who she might have talked to before she "died."

It just made sense that he would change the time and location of the distribution. But Adam didn't know that she knew all the details. A new burst of adrenaline zapped through her as she realized he hadn't told her the location, Burt had.

Adam had already left the bedroom when Burt had told her the where of the distribution.

"Kane." She burst into the bathroom where he stood at the sink, clad only in a towel wrapped around his slim waist. The scent of shaving cream hung in the air.

He turned to face her in the doorway. "Mercer didn't know I knew where the distribution was taking place. Burt told me, after Mercer had left the room. I don't think he changed the location. I think it's going down in one of those warehouses his wife owns just as he originally planned. He's arrogant enough not to change his plans."

She left the bathroom as he reached for his cell phone.

Within an hour they were once again back in Kane's car and headed for the warehouse most likely to be the one Mercer would use.

"Mercer's ex owns three warehouses. This particular one is the largest, large enough to pull a semitruck inside," Kane said as they headed toward the airport.

"I'm mostly playing a hunch," Cassie said. "I don't believe Burt would have told Adam what he'd told me, and if Adam thought I didn't know, then I don't think he would have changed a thing. He would have been confident that we'd probably never figure out he had access to his ex-wife's storage units."

"I've always been a big believer in your hunches, Cassie," he said.

The Kansas City International Airport appeared in the center of acres of fields, the huge buildings surrounded by crops of wheat and corn.

Kane took the exit for the airport, but detoured off

that road and headed back away from the airport to the west. Within minutes she saw a compound of warehouses in the distance.

Kane didn't enter the gates that led to the compound, but rather drove past the entrance. He drove for a distance, then took off on a dirt road. Several more twists and turns later he pulled the car to a halt beneath a leafy oak tree.

"You know, without your information we probably wouldn't have considered these warehouses," Kane said as they got out of the car. "Mercer owns so many buildings around the city we would have focused solely on those. But this makes sense. It's not in his name and more importantly, it's a stone's throw away from the airport."

"So he could distribute the drugs, then the men receiving them could hop a plane and within hours the drug could be all over the country."

"Exactly." He grabbed a rope and a duffel bag from the back seat and slung both over his shoulder. "We'll walk in from here."

"Anything from surveillance?" she asked as they trekked through thick brush and grass. In the west the sun was setting, splashing the sky with a burst of orange and pinks.

"Nothing. We've got a team watching this place, but so far they've reported nothing amiss."

"If Mercer stays true to his plan, then the deal will go down around dawn in the morning. I want to be inside that building."

They fell silent as they drew closer to the compound of warehouses. The only sounds were an occasional plane going overhead and the noise of insects beginning their night songs.

Cassie tried not to think about the bugs that surrounded her. If she dwelled on that she'd be up in Kane's arms, forcing him to carry her the remainder of the way to the warehouse.

When they reached the compound, Kane led her to a break in the chain link fence that surrounded the area. It was obvious that cutters had been used to breach the fence. He held up the fence so she could slither through, then entered the compound just behind her.

There were a total of six big warehouses and he pointed to one of the two on their right. "That's it," he said.

The sun had set but there was still just enough fading light left for them to get to the building. Kane led her to one side of the building where the night shadows were the deepest.

He leaned close to her. "I'm going up," he whispered and pointed to a row of windows that looked to be about three stories up the side of the tin building. "You sit tight. I'll throw the rope down to you when I'm situated."

She didn't argue with him. She had many skills, but when it came to scaling the side of a building, Kane beat her hands down. She was proficient, but Kane was the master.

She stood with her back against the building and

heard only a whisper of movement as he left her side. Seconds ticked by…minutes as she waited for Kane to reach the window at the top of the building and throw down the rope to aid in her ascent.

A flash of light shone from around the side of the building. Cassie's breath caught in her throat. It had been the beam from a high-powered flashlight. Her heart jackhammered a frantic rhythm. She looked up, but couldn't see anything but darkness.

"I don't know how we got stuck on this duty," a deep male voice carried to where she stood. She recognized that voice. It belonged to Sebastian.

"I always get the crap details," another male voice replied. "But this will be all worth it by tomorrow. I'm going to have more money than I know what to do with."

Their surveillance had said there'd been nobody around, nothing amiss. Apparently that had changed in the last few minutes. Hurry up, Kane, she prayed.

She flattened herself against the building, aware that if they stepped around the corner, the light would find her and the reports of her death would be true.

Chapter 17

Cassie pulled her gun out of the waistband of her jeans and waited for the moment one of the two men rounded the corner to the side of the building where she stood without cover.

If they caught her, they'd kill her. She had little illusion that somehow she'd manage to take them both before one of them would take her down.

She intended to shoot first, before they knew what had happened. All she had going for her was the element of surprise. She clicked off her safety and slid her finger on the trigger.

At that moment the end of the rope hit her on top of the head.

She shoved her gun back in her waistband and gripped the rope firmly, then began to climb, desperate to reach the window before she was spotted. Kane pulled from the top, making her ascent easier.

She was three-quarters of the way up the side of the building when the beam of light rounded the corner. Two hulking men followed the beam.

Cassie froze in place. She hung motionless, suspended above their heads and prayed that neither one of them took this opportunity to decide they were into astrology and looked up.

The two men stopped directly beneath her. "I'm telling you the Steelers could take the Chiefs any day of the week," said the man Cassie didn't recognize.

"No way," Sebastian replied. "The Chiefs are going to be contenders this year. You mark my words. We've got the defense and the offense this year."

"Yeah, yeah, that's what I heard last year," the other man said.

Cassie closed her eyes and focused on maintaining her grip on the rope. While the two morons beneath her discussed football, she was dying a slow death.

Her shoulders burned with the effort of hanging on to the rope and not moving. Burn…hotter…on fire. Her arm muscles began to quiver with her effort to hang on…hang still.

She couldn't move. She didn't want to do anything to draw attention. If either of them spotted her she'd be a hanging duck for them to shoot.

One of them lit a cigarette as they continued to talk and argue about football. Go. Just walk on by. Please keep on walking, Cassie thought.

Her heart beat frantically as her sweaty hands momentarily lost their grip and she slid an inch down the rope. She clutched more tightly to the rope, her hands burning from the unexpected slide.

She nearly sobbed in relief as the two men continued walking along the side of the building and rounded the next corner and disappeared. Frantically she continued moving up the rope.

Kane awaited her at the window and pulled her inside and to the loft floor. He quickly pulled in the rope and slid down on the floor next to her. "You okay?"

"I thought you said there was no activity," she whispered.

"There wasn't until now."

She leaned her head back against the wall and drew deep, steadying breaths in an attempt to slow her galloping heartbeat. Her arm muscles still ached and her shoulders still burned, but she knew eventually the discomfort would pass.

That had been too close, far too close for comfort. But at least she and Kane were in and the silence and darkness inside the building were both comforting and profound.

"We'll just sit tight for a little while," Kane said softly from right next to her. "I've got a penlight, but I don't want to use it while those bozos outside are walking around the building."

She nodded, understanding his desire for caution. It would take only a single flicker of light to give them away. If they were busted now, they'd never get a chance to stop Mercer.

For several minutes they sat side by side in the dark silence, listening for any sound that would indicate something amiss. From inside the building they couldn't hear the two men who patrolled the area.

It didn't take her long to notice several things that had nothing to do with sight or sound. The scent of Kane filled her head, the faint scent of soap and male, a familiar scent that made her feel both defensive and vulnerable.

His thigh and shoulder pressed against hers, creating an evocative heat that she tried to ignore. Her skin still retained the imprint of his touch, the feel of him intimately against her. Making love to him had been the greatest pleasure she'd ever had and the biggest mistake of her life.

Unresolved issues, that's what Max had told her she had where Kane McNabb was concerned.

But, as far as she was concerned, there was nothing unresolved about it. They'd been lovers and now they weren't.

Their lovemaking of hours before had been an anomaly, an error in judgment that wouldn't happen again. End of story. What was left to resolve?

Her desire. The answer came unbidden to her mind. What was left to resolve was the fact that spending time with him again, tasting his lips and sharing passion with him again had stirred up a new well of desire for him.

God, she was so pathetic.

She could pin a cockroach to the wall with her knife. She could climb a twenty-foot stone fence. She could go head to head with a burly bodyguard, but she couldn't get one stinking, sexy man out of her mind.

She didn't know how long they sat in the darkness,

in the silence before he stood and touched her arm, indicating she should get up as well.

He turned on the tiny penlight and in the small beam Cassie realized they were surrounded by furniture. Love seats and highboys, sofas and dining-room tables, all unusually ornate and oversized.

The furniture was situated so that there were plenty of hiding places. Kane led her to the middle of the loft and pointed to a small area between a tall bookcase and a six-foot solid wood wardrobe.

Cassie slid in between the two pieces and sat with her back to the wall. Kane scooted in beside her, the two of them like sardines packed tightly in a can.

"Now if somebody comes up either staircase to the loft, they won't be able to see us," he whispered. He shut off the penlight and once again they fell silent.

Minutes ticked by. She was aware of the sound of her own heartbeat, slow and steady now that they were settled in. There had been many times in their past when she and Kane had shared tight spaces, hiding from people who would kill them if they were found, eavesdropping on conversations they weren't supposed to hear.

Always, when on an assignment with Kane, she'd felt the peace of knowing she was with somebody as competent as her, that as partners, they were a force to be reckoned with.

When they hadn't been on assignment their time together had always been filled with passion and laughter, with an intensity of emotion that had been exhilarating. She'd missed it…the laughter…the passion.

"It's going to be a long night," Kane said, his mouth close to her and creating a warm whisper in her ear.

"Yeah, there's nothing worse than waiting for the action to begin. Are we the only ones inside?"

"Apparently so. Somehow the men outside managed to get by surveillance and on guard duty before the team could get anyone else inside. But there's plenty of backup on the outside. They'll come in like the cavalry when the time is right. I'd say your hunch was right. We're in the right place at the right time."

"Let's hope so. Let's hope the guards outside aren't some kind of a diversion," she replied.

They were silence for another long moment. "Tell me the truth, Cassie, you've missed this."

Her first impulse was to deny his words, to tell him that she had been perfectly satisfied with her life before the agency had tapped her for this particular assignment.

She'd thought she'd been happy arguing with her neighbor, tending her lawn, fighting with common criminals and making arrests. But she'd been fooling herself and she knew she'd never be able to fool him.

"Yeah, I missed it," she finally replied grudgingly. "But that doesn't mean I'm coming back," she added quickly. "I agreed to this one assignment and that's all."

He reached out for her hand and his fingers twined with hers. "We were good together, Cassie. We were the best when we were together. We stopped a lot of bad things from happening in the world. We stopped a lot of bad people."

"I know," she replied.

"Why did you quit the agency?" The question hung in the air and before she had time to reply, he continued. "Why did you quit on me? You didn't even come to see me in the hospital."

She heard the emotion in his voice, emotion she'd never heard before and she knew she owed him a real answer, not some smart-ass quip. She was grateful for the cover of the darkness, so he couldn't see her face or read her expression as she replied.

"Yes, I did. I was there while you were still unconscious. I saw you pale and still as death…" Her voice trailed off as she fought the lump of emotion that pressed against her chest. "I thought you would die and it was all my fault."

"Your fault?" He squeezed her hand. "You are so egotistical that you want to take the blame for me getting shot? You got it wrong, Cassie. I took that bullet by choice."

"Yes, to save me." Hot tears burned her eyes and she was appalled that after all the time that had passed this still had the power to hurt. "Kane, if I hadn't been your lover, if we'd just been partners like we were supposed to be and hadn't blurred the lines, then you would have never jumped in front of me."

"Cassie, honey, do you really think I've been trained only to save the lives of the women I sleep with?" Gentle amusement filled his voice. "If you'd had two heads and four legs and turned my stomach every time I looked at you, I still would have jumped in front of you.

I'm trained to save lives, Cassie. It had nothing to do with the fact that we were lovers."

There was a resounding ring of truth in his words, a truth she couldn't deny. She'd never thought about it in those terms before. But she knew it was right.

Both of them had been trained by the agency to save lives. Kane would have had to turn his back on all his training in order to remain still and let her take a killer's bullet. If the tables had been turned, she wouldn't have thought twice about jumping in front of him to save his life.

Years of guilt fell away, guilt she had carried since that day so many years before. But still emotion was thick inside her.

For it wasn't just the fact that Kane had taken a bullet meant for her that had haunted her all these years, it was the realization that she'd allowed him into her heart in a way she'd never before allowed in anyone.

It had been that realization and the woman's intuition that had told her he had been in love with her. It had terrified her and she'd run...run away from the agency...run away from him.

"Cassie, you belong working for the agency. You're one of the best agents SPACE has. You have a gift, a knack for the kind of work that needs to be done. Denying that would be criminal." He hesitated a moment, then continued, "and denying what we had together is a crime as well."

His lips touched the side of her neck and a thrill of

pleasure washed over her, pleasure combined with a strange kind of pain.

"Kane," she protested and pulled away. "You kissing me isn't going to change things."

"Even if I kiss you on the back of your neck?"

His teasing made all her defenses jump into place. She didn't want to have this discussion. He was her past, and the past wasn't supposed to argue with you.

"Surely this isn't the place or the time to have this conversation," she said impatiently.

"It's the perfect time and place," he replied. "We have nothing else to do to pass the time but talk and at least this way I can be assured that you won't run out on me in the middle of the conversation."

He released her hand and uttered a deep sigh. "I've waited five years to have this conversation with you and I'm going to have it. Cassie, you know as well as I do that there's a possibility that one or both of us won't walk out of this warehouse tomorrow. I think this is the perfect time to sort things out between us."

"There's nothing to sort out," she hissed with aggravation. "We were lovers and now we're not...end of story."

There was a long pause. "We were more than lovers and you ended the story." Again there was an edge of emotion in his voice that she'd never heard before. "Cassie, just because your mother threw you away doesn't mean you aren't worthy of being loved."

She stiffened, wishing she could run from him. "That's hitting below the belt."

"But it's there, isn't it," he countered. "Sometimes the past can hurt you, if you give it power over you. Not everybody leaves, Cassie. Max didn't and neither did I."

He put an arm around her and pulled her closer, so that if she leaned her head to the right it would rest against the hollow of his throat.

She refused to lean her head there, remembering too many nights when she'd slept next to him, nestled against his body, her face burrowed in his neck.

How like him, to go for the jugular, to bring her mother into the mix. But his words struck a chord and sent questions chiming through her.

Had her mother's abandonment made her afraid of commitment of any kind? Had that childhood experience tainted her, making her feel unworthy of love from anyone else? Was she allowing the past to hurt her present? Had she run from Kane because she hadn't wanted to chance the possibility of being abandoned yet again?

"I got an address off Mercer's computer for her."

His arm tightened around her. "Here in town?"

"Yes, 1327 Paseo Drive. According to Mercer's records she was living there five years ago."

"What about your brother?"

Cassie thought of Billy and a new ache rose inside her. "There was no record for him. Five years ago he would have been nineteen. I'm assuming he would have been living with her." Unless she'd tossed him out years ago like she had Cassie.

"Where's your father, Cassie? I've never heard you mention him."

"The better question would be who is my father." She sighed. "My mother was only sixteen when she got pregnant with me. She was a party girl, wild and free and according to her my father could have been any of many men."

She had long ago come to terms with the fact that the identity of her father would forever remain a mystery. Besides, she didn't really need a father. She already had one…Max.

"You think she's still there?"

She followed his jump of thought easily. "Who knows. Years ago we never stayed in one place for too long. We were evicted about every five or six months from one place or another. But she's older now. Maybe she's straightened out and still lives at that address. As soon as this is all over I'm going there to find out."

"What do you want from her?"

His question whirled around in her head. What did she want from the woman who had left her to fend for herself in a strange city when she'd been nothing more than a child?

Certainly she didn't need dating advice or motherly wisdom. She didn't need to exchange recipes or celebrate birthdays. It was far too late to forge the kind of mother/daughter bond she'd only read about in books.

"I want answers," she replied. And I want to know if she ever thought about me, worried about me. I need to know if she ever loved me at all.

"I hope you get what you need, Cassie."

They fell silent and it was only then she relented and

leaned her head against him. There was comfort in the familiarity of him.

Who knew what the morning would bring? Kane was right. It was possible one or both of them wouldn't make it out the warehouse alive. The potential for death had always been a part of the assignments for the agency and that had made life that much richer and sweeter.

At the moment she couldn't imagine anything more right than sitting in the embrace of Kane's arm and resting her head against him. It was one last poignant, sweet moment before the uncertainty of life returned.

She awoke when a hand clamped down firmly over her mouth. She instantly became aware of three things. Early-morning sunlight whispered into the windows around the ceiling of the warehouse, male voices could be heard from outside the building, and less than a foot in front of her face a silvery strand of web held the biggest, meanest-looking spider she'd ever seen.

She stiffened, her gaze riveted to the creature that danced mere inches in front of her face. She knew Kane had placed his hand over her mouth to still the scream he knew the sight of the spider would bring to her lips.

The scream was there now, trapped behind his hand. If he took his hand away she wouldn't be able to help the bloody scream that would rip from her.

The blood in her body all seemed to move to her head, leaving her lungs void of oxygen as a rush of light-headedness overtook her. In the back of her mind she knew she was on the verge of a full-blown panic attack.

The spider dangled on the end of the silvery strand, threatening at any moment to drop right on top of her. She was frozen in fear, hypnotized by the sight of the big, eight-legged creature.

"Shh," Kane whispered in her ear as he pulled his arm from around her back.

On a rational level Cassie knew the terror that washed over her was not rational, she knew that a spider couldn't hurt her, but that didn't stop the chill of horror that filled her.

She also knew, on a rational level, what had caused her phobia of insects and bugs. Her fear had been born on a morning when she'd been twelve and had been awakened from sleep by the creepy-crawl of dozens of beetles climbing all over her.

She'd had no idea where they had come from. She'd been sleeping on a slightly damp piece of cardboard in the back of an alley when the bugs apparently decided she was invading their personal space.

They had been everywhere…on her legs, crawling beneath her blouse, creeping over her neck and face. She'd screamed and fought them off, swatting and running out of the alley in an effort to get rid of them.

That's what she wanted to do now…scream and run. She'd rather take a bullet from one of the men outside than allow the spider to fall on her.

"Cassie…close your eyes and listen to me," Kane's whisper was barely audible.

She couldn't close her eyes. If she closed her eyes the spider would get her. It would fall on her and run across her skin with all those legs. It would bite her and make her sick.

She was vaguely aware of more male voices outside the building, as if a crowd was gathering. Within minutes they would be inside the warehouse. But at the moment Cassie feared them far less than she did the awful creature that hung before her.

"Dammit, Cassie. I can't kill it unless I pull my hand off your mouth, and I have to know you won't scream. If you make a single sound, we're dead. Now, close your eyes, keep quiet and I'll take care of it."

His words penetrated through her terror-filled brain. She forced herself to squeeze her eyes shut and bit her bottom lip as he removed his hand from her mouth. She heard a faint clap noise.

"You can open your eyes now," he whispered.

When she did, the web still sparkled in the sunlight but without the spider at the end. She turned and looked at him. "Thank you," she mouthed. She didn't want to know what he'd done with the dead spider.

He grinned and nodded, but the grin fell from his face as they heard the sound of the large garagelike door opening.

A new tension gripped Cassie.

It was show time.

Both she and Kane moved forward, not leaving their hiding place but moving to positions where the floor of the warehouse was visible and they could see the activity taking place.

There was no sign of a semitruck, but there were men

swarming the lower floor. As a Kansas City cop, Cassie hadn't worked any drug details, but she certainly knew many of the drug dealers of the city by sight. She recognized many of those men now, on the floor beneath them.

There were about a dozen men milling about and anticipation screamed in the air. Kane leaned over, his mouth against her ear. "I don't see Mercer."

Cassie's gaze swept the floor, looking for the man who had ordered her death, the man who was the maestro in this orchestration of death. "I don't see him, either," she whispered back to Kane. "Are you sure we have backup?"

"As sure as I can be."

The two of them watched the activity on the floor. Sebastian appeared to be the man in charge at the moment. He took a seat at the desk at the front of the warehouse and the men began to form a line in front of him.

At the front of the warehouse next to the open door, several men appeared to be frisking the dealers for weapons. Cassie assumed the heavily armed men doing the frisking worked for Adam.

Apparently it was a no-weapon kind of activity. Cassie was certain Adam wanted to take no chance that somebody would use firepower to take the drugs away from him without proper payment.

Sebastian appeared to be doing the bookkeeping. As each dealer stepped in front of him, money was exchanged and Sebastian recorded the transaction on paper.

When the cash was given to Sebastian, another man

took it from there and carried it into the heavily guarded inner office.

What was most amazing was that these men were ponying up the money without any sign of the product. She hadn't realized until this moment the utter depth of the desire Adam had spawned on the street for his drug.

At that moment the rumble of a large vehicle approaching could be heard. The men in the warehouse fell silent as a semitruck pulled into the drive that led directly into the warehouse.

Kane looked at her, and in his eyes she saw the fire of steely resolve, of sheer determination and she knew what he was thinking. There was no way they could allow that shipment to leave this warehouse. They should know within minutes if there was backup, or if they were in this all alone.

Chapter 18

The truck rolled into the warehouse and the big door closed behind it. The engine shut off and there was a moment of silence among the men on the floor. The air smelled of diesel fuel, exhaust fumes and excitement.

Adam Mercer got out of the driver's seat and climbed up to stand on top of the hood of the vehicle. At the same time armed guards got out of the truck and took up positions.

Two went to the back of the truck and two more headed for the stairs of the loft. Cassie and Kane both eased back. Farther into the shadows of the furniture as the two guards joined them on the loft at the top of the staircase on either side of where they remained out of sight.

The two men kept their backs to where Kane and Cassie were hidden, their focus on the ground below where cheers had erupted from the crowd.

Adam held up his hands, like a king asking for silence among the unwashed subjects around him. He got it. Cassie stifled a groan. She knew what came next. King Adam would make a speech. She'd never known a man who liked the sound of his own voice as much as Mercer.

"My good friends and colleagues," he began. "This is the day we've all been waiting for. It's the day that Blue will once again be on the streets. And we're going to be the ones to put it out there."

The men cheered. Of course, they probably had no idea that the drugs they were going to distribute on the street would kill their customers.

They had no idea that the drug deals they made this evening would be the last they made. They had no idea they weren't dealing highs, but rather they were dealing death.

Kane touched Cassie on the arm and motioned toward the guard on the loft to her right. She understood what he wanted. He'd take out the guard on the left and she was to deal with the guard at the right.

He reached into the duffel bag and pulled out a roll of duct tape and handed it to her. Good old duct tape, there were a thousand uses of the stuff. You could secure a lid, wrap an air vent, fix a leak and make a fine-looking miniskirt out of the strong, shiny sticky stuff.

As Adam continued to talk to his "troops," rallying responses of cheers with his words about the pure, high-quality dope he was about to deliver, Cassie and Kane crept out of their cover and headed for their respective targets.

Cassie moved in and out of the cover of the furniture, her gaze intent on the man she needed to bring down. The last thing she wanted was for him to hear her approach and cry out an alarm.

Although she knew exactly where to squeeze on the neck to render a man unconscious, it took only one look at the man's thick neck for her to realize that particular form of incapacitation might prove difficult.

This would take less finesse and more brawn, she thought. She pulled her gun from her waistband and crept closer, close enough that she could smell the scent of him…the unpleasant odor of an unwashed body.

No handgun for this man, he cradled an assault rifle in his arms, the barrel pointed toward the warehouse floor. There was no tension radiating from him, rather he looked relaxed.

As Adam continued to drone on from his stance on the semitruck hood, Cassie raised her gun over her head and waited.

When Adam's speech evoked a rousing cheer from the crowd on the floor, Cassie brought the butt of her gun down on the back of the guard's head with bone-jarring force.

He turned around and stared at her. Uh-oh, she thought. His eyes glazed over and he crumpled to the floor of the loft, unconscious from the blow. She breathed a quick sigh of relief, then grabbed him by the feet and dragged him back out of sight.

She used the duct tape to bind his wrists and ankles, then secured a strip over his mouth. God bless duct tape. She then taped him to the leg of a solid wood table, certain that even if he did regain consciousness he couldn't raise an alarm or do much of anything.

She grabbed his assault rifle, then made her way back to the center of the loft where Kane awaited her. "Where's our backup?" she asked. "Dammit, Kane, where the hell is our backup?"

His eyes were darkly troubled as he gazed at her. "I don't know."

She looked back to the floor, where Adam still held court. "Sooner or later he's going to stop blathering and they'll begin the distribution. We can't wait any longer. We've got to do something soon."

She watched as Kane returned his gaze to the warehouse floor. She could almost smell the wheels in his brain burning as they turned in his head to come up with a viable plan.

"I need to get down to the main floor," he whispered to her. "I want to get to Mercer. If I can get to him maybe we can stop this thing from happening."

"I can't go down there to help you. Somebody will instantly recognize me."

He nodded. "You'll have to cover me from up here. I'm going to try to make my way down and blend in with the others."

It was a dangerous plan. If Kane was identified as an interloper, he would be in deep trouble, and there was no guarantee that Cassie would be able to do anything to help him from her position in the loft. There were too many of them and not enough of her.

If they didn't do something fast, then the drugs would be out of their control and onto the streets, and that was simply not an option.

Where in the hell was their backup? She'd understood why none had appeared before the truck had arrived, but where were they now? She couldn't believe she and Kane were going to have to do this all alone.

She watched, heart thudding, as Kane took off his ammo belt and placed it next to her. He tucked his gun in his waistband, then pulled his shirt out so that the shirttail covered the butt of the weapon.

He leaned over and kissed her, a quick, fleeting kiss. "See you when this is all over." With a brief look of searing intensity, he made his way to the stairs that led down from the loft.

He paused at the top and she knew he was watching, waiting for the moment that he could get down the stairs without anyone seeing where he'd come from. Thankfully all attention from the men on the floor was still focused on Mercer.

In the blink of her eye he was gone from the loft and she leaned forward and peered over the edge to see where he was on the floor.

She held the assault rifle ready as she spied Kane drifting toward the semi. Nobody seemed to be paying any attention to him. But Cassie would shoot the first person who threatened Kane in any way.

"This will be an Independence Day to remember…the day Blue hit the market once again after months and months of inferior product." Adam continued to drone on and Cassie sensed the growing impatience of the men who awaited the moment when they could get their hands on their share of the drug.

Her heart raced and she knew most people under these circumstances would be feeling fear. She didn't. No fear. She welcomed the cold calm that overtook her, recognized it as a familiar friend who always visited her when in the center of the storm of an assignment.

The calm held the calculation of intelligence without the messiness of emotion. Emotion was dangerous, emotion made mistakes. She had to remain cool and calm in order to do what needed to be done.

Her heartbeat accelerated just a notch as she lost sight of Kane in the group below. She was comforted by the fact that nothing had changed among the men. No cries of an intruder, no scuffle indicating trouble.

Still, she wanted to find him. Where was he? How could she cover him if she couldn't find him? Her gaze swept the floor, finding far too many dark-haired men, yet not the one she sought.

Where are you, Kane? Her finger quivered over the trigger of the gun, ready in an instant to fire if necessary.

She sensed Adam coming to the end of his spiel and knew the moment of truth was at hand. The men began to move restlessly, paying less and less attention to the man on the hood of the truck.

She gasped as Kane appeared like a magician on top of the truck hood behind Adam.

Before anyone could react to his bold move, Kane

had an arm around Adam's neck and his gun to his head. "Speech is over, Mr. Mercer." Kane's voice rang out in the sudden tense silence that fell over the warehouse.

"Well, well, what have we here?" Adam's voice held no fear, only a frightening amusement.

"I'm the party pooper who has come to ruin your party. Tell your men to drop their weapons," Kane commanded. "This party is over and the contents of this truck aren't leaving this warehouse."

Cassie held her breath. Every gun in the place was now trained on Kane. Tension snapped and crackled in the air. For a moment nobody moved.

"Call off your goons, Mercer," Kane commanded. "Tell them to drop their weapons or I swear I'll blow your head off."

"I don't think so," Adam replied. He grimaced as Kane's arm tightened around his neck, then suddenly he laughed. The sound, so unexpected, so out-of-place, sent chills up Cassie's spine.

"Do you really think these men care if you blow my head off?" Adam asked. "There's no honor among thieves. They will do nothing to save my life. All they care about is the drugs. I'm afraid you've put yourself into a no-win situation here. You shoot me and they all shoot you and the drugs will make their way into the streets."

At that moment the warehouse door opened and dozens of Kansas City's finest rushed in. "Police...freeze!"

Shouts filled the air, angry curses and frantic yells as the men scattered to all four corners of the warehouse.

Finally, Cassie thought with in relief. Backup had arrived, and not a moment too soon. A gunshot rent the air. She had no idea who fired the first shot, but it ushered in a new chaos as men ran for cover.

More shots rang out and she lost sight of both Kane and Adam in the fracas. Frantically she searched for them, but couldn't find them in the swarm of men.

A firestorm resulted. She backed away from the loft edge as bullets ripped through the air. Dozens of guns delivered their payload. Shouts rang out, curses and cries filled the air and Cassie frantically tried to find Kane or Adam in the melee below.

She lay down on her stomach and inched toward the edge of the loft, knowing that she could pick off the bad guys from this vantage point. She laid the assault rifle aside. She couldn't take a chance that she might hit a cop with a stray bullet. She would do much better at precision shooting with her handgun.

Before she could get into position, the firefight was over and the police had control of the situation. However, she didn't see the man who had orchestrated this entire debacle.

She wanted Adam.

Where in the hell could he be? And where was Kane? She was afraid to study the bodies on the floor too closely, afraid she might see Kane's lying there. Deep in her heart, she knew that this would be the way Kane would want to die…going down in a blaze of glory, fighting to keep the world a safe place for the innocent.

She didn't know how long she remained there, on her stomach looking for Kane, looking for Adam, when she heard a sound to her right.

She turned and saw a flash of movement, but could do nothing to deflect that kick that caught her gun hand. The gun flew from her grip as another kick caught her in the stomach.

A cry ripped from her. Pain rocked through her, but she mentally forced the pain away and tried to focus on her attacker.

"You!" a familiar voice cried in rage. Mercer kicked her again and she rolled away from the kicks and quickly gained her feet.

She crouched, prepared for another attack. He faced her, his handsome features contorted with uncontrolled fury. "You're supposed to be dead," he said.

"Sorry to disappoint you," she replied. He had no weapon and for that she was grateful. In hand-to-hand combat, she thought she could take him. "It's over, Mercer. Why don't you just give it up?"

"It's not over until I say it's over."

She saw the cold hatred in his eyes, knew that at least at this moment he'd lost all sight of anything but his desire to see her dead. Cassie smiled grimly. "Bring it on, big guy."

With a surprising speed, he lunged forward and tagged her with his right fist on her already sore jaw. She sucked air through clenched teeth as sheer agony rocked through her.

She countered with a left, landing a glancing blow

off his chin. All thoughts of the action below them fell away as Cassie focused intently on her adversary.

She kicked, a high and powerful leg blow. He caught her leg at the height of the kick and pulled her other leg out from under her. She fell to the floor, stunned by his agility and speed.

He wasted no time giving her an opportunity to recover. He pushed at her body, moving her toward the edge of the loft. She struggled for a grip against the floor. If she went over the edge, the fall would be bone-shattering. If death didn't immediately occur, she would wish for it.

She kicked and swung at him as she remained on her back like an overturned turtle. She struggled to get to her feet, but he used his body and strength to keep her down and move her closer…closer to the edge.

She was no longer on the attack, but rather was in the defensive mode of trying to protect herself and keep from going over the edge of the loft.

To underestimate an opponent was a terrible mistake, and it was one she had just made with Mercer. She'd thought that even though he appeared to be in good physical condition he was probably soft, accustomed to leaving physical fights to his hired help. But that wasn't the case. He was fit and strong and there seemed to be nothing soft about him.

If she managed to gain her feet once again, she wouldn't make the same mistake twice. Her heart ripped beats in triple time as she tried to find something…anything to stop from being shoved from the loft.

But, despite her efforts, she felt herself sliding off the ledge. At the last moment she jackknifed her body and managed to swing one leg up and over the iron railing that provided a barrier from the edge.

With one leg hooked, she swung out over the warehouse floor, then cried out as Adam smashed his fists against the leg that held her safe.

Once…twice…three times he mashed her leg with his fists in an attempt to dislodge her. Her leg quivered and excruciating pain tore through her.

Before he could achieve his goal, she swung her other leg over the railing and pulled herself up. From there, she leapt back onto the loft and faced him once again.

He jabbed at her, using his left hand like a boxer. Jab. Jab. Jab. Then a right hook that nearly caught her. She managed to evade the blow and returned with a volley of her own punches.

Like two prizefighters, they jabbed and hammered at one another with deadly intent, each looking for a knockout blow. As the fisticuffs continued, Cassie's strength began to flag.

She began to use her legs as well as her arms. She pounded at his chest and stomach with powerful kicks, afraid to aim so high that he might have another opportunity to grab her foot once again and pull her off balance.

Her nose had begun to bleed and she grunted with pleasure as one of her fists caught him on the lip and split it open. It was only fair that if he drew blood from her, she returned the favor.

Cassie felt herself growing weak and she pushed herself harder in an effort to take him down. She was no longer breathing through her nose, but rather gasped openmouthed to draw in oxygen. He seemed to sense her weakness and doubled his efforts to take her down.

She saw her death in his ice-blue eyes, saw there his desire to destroy her. He would fight her until he killed her. With each blow he landed, she saw the glee that lit those cold eyes of his, saw that he enjoyed inflicting pain on her.

Her arms began to feel like they weighed fifty pounds a piece and her kicks were growing less powerful. She knew trouble when she felt it, and she was definitely getting into trouble.

In an effort to regain a second wind, she tucked and rolled away from him. His laughter rang out and she knew he laughed because of what he perceived as her retreat. She was vaguely aware of the activity on the floor beneath them. The police were in control, but everyone seemed too occupied to see what and who she faced.

When she regained her feet, she was about fifteen feet away from him. "You should have let it go," he said, his chest heaving from their exertions. "You should have just let the drugs hit the streets."

She was grateful he wanted to talk. The momentary respite would give her an opportunity to catch her breath. "It's murder, Adam."

"Murder of society scum," he cried. "Murder of people who deserve to die."

"If your daughter was alive today, you'd be dealing death to her. Tell the truth, Adam, this isn't about your daughter anymore. It hasn't been for a long time. It's about the money, and the power. You've become what you once abhorred, just another drug dealer."

He stared at her for a long moment, his eyes darkening with a new torment. "Maybe you're right," he said softly.

Before she could guess his intent, he dove over the railing of the loft.

"No!" Cassie screamed. She gripped the railing and looked below, where Adam Mercer lay lifeless on the concrete floor. She squeezed her eyes tightly closed and turned away. She hadn't wanted it to end this way. But it was over.

"Cassie."

She turned to see Asia standing nearby. In three long strides he had her wrapped in his big strong arms. "God, girl, I thought you were dead."

"I will be if you don't stop hugging me so hard," Cassie replied in a half laugh, half sob.

He released her, but then pulled her back against him for another tight hug. When he released her the second time his dark brown eyes were shining with emotion. "I've never been so glad to see anyone in my whole life," he exclaimed. "I'd hate like hell to lose a partner who kicks butt better than me." He pulled a handkerchief from his pocket and handed it to her. "You gonna tell me why a woman who's supposedly on vacation is in a warehouse kicking the butt of a bunch of dope dealers?"

Cassie's heart swelled with love for the big man. "Probably not. But we'll talk later."

"You'd better believe we will."

"I need to go downstairs and check on someone," she said as she used the handkerchief to dab at her bloody nose.

"Go. I'll take care of this guy."

She started toward the stairs, then turned back to her partner. "Asia, is our patrol car here?"

"Yeah. You need wheels?" She nodded and he pulled a set of keys out of his pocket and tossed them to her. "Go on, I can catch a ride from somebody."

"Thanks." Cassie turned and hurried toward the stairs that would take her down on the warehouse floor. There police officers were busy making arrests, securing the scene and tending to the wounded.

Kane.

His name reverberated in her head. Where was Kane? She moved among the wounded and arrested on the floor, heart pounding as she searched for him.

She hadn't seen him since the police had burst in, was afraid that somehow he'd gotten caught in the crossfire. A dull ache filled her heart as she continued the search for him.

She worked up one side of the warehouse and down the other, but there was no sign of Kane. He wasn't among the living and he wasn't among the wounded or dead. He was just gone.

At least she knew by his absence that he was all right. She shouldn't be surprised that he was gone. He wouldn't have wanted to tangle with the local authorities and blow his cover.

And now she needed to get out of here. The job had been a success. The tainted drugs would be destroyed before they could harm anyone and Adam's dope-dealing friends would go away for a very long time.

She probably wouldn't see Kane again until a new assignment came up that required her kind of talent and that might not be for months…for years.

Afraid to linger too long, afraid that she'd get hung up in red tape that she didn't want to be a part of, she slipped away from the warehouse and to the patrol car.

There was only one place she wanted to go…one place she needed to go. As she drove away from the warehouse, she felt the glow of a job well done coupled with a physical and mental exhaustion.

She held on to the glow. There would never be any public awareness of what they had accomplished. She knew any news story that broke about the big drug bust would not contain any mention of the undercover operation that she'd been a part of.

The local police department and DEA would be heralded as heroes, taking down a nasty operation before anyone could get hurt. That was fine with her. She didn't want public adulation. She just felt good, knowing she had done well and justice would be served.

It was just about noon when she pulled into a parking space in front of the Good Life Gardens. Every muscle in her body ached and she wanted nothing more than to go home to her house and soak for about five hours in a hot tub.

But, in the fray of things, she hadn't had a chance to contact Max and tell him that the newscast about her death had been bogus.

She had a feeling Max was going to be very angry with her when he saw her. She hoped the shock of seeing her alive and well didn't make him have a heart attack. She also hoped he'd forgive her when he stopped cursing at her.

She knocked on his door and when she heard his voice yell "come in," she entered. He sat at the kitchen table working a crossword puzzle. He looked up at her and frowned.

"About time you showed up."

She breathed a sigh of relief and sank into the chair opposite him. "You didn't buy the news story?"

"Nah." He grinned at her. "I knew it would take more than one moron to bring down my girl." He pushed the crossword puzzle aside. "How about you go clean up and I'll make us some lunch."

With these simple words, Cassie's life returned to normal.

Chapter 19

It was after three in the afternoon when Cassie left Max's place and headed toward her house. As she drove she continued the decompression process that always occurred after an assignment.

The process had begun with lunch with Max. Although she didn't tell him about her conversation with Kane in the middle of the night and she certainly didn't share with him the fact that she'd been intimate with Kane, she did tell him all about the operation and how it had gone down.

Now it was back to real life…normal life. She'd go back to bickering with Ralph Watters, working the streets as a cop and contemplating redecorating her living room. Maybe eventually she'd believe that could be enough, but she didn't think so.

Kane had been right. She loved working for the agency and this latest assignment had made her realize it was where she belonged.

Maybe safe lifestyles were for some people…for

most people, but not necessarily for her. She'd cut her teeth on the streets. Her nighttime lullabies had been sirens implying danger and the scuffles and cries of survival. Maybe that experience had twisted her somehow, making it impossible for "safe" to feel real to her.

She had no idea what the psychological forces were that drove her, she only knew that she felt most alive when she was working for SPACE and partnered with Kane.

Kane. Her time with him, her feelings for him were too fresh, too raw to contemplate. She didn't want to think of him and she couldn't go back to work for SPACE unless it was with the understanding that she would not work with Kane. She couldn't risk the emotional investment he demanded of her.

As she turned onto her street her thoughts jumped from Kane to the address that was burned into her brain—1327 Paseo Drive. Maybe the family she missed, the family she needed was there at this very moment.

She could drive there right now. But did she want to meet her mother and brother after all this time wearing the clothes she'd worn all night and sporting the remnants of a bloody nose?

No, she'd shower and clean up first and then drive to the address and see if there would be a family reunion.

She pulled into her driveway and saw Ralph Watters digging in the flower garden in front of his house. As she stepped out of the car she stifled a groan as he approached.

"Ms. Newton, I've been wondering where you've been. I haven't seen you for a while."

"Work, Mr. Watters. I've been working."

He leaned toward her and frowned, the gesture pulling his nose and mouth almost together, making him look like a caricature of human emotion. "Are you all right? You look kind of banged-up."

"I'm fine. I'm just tired."

"I took the liberty of mowing your lawn while you've been away. Don't worry, I didn't touch your tree."

For the first time Cassie noticed that, indeed, her lawn was neatly clipped and her flower bed looked as if it had been recently weeded. "Thank you, Mr. Watters, I appreciate it."

He nodded curtly. "Can't have the neighborhood blighted by one unmowed lawn." The implication was that he'd not done it to help her, but had done it to maintain the well-being of the neighborhood. "Next time you need help with things, you call me. A woman alone, it's probably hard to keep up with everything."

A burst of hysterical laughter bubbled to her lips but she managed to suppress it. In the last three weeks she'd gone head-to-toe with an ex-con, had scaled the side of a warehouse and had nearly been thrown to her death from a loft. And her neighbor was afraid doing yard work might be too much for her.

Still, she recognized his words for what they were— old cantankerous Ralph had offered an olive branch.

"I'll keep that in mind. Thank you." She'd almost reached the front door when she turned back to him.

"Mr. Watters, maybe one day this week you could help me take out this bush." She pointed to the dried brown bush. "It's dead, you know."

He nodded, his eyes lighting up. "You just name the time and I'll be here to help."

It was time to get rid of the bush. She wasn't sure why she'd been so reluctant to have it removed before now. She entered her house and locked the door behind her. She knew her car would be in the garage and her keys would be on the kitchen table. Somebody from SPACE had made sure that things were once again the way they had been before she'd started the assignment.

But of course things weren't the way they had been before. Before the assignment she hadn't had an address for her mother. Before the assignment she'd been able to fool herself into believing that Kane meant nothing to her.

The bathtub called and she heeded the call. She started the water running, added a healthy dollop of bath oil, then stripped off all her clothes.

As she waited for the bathtub to fill she studied her nude reflection in the mirror on the back of the bathroom door. New bruises were beginning to show along with the old ones.

The most vivid was on her knee, where Mercer had hit her over and over again as he'd tried to get her leg off the railing when she'd gone over the edge of the loft.

Yellows and purples decorated her jaw on the lower side, and all over her body what wasn't bruised ached. A long hot soak would do her a world of good.

Minutes later she eased down into the water, sighing with pleasure as the steamy hot water soothed muscles.

1327 Paseo Drive.

1327 Paseo Drive.

The address thundered in her brain, momentarily stilling the hollow emptiness in her chest. The address flashed like a neon sign piercing the darkness of a long, lonely night. It was like an itch that had to be scratched.

She dressed carefully, choosing a pair of navy slacks and a red blouse. As she dressed, her thoughts once again went to Kane. She didn't expect to see him again. The conversation they'd had in the warehouse had offered him no resolution, no hope that they would ever again share a relationship of any kind.

Kane was a proud man. He wouldn't come begging for her. No, it was time for her to readjust to her life…the safe life she'd chosen.

By the time she walked out her front door, the Escort that had been her wheels for the past couple of weeks had disappeared from her driveway. Moments later back in her shiny red Mustang, she headed south toward the Paseo Bridge and the address where her mother lived.

The cool, calm that had always been a companion when faced with difficulty deserted her. With each mile that took her closer to the address, anxiety gripped her.

Her stomach began to ache. Maybe she was coming down with the flu, she thought. Maybe she should wait and do this another day.

"Yeah, right," she said aloud. "Maybe you should

wait until you grow hair on your chest, or get a tattoo or eat a spider."

It would be far too easy to turn around and forget the whole thing, but she knew if she didn't do it now, she might never do it at all, and it had to be done. She had to see if her mother was there. She had no idea exactly what she wanted or what she needed, but she knew it was something.

She parked her car two blocks from the address. For a long moment she remained in the car, fighting an overwhelming feeling of nausea and the worst case of nerves she'd ever experienced in her life.

She gripped the steering wheel tightly, her hands sweaty. She was thirty years old. She'd lived almost twenty of those years without the benefit, love, or protection of her mother. So why did any of it matter now?

She had no answer. She only knew it did.

Her legs trembled as she got out of the car. She sensed eyes peeking out of windows, saw in her peripheral vision several gang members veer off the sidewalk and disappear into a nearby house.

She kept her gaze focused straight ahead, knowing the house she sought was in the next block. Where was the calm, rational frame of mind that always overtook her in times of stress? Why did she feel as if she were about to splinter into a thousand pieces?

1297. 1391. 1303. She began to watch the addresses as she continued walking, although her footsteps had slowed as her heartbeat raced faster.

The houses were old, two-stories in brick and wood.

Some had been renovated and shone with new paint and the tidiness of care. Others had fallen to near-ruin, with sagging front porches and boarded-up windows.

1305. 1307. 1309. Closer…closer she moved toward the past that had haunted her for so long. Closer…closer she moved to the answers to questions that had tormented her throughout the years.

1311. 1313. 1315. Sweat trickled down the small of her back, a nervous sweat that chilled her to the bone. She wished she had her necklace to clutch in her hand, the necklace with the locket that contained the picture of her mother and of Billy.

Would she even recognize her mother? Would her mother recognize her? Cassie knew better than to think her mother was still the woman in the tiny photograph. Almost twenty years had passed since that photo had been taken.

1327.

Cassie stared at the house and fought a surge of hysterical laughter that threatened to erupt from deep within her. Boards were nailed up across the front door to prevent entry. The windows were all smashed, leaving gaping maws in place of glass. A sign on the door warned trespassers not to enter, that the place had been condemned.

Her mother didn't live here. Nobody had lived here for a long time. She hadn't realized how high her hopes had been until this moment. She hadn't realized how badly she'd wanted a reunion with the woman who had given her birth and little else.

In all the years since she'd been left behind, abandoned on the streets, she'd never cried. Now emotion clawed its way up her throat, almost choking her. Tears blurred her vision as a small sob ripped from her.

All she'd wanted was her family, the connection of blood and love that had been absent for so long. She closed her eyes against the stinging tears that flowed down her cheeks.

Time to let go, Cassie, a little voice whispered in her head. Time to stop yearning for something she would never have. Like that dead bush in her flower garden that she'd finally decided to let go of, it was time to put away her dream of ever having a family who loved her.

She opened her eyes and cast one last look at the house, then turned and started to walk back toward her car. She'd only taken a couple of steps when Kane stepped out from behind a tree.

"What are you doing here?" she asked.

He leaned against the tree, looking as handsome, as sexy as she'd ever seen him. "Waiting for you." His dark eyes lingered on her face where she knew the remnants of her tears were still probably visible.

"How did you know I'd be here today...now?"

"Because I know you. I knew the first thing you'd do when the assignment was over was come here."

She turned and looked back at the house. "Did you know nobody was here?"

"Not until I got here." He shoved off from the tree and approached her. She stiffened, afraid that if he touched her, she'd shatter into a million pieces. He

ATHENA FORCE

Chosen for their talents.
Trained to be the best.

Expected to change the world.

The women of Athena Academy
share an unforgettable experience
and an unbreakable bond—until
one of their own is murdered.

The adventure begins with these six books:

PROOF by Justine Davis, July 2004

ALIAS by Amy J. Fetzer, August 2004

EXPOSED by Katherine Garbera,
September 2004

DOUBLE-CROSS by Meredith Fletcher,
October 2004

PURSUED by Catherine Mann, November 2004

JUSTICE by Debra Webb, December 2004

**And look for six more Athena Force stories
January to June 2005.**

Available at your favorite retail outlet.

shoved his hands into his pockets as his gaze lingered on her.

"You're the strongest woman I know, Cassie. I'm not just talking about your physical strength and agility, I'm talking about your single-mindedness and focus, your inner strength that allowed you to survive fairly well-adjusted despite your background, but the worst thing your mother did to you wasn't leaving you on the streets of L.A."

She looked at him in surprise. "What do you mean?"

He took another step toward her, his gray eyes holding a hard edge. "The worst thing your mother did to you was teach you to be afraid to love and in your fear you're hanging on to ghosts."

"I don't know what you're talking about." She would never admit it, but his words frightened her for some reason.

"You have the family you need," he said softly. "Oh, they aren't blood related, but who says family is about blood? You have Max, who absolutely, positively adores you, who would do anything to keep you safe and make you happy. And whether you know it or not, Cassie, you have me. You've had me since the moment I met you. I love you, Cassie and I'd love to be the family you need, the family who loves you and makes you feel safe."

His words made something break loose inside her. The pain, the sense of betrayal that had forever burned a hole in her heart seeped away. Tears once again burned in her eyes and this time he touched her…he pulled her into his arms and held her as if to keep her from blowing away in a storm.

"Let it go," he said softly as she cried into his chest. "Let them go."

As the sobs ripped through her she realized that's exactly what she was doing. Like that dead bush in her yard that she'd clung to for far too long, she'd been holding on to ghosts...the ghost of a mother who never was, the vision of a family that had never existed. It was time to let go.

As she let go of the dreams of a child, the desires of a woman filled her soul. She realized she'd been so busy seeking what she'd never had, she hadn't realized what was right in front of her. Max...and Kane...her family.

She raised her face to Kane, whose gray eyes held the welcome of homecoming. "I love you, Kane."

"I know. I've just been patiently waiting for you to figure that out. Come on, let's get in that shiny red Mustang of yours and go home to your place."

"Yes, I'd like that."

He smiled at her, his eyes lit with pleasure. "Want me to tell you what I intend to do with you when we get there?"

"No, don't tell me," she said with breathless anticipation. "Surprise me."

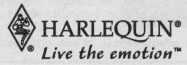

BOMBSHELL

COMING NEXT MONTH

#5 KISS OF THE BLUE DRAGON—Julie Beard

Angel Baker wasn't your typical twenty-second-century girl—she was trying to rid the world of crime and have a life. Then her mother was kidnapped and Angel was forced to rely on powers she didn't know she possessed, and was drawn to the one sexy detective she shouldn't be....

#6 ALIAS—Amy J. Fetzer

An Athena Force Adventure

Darcy Steele was once the kind of woman friends counted on, until her bad marriage forced her to live in hiding. But when a killer threatened the lives of her former schoolmates, she had to help, even if it meant risking her life—and her heart—again.

#7 A.K.A. GODDESS—Evelyn Vaughan

The Grail Keepers

Modern-day grail keeper Maggie Sanger was on a quest, charged with recovering the lost chalices of female power. But when her research was stolen and suspicion fell on her ex-lover, Maggie was challenged to uncover the truth about the legacy she'd been born into—and the man she once loved.

#8 URBAN LEGEND—Erica Orloff

Tessa Van Doren owned the hottest nightclub in all of Manhattan, but rumors swirled around that she was a vampire. Little did anyone know this creature of the night had a cause to down the criminals who had killed her lover. Not even rugged cop Tony Flynn, who stalked her night after night....

SBCNM0704